ADVANCE PRAISE FOR
HIT THE GROUND RUNNING

"The characters may be moving constantly, but the story allows readers to get to know them, their flaws, and their motivations. There's parkour, science, cool tech, and even a paranormal element."
— Sarah Monsma, *Middle Grade and Young Adult Book Reviews*

"The first instalment of this Young Adult trilogy is a fascinating and compulsive read."
— Brigitte HF, *Mes Livres*

"I highly recommend this book for YA... Buckle up because a fast paced adventure awaits you!"
— Jacqui Corn-lys, *Finishing Touches*

"A must read for YA readers, especially if you like action and adventure, along with mystery."
— Fizza Younis, *Book Eater*

"*Flow Like Water* is an exciting sequel to Hit the Ground Running, and the fast-paced action that readers enjoyed in the first story continues. In this novel, much of the story centers around Rome, the Vatican in particular. Mature readers will enjoy the detail of the city and culture as well as the links to history that are peppered throughout."
— Libby McKeever, *Canadian Review of Materials*

"Highly entertaining, this story is full of action and enough suspense to be a page turner with a perfect cliffhanging ending. The story has a little bit of everything to appeal to YA readers."
— Arlene Arredondo, *Arlene's Book Reviews*

"This book has action, adventure, anthropology, archaeology, and a mixing in of various mythologies and legends.... The pace of the action is also excellent, and the descriptions during some of the scenes, especially Eric's parkour, are thrilling."
— Steven McEvoy, *Book Reviews and More*

TAKE FLIGHT

Book Three of the Hit the Ground Running Trilogy

Mark Burley

COPYRIGHT INFORMATION

TITLES IN THE
"HIT THE GROUND RUNNING"
SERIES

CONTENTS

In memory of
Aidaen Mae Mitchell

1

PASSAGE

Eric Bakker leapt down from the railing and sprinted the short distance along the metal walkway. He approached another rail, dash-vaulted it, and landed without stopping on the flat expanse that was the container stowage area of the ship. The space was empty because the ship didn't have its cargo yet; this would happen after it returned to Palermo. It was late, and the sky was very dark, but the sea air was not as cool as he'd expected. The deck was lit by bright lights mounted outside the bridge high in the stern and by others near the bow. The darkness in between added a challenge Eric found appealing.

He wall-climbed a pillar that rose above the hull — one of several that appeared to be brackets for shipping containers — topped out, and immediately did a standing precision to the outside rail below. Arms back, feet extended, a perfectly balanced landing. He looked down at the churning water for a moment then jumped backward to the deck before sprinting easily to the next pillar and topping out again. He was near the bow now, the deck hardly shifting as it powered through the gently moving waves. He jumped as far as he could from the top of the pillar, slapped out his landing, and rebounded to climb a bulkhead at the end of the cargo area. He swung around some guide wires that stabilized a short mast on top of the compartment there and stood looking out at the dark sea ahead.

He would need some sleep before they arrived in France, he knew, and his opportunity to do that was slipping away. But he also knew his mind wouldn't be quiet enough if he tried. Not yet. Another lap, then he'd see how he felt.

When they'd left Sicily, they planned to go to Sardegna, where they could get on a plane to Norway, but that was before Seth and Lakey had found what they found. Now they were headed for Nice, where flights were arranged for everyone except Eric, Michael, and the twins, who had something else to do first. It involved a plan, which, like most of the plans they'd made in the last two weeks, would probably go sideways.

He waited a few more minutes before his legs started twitching, urging him to move. He swung around another guide wire and dropped back to the deck, port side this time. As he landed, he rolled forward and was quickly on his feet again, moving smoothly as he tried to clear his mind. It turned out that one more lap was all he needed, and he felt himself relax to the point where he thought about rest. By the time he reached the high bulkheads aft, he was satisfied. He retrieved his jacket from the railing where he'd left it and made his way back inside. Feeling better, he decided to hit the galley on the way to his bunk. The captain's wife had a special talent for pastry.

The tight, practical passages in the ship were dimly lit and empty. The captain and his family had found makeshift bunks for everyone, despite the limited space and absence of passenger accommodations, but everyone was comfortable. It had taken a long time for Eric's parents to take a break from preparations, but considering what they were about to do, it wasn't clear when they would get another chance to rest. And if sleep were part of the preparations, Clara Bakker would see that it was done.

As Eric made his way down one passage, a light shone ahead of him from a doorway. When he reached it, he saw Ada sitting in a chair next to the bunk where John Williams lay. She had a book open in her lap and looked up at Eric as he came into view.

"How is he?" Eric asked.

"The same," Ada replied without looking at her husband. Her expression showed resolve without a trace of arrogance. The extent of the burns Williams had sustained in the fire at the lab in Palermo — and the fact he'd been unconscious since then — had left everyone with fading hopes. Everyone except Ada.

Regardless, if it hadn't been for Williams, Eric's parents, Gabriel and Clara, would have died when Captain Falco's men locked them in the lab and ignited it. Eric's brother, Michael, would have been killed in Montana at Gilroy Stockton's research facility if Williams hadn't been there. And for Eric, Williams had been directly responsible for saving his life on three separate occasions. Two years earlier, although Eric didn't know it at the time, a small transfusion of dreylagr — the lifeblood of Williams and his people — cured Eric of what would have been a fatal infection. In Montana during Michael's rescue, Eric would have been killed by hired gun Olaf "The Butcher" Meszaros if Williams hadn't intervened. And in Chicago, when Eric recovered the book that would lead him to the Vatican, where they found Ada and eventually his parents, Eric would have been killed by the Vidi if Williams hadn't fought them off and given Eric time to escape.

The Vidi. Three-thousand-year-old mummies whose sole purpose was to find and destroy the People Under the Mountain — and anyone who came into contact with them — wherever they were in the world. For all Eric knew, Williams and Ada could be the last of the People left alive.

Under the circumstances, if there were any chance to save Williams, Eric and his family would do whatever was necessary.

Eric gestured to the book in Ada's lap. "What are you reading?"

Ada folded the battered cover closed, keeping a finger inside to mark her place, and held it up. The words were Italian. "Umberto Eco," she said. "*Il nome della rosa.*" She motioned in the general direction of the captain's quarters. "*Madam* has excellent taste in literature."

Eric considered his own collection, recalling that he'd been in the middle of James M. Cain's *Double Indemnity* in the caf at school when he received his brother's message and all this started. He couldn't remember where he'd left it now. He glanced toward the glowing fixture on the bulkhead above her. "You prefer having the light?" he asked, knowing she didn't need it.

"It lets others know I am here," she said. "And there is a warmth to it I find appealing."

Eric nodded. "John told me about your love of libraries, of books. Considering the collection you had at the Vatican — I only saw it for a moment when we found you, but it was impressive — I imagine there must be quite a library at the place where you're going." Eric thought back to the shelves of books lining the cell where Ada had been kept beneath the Tower of Nicholas V. There were thousands of books, many of which she'd made herself over centuries of confinement.

"There was at one time, yes. Though now, I do not know."

"You must be excited about returning to the Mountain, about going home."

Ada smiled kindly. "It is not my home. I go because it is the only hope for Johannes; no other reason would take me there."

"What about your father? You must be looking forward to seeing him."

"No," she replied, her expression closer to sadness this time. "No, I am not."

There was no intention toward Eric in the comment, none that he could see, anyway, but she didn't elaborate, and rather than pursue it, he decided to leave her to her novel. She had already dealt with so much, there was no need to describe it to him. They parted, Ada to continue her vigil, and Eric to go in search of baklava.

2

NICE TO BE IN NICE

Lakey Sawatzky pushed open the glass door and stepped into the small mobile phone repair shop. The store was one of several that lined the street on a block that seemed typical for the area, as far as Lakey could tell, with storefronts below and balconies and shuttered windows above. The buildings were tight to the street and continuous, five storeys high, and covered with stucco, mostly pale yellow. The outside of the repair shop had large, brightly coloured signs, metal door frames, and floor-to-ceiling windows, a more modern look than the cardio gym next door and the barbershop on the corner, normal places you would find in a lot of cities back home, except Lakey figured the *shutters* on the upper levels here were probably older than Vancouver.

An electronic tone sounded from somewhere deep in the store. The door behind the dull white counter was closed, and there was no one out front, but Lakey knew that most of the real work happened in the back. The customer area had a few lame displays of cheap phone and tablet cases and accessories, and all the signs were in French, but Lakey figured they weren't that different from what she'd seen in shops in San Diego or Manhattan Beach.

Lakey walked to the counter and peered behind it. There were white, enamel-covered cabinets and drawers, streaked black in places by grimy hands or careless feet, and the white floor tiles were scuffed and dusty. She draped herself over the counter and tried a few of the drawers. They were filled with random wires, accessories, bits of paper, and the odd old, dead-looking device. Nothing that looked familiar. She glanced contemplatively at the computer near her then started toward it when she heard movement behind the battered white door. She slid off the counter and wandered casually toward a collection of tablet cases mounted on one wall.

A guy came out, thin and not very tall, maybe late twenties. His face was covered with two weeks' worth of dark stubble, and his eyes were bleary and tired. *"Bonjour,"* he said blandly. *"Puis-je vous aider?"*

Lakey beamed a massive smile. "There you are!" she said brightly, appearing to assume the salesperson would have no problem with English. "I was starting to worry you weren't open and you'd just left the door unlocked or something." The weary eyes narrowed, but Lakey didn't seem to notice. She pulled a phone out of her pocket, an old BlackBerry Bold provided by Captain Khoury. He'd given it to her from a stash on his ship during the crossing from Sicily to France. It was a kind gesture, and Lakey had thanked him before carefully breaking the screen on a pipe.

"I need you to fix this. My idiot brother dropped it in the street, and it was run over by a bus." She held the phone out to the man, who balked at taking it. Lakey held it out farther and gestured impatiently. "Come on! This phone has exceptional personal value to me, and I need it fixed!"

The man reluctantly took it, glanced at it, then started talking rapidly in French while shrugging in exasperation.

Lakey cut him off. "Well, do you fix phones here or not? It says so on the sign outside."

The man sighed and looked at the phone more closely, mumbling irritably. Lakey couldn't tell what he was saying. Finally, he set the phone on the counter. *"Revenez dans une semaine."*

"What?" Lakey asked.

The man held up a finger and spoke haltingly. "One week."

Lakey shook her head. "No, no, no. I need this done now. Today. I'm only here for one day, and I need it fixed now."

The sales guy shook his head dismissively. *"Non, ce n'est pas possible,"* he said. "Order piece."

"Parts? You mean you don't have screens here?"

He gestured impatiently at the phone. "Too old!" he said and continued mumbling.

Lakey rolled her eyes. "Ridiculous. Well, what else do you have?"

"*Quoi?*"

Loudly and slowly, "WHAT-ELSE-DO-YOU-HAVE?"

He pointed at the phone. "*Comme ça?*" He shrugged again in a you-have-to-be-kidding kind of way.

"Anything."

He looked at her impassively.

"Show me."

∞

At the sound of the electronic tone behind the door in front of him, Seth Sawatzky, Lakey's twin brother, silently pushed his wheelchair closer and listened. He was near the service entrance behind the phone repair shop, having taken the alley that snaked in from a side street. The alley was narrow, covered in some places, and partially blocked by vehicles randomly parked everywhere. The buildings were all connected, some at sharp angles to one another like they were packed in to the space made available by the surrounding streets. The arrangement created tight corners that were also cluttered with waste bins and air conditioning units. If they had to get out quickly, it wasn't going to be easy.

It took a while, but he eventually heard an inner door open and close. He heard his sister's voice through his earpiece. *There you are!* He waited a moment longer, glancing back down the alley to make sure no one was there, then quietly opened the outer door and went in.

It was dark inside, the fluorescent lights on the ceiling lifeless. There was a metal overhead door next to the one Seth had used, now closed, with wooden pallets sitting on the concrete floor just inside. The pallets were covered with boxes, and one load was wrapped entirely in plastic. Metal shelves lined the far wall and contained several boxes similar to those on the pallets, some broken and dented. Most of the light came from a workbench near the inner door where an under-cabinet fixture and a couple of clamp-on lamps on long arms were directed onto the pile of tools and equipment that covered the surface. One of three computer monitors glowed, though he couldn't make out what was on it from where he was. The soft *thump-thump* of dance music playing at low volume came from speakers next to the monitor.

Seth checked his phone to confirm the location of what he was looking for. It was over by the workbench. He pushed his chair around a stack of boxes, caught a wheel on a cable he hadn't seen in the dim light, and rubbed a precarious stack of boxes with the frame of his chair, causing it to teeter and fall with a crash. He froze, looking at the door to the front of the store and listening through his earpiece. *WHAT-ELSE-DO-YOU-HAVE?* Lakey seemed like she still had things under control, her version of it, at least. Seth partially cleared a path toward the workbench and made his way there.

He found plastic crates on the floor next to the bench, with several devices of different brands, mostly phones. He rooted through them, found none of them had cases, and so he couldn't locate the one he was familiar with. He began looking for the make instead and found more than one. He touched each to try to wake it from sleep. Most didn't come on, but he found the one he wanted when the screen showed a photo he recognized. It was a tall, leafy tree, with thick branches and clumps of berries, the arbutus tree that grew out of the bank down by the water on campus at Brentwood College School on Vancouver Island. The phone belonged to Tess Edwards. Seth set it in his lap and started out the way he had come in.

"Got it," he whispered, "heading out now."

At that moment, the overhead door started to open, and light from outside gradually filled the space. A truck slowly revealed itself, its back end toward the opening and its brake and reverse lights showing red and white. The truck filled the gap entirely. Seth slowly wheeled backward until he bumped another pile of boxes, knocking it over and spilling phones and other equipment out over the floor. The noise was muffled by the sounds of the door going up and the engine outside. When the door was high enough, the truck moved slightly into the space, the taillights went out, and the engine stopped. Seth rushed toward the door he'd used earlier, which was still closed. He grabbed the handle and pulled, but it opened more easily than it had the first time. He understood why when a girl wearing a leather jacket, an elaborate scarf, and combat boots lurched forward, tripped on the threshold, and fell into his lap.

"Aw, *putain*," the girl said, struggling to get up. She stared angrily at Seth. He managed a weak smile, which only seemed to piss her off more. "*Qui est-tu?*" she spat, glancing at the two phones in his lap and rubbing the side of her head where one of them had collided with her.

Seth mumbled something and gestured back toward the work area inside the store. In the moment when his head was turned, the girl snatched the phones away. Seth tried to grab them again, but she took a step back and held them away from him, staring menacingly. From outside the doorframe, a hand reached in and picked the phones from the girl's grasp. She turned, furious, then backed up immediately as Michael Bakker's huge shadow filled the doorway. He came in slowly and closed the door.

"These don't belong to you," he said firmly. The girl started to protest loudly and rapidly in French, but Michael held up a hand and shook his head. "Now, just a minute. You and I both know what kind of operation you're running here." He glanced around the workshop. "Not your average mobile phone repair shop to handle so many units at one time." He stared hard at the girl, whose eyes were narrow and burning. "We know that stolen gear from all over France comes through here on its way out of the country." He nodded at the plastic-wrapped pallet. "We know this load is on its way to a ship at port, part of your regular shipment to Brazil. One phone call and this place is swarming with cops in three minutes." He nodded at Seth. "My friend here has connections at Interpol."

The girl was still smouldering but said nothing, clearly understanding every word.

"You get what you came for, brah?" Michael asked Seth.

Seth looked at the girl again. Her eyes were boring holes through Michael's skull. *Man, she's hot*, Seth thought. He nodded at Michael and wheeled past both of them to the door.

Michael turned toward the girl before leaving. He held up a finger. "One call." He held up three fingers. "Three minutes." He pointed at her and followed Seth outside. "We're out," he said into his mic.

∞

Eric acknowledged his brother through the mic hidden in his clothing. He was standing at a display of magazines inside a pharmacy across the narrow street from the phone repair shop. He replaced the magazine he'd been flipping through and walked outside, paused briefly to allow a bus to pass, then crossed to the shop entrance. Lakey was still talking animatedly with the associate. She had arranged a row of phones and several rows of cases he had provided for her on the counter, examining each possible combination with a level of contemplation that had to be pushing the associate close to the breaking point. A chime rang as Eric entered, and at almost the same time, the door to the back of the shop opened and a girl came out looking mildly homicidal.

"There you are!" said Eric loudly. "Come on, we have to go. Mom's going to have one of her freak-fests." He looked at the equipment on the counter. "What are you doing?"

"I'm not leaving until I replace the phone you broke," Lakey said flatly. The girl who had entered looked from the array of phones and cases on the counter to her partner, who shrugged in an exasperated way.

"Seriously?" Eric exclaimed.

"Well, you're the one who threw my baby under that bus!"

Eric did his best to look indignant instead of laughing. "You're blaming *me* for that?"

"Because it's *your* fault!"

Children, said Michael, *stop fighting and come along.*

"Is not."

"Is too."

"Is not. And Mom's still going to freak." Eric started for the door. The man and the woman behind the counter stood watching wordlessly.

"Is too!" Lakey grabbed the BlackBerry and followed Eric. They continued arguing until they rounded the corner outside and started up the narrow street.

They met Seth and Michael on the next street and continued walking back toward the Nice Port, where Captain Khoury's ship was waiting. A high stone wall stood above them on the right, with trees rising up from higher on the hill, and cars ran end-to-end on the sidewalk. Lakey, not one to dwell on what they'd just done, did a double-take next to a boxy blue hatchback.

"Oh, look, Sethie! Another Panda." She turned toward Michael. "Might not look like much, but it's got it where it counts." This Fiat was a little smaller than Francesco Azzarà's, which she'd flown through the streets of Palermo from the lab to the ship the previous day, the Carabinieri screaming along behind them. "Might not be up to the Prez back home, but give me a few weeks to Lakefy it and see what happens."

She turned and looked at the wall opposite the Panda. It was ancient stone, smoother along the bottom but much rougher higher up, worn by centuries of weather and now filled with weeds and grasses that grew out of the crevices. The height was around fifteen feet, not quite as tall as the Passetto around Porta San Pellegrino at the Vatican but with a similar feel. There were small, rectangular openings at intermittent levels over the face, though it wasn't clear what they were for. They looked too small to be windows or weapon ports. Just drainage, maybe. But in the split second it took for Lakey to see them, she came up with another purpose.

"Hey, Rico — check it!" She ran toward the wall, launched herself upward by planting her foot against the stone, and grabbed for one of the openings partway up the surface. Her hand found one, and she tugged hard while kicking with the opposite foot, continuing up until a foot found the same opening. She didn't stop her momentum, moving sideways slightly as she reached for more holds. She almost made it to the top, but she hadn't calculated well enough and ended up in a large clump of weeds, long ones with purple flowers. Blinded, she grabbed at the plants, pulled them from the wall, and started to fall. Michael reacted with lightning speed and caught her around the waist just as she reached the ground.

She turned to the others then looked up at the wall. "Whoa, did you see that? I almost made it!" Seth shook his head and started wheeling. Michael gave Eric a knowing look. Eric had spent some of the time on the ship teaching Lakey parkour. She was still figuring out her limitations, though Eric suspected she didn't think much about limitations in general.

The wall became gradually lower as they walked, eventually ending at more buildings that followed the curve of the street.

"So what's the play?" Michael asked. No one had spoken to Tess since the airport in Montreal, and Eric had only received one text. "We've got her phone, and assuming someone just lifted it, she could be anywhere."

The Interpol Command and Coordination Centre in Lyon had become Tess's destination after a phone conversation with an agent made her question what she'd known about her father's death. Seth's hack of Interpol's systems hadn't found any record of her arrival.

"I don't think we have any choice," Eric replied. "We need to go there."

"To Lyon?"

Eric shrugged. "Someone would remember her." He started tapping the screen on his phone.

"Texting Mom and Dad?" Michael asked.

"Yeah."

Michael had given his phone to their parents, since theirs had been taken while guests of Captain Falco and Cardinal Abito in Rome. He looked at his watch. "They won't be in Oslo for another three hours."

Eric put his phone in his pocket. "We'll get our stuff from the ship, check the train schedules and the flights, see if we can get something out right away." Michael frowned and nodded.

They walked down the hill toward the water, past picturesque blocks of square buildings with rows of shuttered windows and wrought iron balconies, and emerged near the docks. Nice Port was small and very orderly, a constructed rectangle that pushed straight inland from the coast and was protected by a long breakwater. Ferries and larger commercial vessels were tied to the wharf near the entrance to the port, while private boats, some of which were floating mansions, were neatly arranged farther in.

The ship that had brought them there, the small cargo vessel with its blunt face and beaten, rust-streaked hull, was docked near the breakwater next to a short crane. It stood out among the pristine boats around it like an Oakland Raiders fan at a golf tournament, but the ship, like its captain, appeared not to care. Captain Khoury had brought them from Palermo to Nice out of respect for Williams, to whom he owed some debt. Eric hadn't discovered what it was, but he could relate, considering his own circumstances. The ship had remained at port while Eric and the others went to the phone repair shop, just in case they were needed, but Eric knew the captain was anxious to be underway.

The crossing from Sicily had taken several hours, but no one — not even Ada — was sure how much time they had. Williams still hadn't shown any signs of life, but he hadn't shown any signs of death, either. And since he hadn't had any vitals when he was walking around, it made sense he wouldn't have any when he was unconscious. Ada's plan was their only option.

When they left Palermo, they were headed for the airport in Cagliari on Sardegna, but while on the ship, Seth and Lakey located Tess's phone, so they went to Nice instead. Eric had hoped this meant they'd found Tess, but once they determined the phone was at a repair shop, and especially after a little digging showed the repair shop was part of a network sending used phones to several countries under sketchy circumstances, they knew it had been stolen. The chances that the people at the shop would know where Tess was — or even who she was — were slim, but they had to try.

Captain Khoury's tech setup was a lot more advanced than Eric would have guessed, looking at the ship. But apparently not all the shipments they handled were legal, strictly speaking, so certain capabilities were necessary.

Seth and Lakey were almost disappointed when they arrived in France and had to leave.

The captain had been to the port many times and knew people in customs who wouldn't raise issues for them, but this didn't extend to getting on a plane and flying to Norway. Travelling across international borders with someone who appeared to be dead was actually harder than you might think. However, thanks to the Council of Europe's European Treaty Series No. 80, *Agreement on the Transfer of Corpses* (Strasbourg, 1973), some very official-looking travel documents, and some equally official-looking Interpol credentials, they were able to arrange travel on a commercial flight out of Nice Côte d'Azur International Airport. Captain Khoury provided a suitable container that would meet treaty regulations, basically a sealed coffin, so Ada, according to her Interpol documents, could repatriate the remains of her late husband to his homeland. Gabriel and Clara had gone with her, along with Owen Yancey, their friend and colleague from the Field Museum in Chicago — also saved from the fire by Williams — and Angel, his daughter.

Eric had come to know Angel since he met her in Chicago. She was brilliant, and though she didn't make a big deal of it, she didn't have much tolerance for people who weren't. She was also a Wing Chun expert with a fairly serious case of claustrophobia. She might have been more of a challenge for Eric than the others, but they wouldn't have been able to get this far without her. She'd made it possible to find the book and track it to Ada, which ultimately led to finding Eric's parents. She'd also taken out one of Falco's men who might have killed them at the lab in Palermo. Having her with his parents while he went looking for Tess made Eric feel better about their chances.

Captain Khoury greeted them as they approached. Sallah el-Kahir, another research team member who, along with Williams, had saved Gabriel, Clara, and Owen from the fire in Palermo, stood beside him, looking grave. The captain smiled broadly and held out his arms. "Welcome back, my friends! You had success, yes?"

"Yes and no," Eric replied. "May we come aboard?"

"Of course!"

Eric led the others up the short ramp onto the ship. After explaining what they had found and what they intended to do, they gathered their things, said thanks and goodbye to the captain and his family, and made to leave again. As they approached the ramp that led down to the dock, Sallah met them. He stood leaning on the railing, his eyes heavy from lack of sleep. Seth and Lakey acknowledged him as they passed, and when Eric and Michael approached, he stepped forward.

Eric hadn't heard much from the Egyptian during the crossing, though he had been involved in lengthy discussions with Eric's parents. He struck Eric as a private person, confident and intent, but withdrawn, as though his thoughts and work were deeply personal. Both Sallah and Owen had only then become aware of who Williams really was, and while Owen was clearly blindsided, Sallah seemed unaffected. Eric got the impression it wasn't out of some need to protect an ego, not wanting to show some insufficiency, more that he just didn't rattle easily. He'd chosen to stay behind when the others went on to Norway because he wanted to return to Sicily; he had connections at the university in Palermo which might help keep the authorities off their trail, but he also felt he owed it to Francesco. He'd been missing for some time, and someone would need to start dealing with his affairs.

"You have everything you need?" Sallah asked, his voice low and penetrating.

"Yes, I think so," Eric answered. "The next flight isn't until tonight, but there's a train that leaves in about half an hour. They both arrive in Lyon around the same time, though. We'll probably take the train, just so we're not sitting around all afternoon."

Sallah nodded and looked out over the rail at a passing boat, one of the smaller yachts that was making its way out of the port. "I know you do not need me to remind you to be careful," he said. He looked back at them. "There is clearly more to this than we are aware."

"No question on that point, Sallah," said Michael. "We've had to be careful. But our friend hasn't been involved enough to be a target for anyone, and the people who had their fun with me in Montana are out of the picture now. She's not even looking for anything related to the project; she's trying to find out what happened to her father."

"You are right, of course," said the archaeologist, "and I do not think there is enough concern for whoever is behind this to consider your friend, even if they are aware of her. But you must realize there may be others who have yet to appear. You have had no choice but to leave a trail behind you, and I do not believe it possible for your actions — or your movements — to have gone unnoticed."

"What do you mean? Are you suggesting this is bigger than Abito and Falco?"

Sallah pursed his lips and shrugged slightly. "I suggest only that something as important as this may attract others. We endeavoured to keep our work secret, but this is much harder to do when people die because of it."

"We'll be careful," Eric said. "You have my number; please contact me if you hear anything in Palermo."

Sallah shook hands lightly with the brothers, saying, *"Fi Aman Allah,"* to each of them as he did so.

Eric held his gaze for a moment, then he and Michael joined Seth and Lakey on the wharf, and the four of them made their way back into the port city.

3

BUSTED

Eric and the others walked up the hill from the harbour, headed toward the tram that would take them to the train station. They each carried their gear in backpacks; Seth's pack was smaller and strapped to the back of his chair. A second bag, a travel case for his tech, spanned two posts that extended off the front, a position that helped both for easy access to its contents and to balance his weight. The extra effort to push up the hill was obvious, but he didn't request any help, and everyone knew better than to offer. It was cooler on the Côte d'Azur than in Palermo but still mild, and the sun was warming when it emerged from intermittent clouds. Activity flowed around them, but the pace was different, like it was more casual, almost leisurely. They passed several food establishments as they went, from small bistros, bars, and sidewalk cafes to wide, glass-fronted restaurants specializing in local French Mediterranean fare, Italian, even American. Every time one came into view, Lakey became more insistent.

"Come on, please? How about this one? It's Indian. You like curry, right? We might not see another place before we get to the station."

"Gidge, every second place sells food," Seth responded. "This is France. Most people here don't even *have* kitchens."

"I know." Lakey sighed. "I could so live here forever."

"They'll be food services on the train," Eric suggested.

"Yeah, but train food is like airplane food; they keep it hot too long after it's cooked, and it's like squirrel-sized portions. We have time, don't we?"

Lakey trailed sullenly behind the others. The next place they passed had a wide black awning that extended out over the sidewalk, where three high metal tables stood along the wall, each with bar-style black chairs. A sign above the awning said "WOKSHOP" in a two-tone orange made to look like flames. The wall outside was covered with photos from the menu, Asian fusion cuisine. Lakey, predictably, stopped and stared. The others turned toward her.

Lakey made a defiant face and gestured toward the restaurant. "It's *noodles*," she said. "It takes twelve seconds to make, and I can eat while I walk. You guys keep going; I'll catch up."

Before anyone could stop her, she disappeared inside. Eric looked at Seth, who shrugged and looked back expectantly. Eric sighed and nodded. Seth immediately turned and beat a line to the door, forcing another customer to jump out of the way as he bounced over the small threshold.

Eric looked at Michael, who also shrugged, grinning. Eric shook his head and laughed. He checked the time and let out a breath. "We might not make it."

"The stop for the tram is just around that corner," said Michael, nodding up the street. "With a four-minute interval, we won't have to wait. But don't worry about it; if we don't catch that last train, we can always fly instead and not lose any time in the end. And we'd still have to go to the train station to get to the airport."

The twins emerged a few minutes later, each with two boxes of something that smelled a lot better than Eric had expected. It made him hungry, and he had a moment of regret that he hadn't gone in himself. Lakey had two chopsticks and most of her face buried in one of her boxes as she walked, while Seth had his in a bag on his lap, likely intending to hit it as soon as they got on the tram.

They made a right at the corner and entered a large square filled with leafy trees and park benches. One end of the square had rows of tables beneath a series of large white umbrellas that made a kind of canopy. People sat in small groups, and others drifted through the area, talking. Michael had to guide Lakey through the sparse crowd to keep her from running into people. They turned again onto a street designated only for tramcars and approached the stop. The street was separated from the square by rows of young palm trees in brown planter boxes. The trams themselves were not the clunky streetcars of San Francisco; they were sleek and modern, like something you'd find in a Philip K. Dick novel. Or in Tomorrowland at Disney.

The Disney connection made Eric think of Tess and her improv performance at the airport in Oakland. Eric wouldn't have made it off Vancouver Island without her. Here was someone who had only been to the mainland a few times, and never out of the country, but she'd jumped in when he needed her in San Francisco and made sure they came back again. She'd brought them together not only with Seth and Lakey but also with Williams, and she'd played a key role in getting into Stockton's research facility in Montana to save Michael. Eric was sure the trip so far had been difficult for her; she'd broken up with her boyfriend when she saw him in Toronto while they were on their way to Montreal, which Eric hadn't handled well. And he'd done worse when she went off on her own to France looking for information about her father's death.

Eric was frustrated that he couldn't talk to Tess, and he was uncertain whether he was going in the right direction, which made it worse. He'd managed to get his brother back, and his parents, but now he found himself searching yet again for someone he cared about with little or no information on where to find them.

The next tram glided up just as they reached the boarding area. It was so quiet, they couldn't hear it until it was right in front of them. The doors parted, and they stepped on, along with a few others. There was plenty of space. As soon as they were in position, Seth threw on his wheel locks and ripped open the bag on his lap. Lakey was nearly finished her first box, and Seth obviously felt he was behind. His chopsticks materialized as if summoned magically, and he had his first mass of noodles halfway to his mouth when his phone rang. He paused midshovel and looked at the others. Eric and Michael were grinning at him, but Lakey didn't seem to have noticed. Seth sighed, stuck the chopsticks back in the box, and pulled out his phone. He held it up for them briefly. "No ID," he said, unimpressed. He gazed at his lunch as he put the phone to his ear. "Yeah?"

Eric and Michael glanced at each other, still grinning. They stopped as Seth's expression changed. He sat up, and his eyes widened.

"Mom! Hi!"

"Uh-oh," said Michael.

"No, you didn't wake me. We're up! Just getting something to eat." Seth looked at his noodles then over at Lakey, who hadn't noticed her brother's conversation. He picked a piece of broccoli out of the box and threw it at her. She scowled at him, protecting her food, but when he mouthed the word "Mom," her face paled. "Yeah, thought we'd get an early start," Seth continued. He looked at his watch. "How's Oahu? You see Kekoa since you been there?"

He paused. "I'm not trying to change the subject; I'm genuinely interested. How's the weather? You should be seeing the tail end of a system I've been tracking... No, we had to jet. School's in a bit of a low-swing phase anyway, so we aren't missing much. It's this system... Yeah, took the rig up to Chesterman. Sun's up and the lineup's sparse. The wave should be just what we're looking for. Couldn't pass it up... She's here; she's right beside me. She's good. Really good. Best trip ever. She hasn't broken anything all day. It's like the best day ever... No, it's cool. After today, we'll be tapped. We'll just DL the vibe from there and pack it in. You're still back Friday, right? We'll see you when you get home."

He listened for a long time, nodding frequently and adding the occasional "uh-hunh." Eventually, he said, "Okay, thanks, shaka to Dad. Love you. Bye." Seth ended the call and sat stock-still for a full ten seconds.

"Dude, we are so busted," said Lakey solemnly.

"Ya think?" Seth replied. "It's like 3:00 a.m. in Hawaii right now. She knows something's up."

"What do we do?"

"There's only one thing we *can* do. We have to get home before they do. And for us, that means flying to Montreal and driving across the country. By *Friday*."

"Oh, man," Lakey mused. She folded her box of noodles closed. Eric thought her appetite must have been affected by the news. But then she opened the second box, and he realized that the first one was just empty. She started in on her second course with a thoughtful look.

Eric also saw acceptance creep in to Seth's expression as he reached for his chopsticks again.

The tram had made one sharp turn to the right early on but had otherwise moved in straight lines, making occasional stops. The ride was very smooth, and they hardly noticed the speed changes.

"Our stop's just up ahead," said Michael as he looked out the window.

Seth seemed inspired by this and focused more intently on his food. He lifted another mass of noodles, larger than the first, but before he could get it in his mouth, his phone rang again. "You have *got* to be kidding me," he said as he shoved the chopsticks back in the box and looked at the screen. "No ID," he added. Lakey continued to eat, though she appeared to be listening this time. Seth swiped the screen to answer. "Look, Mom, I'm really sorry..."

Eric and Michael watched him again, trying to show more sympathy than amusement, though they weren't that successful. Seth's eyes widened again.

"Tess?"

Eric and Michael reacted with stunned silence. Lakey's reaction was muffled by noodles that seemed to come at least partway out of her nose and was followed by fits of coughing that drew looks from other passengers. Seth put a hand to his opposite ear as he strained to hear.

"Are you okay? Where are you?"

"Turin?" He looked at Eric. "As in Italy?"

Seth leaned to the side, resting an elbow on one of his wheels.

"We're good. We're in France, actually. Looking for you."

"That's the one. We arrived in Nice a couple of hours ago. Hey, I have your phone here."

He switched his phone to the other hand, listening.

"Well, there's a funny story behind that."

He looked at Eric again.

"That's quite a story, too. I better let him tell it."

Seth listened for a moment longer then held the phone out to Eric, who took it and looked at the floor as he put it to his ear. "Tess?" He felt his face flush.

"Hi, Eric."

"You're okay?"

"Yes, fine. I would have called sooner, but someone stole my phone."

"Yes, I know. We got it back for you."

"Seth told me. That's amazing! I hope you didn't go through too much trouble. I didn't have anyone's number without it, so I called the school and spoke to my roommate, Jane. She was able to get Seth's number for me. How did it go in Rome?"

The conversation felt so casual and plain, like a pleasant call between friends who don't have much in common. Eric felt irritated with himself. "Tess, I'm really sorry," he said. He turned away from the others, keeping his eyes on the floor. "I've been such an idiot. You were right; I have no people skills, and I shouldn't be calling the shots in any kind of situation, let alone one that could mean people I care about might get hurt. I should have been more understanding and supportive in Toronto, and I should have paid more attention to what you were going through." He tapped his foot against the base of a pole. "I'm sorry," he repeated.

"It's all right. I understand. There's no way anyone can do or say all the right things in the kinds of situations we've been in. It's not like either of us does this kind of thing every day." She paused. Eric pictured her tilting her head to the side, like she did when she was about to ask a thoughtful question. "How's Angel?"

The tram pulled in to their stop near the train station. Michael gestured to Eric to direct him.

"Uh, good … she's good. I think." Eric was caught off-guard by the question, and he was trying to stay with the others amid the people around the tram. "She's not here."

"Not there? Did something happen?"

"She's fine. She's with her father. They went with my parents to take John and Ada to see Ada's father."

"*WHAT*" Tess exclaimed. It came out almost as a scream. Eric reflexively pulled the phone away from his ear.

He shook his head, snapping out of it. "It's a long story. I'll tell you as soon as I see you. Are you travelling? Can you meet us?"

"Did you say '*Ada*'?"

"Yes, sorry. I'll explain, I promise. We'll need to check the train schedules to see how soon we can be in Turin, but we're on our way to the station now. We'll know shortly. Where can I call you? Your number didn't come up on the phone."

Tess hesitated. "I'll come to you," she said. "I'm travelling by car. Seth said you're in Nice, right? Just a minute." She paused again. Eric couldn't hear anything and wondered whether it was because there was nothing to hear or because Tess was covering the mouthpiece. When she came back on, he still couldn't tell. "Meet me in Monte Carlo. There's a church not far from the train station, the Chapelle Sainte-Dévote; you just have to walk down the hill toward the water. Your phone will tell you where. I'll be there in just over two hours."

"We can do that, no problem," he said. "How do you know about this place?"

"My dad told me about it."

"That's right, you mentioned — Grace Kelly and Monaco. Did you find out anything about him?"

"I did, actually. But it would be better if we didn't talk about it over the phone."

"You're starting to sound like everyone else I've talked to over the phone in the last ten days."

"Well then, you know what to do, don't you, Runnerboy?" He could tell she was smiling. He thought of her smile, could see her face in his mind, and willed time to move faster.

4

GRACE KELLY WAS HERE

They missed the 2:08 high-speed train to Monaco and had to wait nearly an hour for the next regular train. It wasn't far — the trip only took twenty-five minutes — and they arrived more than half an hour before Tess was supposed to get there. Seth and Lakey had postponed their emergency evacuation, deciding instead that they couldn't pass up the chance to go to Monte Carlo. "Are you kidding me?" Lakey had asked incredulously. "Monaco Grand Prix! Ring any bells? Only the best F1 race in the world. S'all right, though, you go. Sethie and me, we'll just fly home. Are you crazy?"

They left the underground train station — the only station in Monaco, actually — from a lower level and walked the short distance down the steep slope to the Sainte-Dévote Chapel. Monte Carlo was unlike any place Eric had ever seen. High buildings, most very old but in perfect condition, were stacked tightly around each other everywhere. The land was steep, and the roads were so tight, it seemed impractical to get around by car, which made the idea of an F1 race here seem incredible. Driving from the train station to the church would have involved several switchbacks through such narrow streets that it might actually be faster to walk. The entire city-state was only two square kilometres, a little larger than the Vatican but much more populated. From checking it out during the train ride, Eric found it was the most densely populated country in the world, and according to Wikipedia, thirty percent of the people were millionaires. It showed. The area in front of the church was close to the marina, and jammed together to fit them all in were the most ridiculously expensive-looking yachts Eric had ever seen.

It actually made him laugh. They were ships, really, with designs he hadn't even known existed.

"It's here!" Lakey exclaimed. "Right. Here." She and Seth had continued through the square in front of the church to the narrow street that ran in beside it. "The Grand Prix, Sethie! Right here!" She knelt down and touched the pavement. Seth had to tug her backward as a van flashed by. "Look!" she added, unfazed. She pointed at a monument on a small grass island. It was a statue of an old-fashioned racecar and driver. "William Grover-Williams! The first winner in 1929. Oh, I'd love to get my hands on that Bugatti." She walked across to it. Fortunately, there were no cars passing at the moment. Seth followed her over while Eric and Michael turned back toward the church.

Sainte-Dévote Chapel was eleventh-century, nestled in what seemed like a ravine with cliffs rising up on both sides, the rock faces giving way to ancient stone walls in some places. The design was Neo-Greek, which meant it was probably overhauled in the nineteenth century. It was small, with smooth, cream-coloured walls and a dome-covered bell tower that rose high above the peak on the right side. Arches supporting roadways passed overhead in front and behind, framing the church from above. Trees covering the slopes on both sides offered contrast, softness, and acoustic dampening. A few wide steps that extended the width of the building were all that separated it from the courtyard, with its tightly packed cobblestones in arching patterns. In a place where buildings were piled around each other, the way the church was situated gave it a rare and notable feeling of seclusion.

Eric and Michael sat on the steps, setting their bags beside them. It wasn't long before Tess arrived. When she did, she wasn't alone.

A small, beaten white van, twenty years old at least, made a right, went past a "Do Not Enter" sign, and stopped next to a series of concrete posts about fifty metres away. It was a Citroën, French-made, with a long hood like a car and panels on the sides instead of windows. Tess got out of the passenger side, her eyes already on Eric, apparently having seen him before they'd stopped. She started toward him immediately. The driver stayed inside the van with the engine running. As Eric and Michael stood to meet her, she hurried the last few steps and hugged Eric warmly.

"It's so good to see you," she said. She moved on to Michael and hugged him as well. "Where are Seth and Lakey?"

"Out playing in traffic," Eric replied. "I haven't heard any screeching tires, so I don't think they've been clipped yet." He shifted his gaze. "Who's in the van?"

"Eric," she took his hand, "the most wonderful thing has happened. I found my *father*."

"*What?*" Eric looked back toward the driver. He couldn't make out any features. "He's *with* you?"

Tess looked expectantly toward the vehicle. The door opened, and a man got out. The situation felt oddly similar to the one at the airport in Oakland when Tess introduced Eric to Williams. Eric's guard went up instinctively.

Eric had talked to Tess about her father, but he'd never seen a photo. Eric didn't know what he looked like. The man coming toward them was not as tall as Eric, and he seemed both unimposing and unremarkable. Still some distance away, Eric could easily see the family resemblance in the shape of his face and the colour of his hair, and his eyes were identical to hers.

"Mr. *E*?" Squealed a voice from across the parking area. It was Lakey. She and Seth were on their way back from the street when she'd seen him get out of the van.

The man didn't startle. Tess had probably told him the twins would be here, so he may have been somewhat prepared. "Hello, Lakey," he said. "Hi, Seth."

"Holy crap!" Lakey turned to her brother. "Look, Seth!"

Seth and the man gave dap handshakes. The wheelchair thing would have been new to him, but he gave no notice of it.

"Eric, check it!" Lakey called. "Tess's dad!"

Eric glanced around awkwardly but didn't see anyone paying special attention to them. When they met, introductions were rather anticlimactic, thanks to Lakey. Sam Edwards shook hands warmly with Eric and Michael, but for Eric the meeting felt odd, and not just because he had previously thought the man to be dead.

"It's nice to meet you," Sam said. "I understand you've had quite a trip."

"We have," answered Eric. "But I have to say seeing you is up there in the Biggest Surprises category."

"Yes, I know what you mean. It was the same for me." Sam glanced at Tess. "Why don't we go somewhere to get acquainted? We could go inside the church; I'm sure we won't be disturbed there."

"How about the airport?" Eric suggested. "I want more than anything to hear about everything that's happened," he looked at Tess, "and we have a lot of catching up to do, but as much as I'd love to stay a really long time in Monte Carlo, there's someplace else we need to be. We can talk on the way, and once you've heard what I have to say, you can decide what you'd like to do."

After some discussion, they decided to pile into the van, Sam driving, Seth in the passenger seat, and the others on the floor in the back. Eric's side spoke first, giving Tess and Sam a description of everything that had happened since they'd left Montreal: the first trip to the Vatican when they arrived, their conversation with Father Bourke and Angel's follow-up with him, their second visit the next day and how they found a secret chamber beneath a tower and with Ada in it, how they travelled to Palermo to Francesco Azzarà's lab, where they found Eric and Michael's parents, about Williams and Sallah's heroics, and how Williams had been injured. They spoke of the catacombs where Falco had taken Gabriel and Clara, and how two of their research team had died in the fire that was intended to kill them all. Their story ended with their trip to Nice, their recovery of Tess's phone, and their plan to meet everyone in Norway.

Sam knew something about the people involved already from what Tess had told him. He showed a lot of interest in Cardinal Abito and Brother Marcus, and also in Falco, though Eric wasn't able to give him much, just the few details his parents had provided.

Tess went next, describing her arrival in Lyon, getting stonewalled at Interpol, her decision to go to Switzerland, and the people she met along the way. She talked about Joëlle and her trip to La Breya to see the place where a plane crashed five years ago. She told them how her phone was stolen on the train, how she overheard a conversation about nymphs that later compelled her to get off the train and go looking for them, and about finding her father instead.

When questions turned to Sam, he downplayed his situation. "Let's just say the rumours of my death were greatly exaggerated." He had a way that was both engaging and dodgy, like someone who liked conversations that involved funny answers to serious questions. They arrived at the airport before anyone could press him further, and opportunities to talk to Tess were lost in the bustle of moving as a group. Tess seemed to be enjoying watching her dad in action, and Eric could feel she was picking up on her father's lead. He would have to wait until they had more time.

Seth had scouted flights during the drive. It turned out to be a good thing they'd left for the airport right away. Seth was able to get Eric and Michael on the last flight out of Nice that would still get them in that night to Trondheim, the city in the Trøndelag region where their parents had gone, a 5:20 on KLM with a stop in Amsterdam. They had to hurry to make it in time. He booked seats for himself and his sister for the following day, a 1:15 nonstop to Montreal, their best option to try to get home before their parents, which they had to admit looked unlikely. The twins didn't seem too upset. "Looks like we'll have to suffer through a night in Monte Carlo without you, Rico," said Lakey with a sigh. As much as Tess wanted to go to Norway and see it through to the end, she and her father made plans to return to Monaco. The decision was an obvious one, but she still appeared to struggle with it.

They drove around to the far side of Nice Côte d'Azur Airport to Terminal 2, the newer and slightly larger of the two terminals, to a parking structure labelled "P5." The sun was setting, and traffic away from the airport was heavy, but the routes around the terminal buildings seemed to flow well. Sam sent everyone ahead, saying it would be better if he stayed with the van and suggesting they say their goodbyes quickly so they didn't miss their flight. Everyone else left the parking structure from the upper level, crossed two walkways that spanned roads below, and entered the terminal.

The inside of this section of the airport was a long, straight corridor with ticket counters on one side and retail outlets on the other. Angled windows with horizontal slats let in what remained of the natural light, casting dim, lined shadows on the tile floor. The ceiling was low, with black metal grates and simple lighting, giving the space a caged-in feel. Michael found a check-in kiosk to print his boarding pass, since he didn't have his phone, and they headed for security.

The security screening area was halfway along the corridor. Retractable blue ribbons attached to metal poles made a maze for passengers to walk through as they approached one of four scanners, two on the left and two on the right. There were less than a dozen people in line, and the scanners on the right side were closed, blocked by grey screens with the airport logo along the top. People were talking in different languages, mostly French, and the atmosphere was subdued.

The entrance to the maze was marked by a large blue archway. When they reached it, Eric and Michael stopped and turned to the others.

Eric looked at Tess and then at the floor. "Strange day, wasn't it?"

Tess smiled. "That's one word for it."

"I have a feeling it's only going to get weirder for you, where you're going," said Lakey.

"He carries the weird wherever he goes," Michael clarified.

Seth checked his phone for the time. "Your parents and the others would have landed in Oslo about half an hour ago. They're scheduled to take off a few minutes after you do, if you want to check in with them."

"I'll give them a call after we go through security."

Tess stepped forward and put her arms around Eric. He bent down so his face was next to hers. "Good luck, Eric," she said softly. "And please be careful. After everything, I really want a chance to meet your mom and dad. Make sure that happens, okay?"

"I will," he replied. "You be careful, too. There's still a lot we need to say."

Tess moved to Michael and hugged him as well. Eric slapped hands and touched shoulders with Seth and hugged Lakey, and Michael did the same.

"After Christmas, we surf The Wharf in Santa Cruz, as discussed, yes?" Michael said.

"You're on, brah," Seth responded.

The brothers passed through the blue archway and joined the short line. Eric looked back toward Tess. A small, impulsive part of his brain was telling him not to go, that leaving was a bad idea. The more rational part — the part committed to catching up with his parents and helping Williams — was calling the shots. There would be time to spend with Tess when both of them had done what they needed to do. *How about now?* thought the impulsive part. *Now's good, too.* He was still contemplating when a small herd of people moved into the maze behind them and blocked his view. Tess, Seth, and Lakey had had to step aside to keep from getting run over.

They appeared to be one large family, four adults and six children of various ages. Eric wasn't entirely sure where they were from, but if he'd had to guess, he would have said Spain. They were loud and excited and used their hands when they talked. They sounded Spanish, but they were talking so fast, he couldn't tell. Another couple, apparently seeing them off, had taken positions next to Seth and Lakey and were waving and calling to the others in a very animated way. Lakey, not to be outdone, started to call and wave to Eric. Seth whacked her in the arm and whispered something to her. Michael laughed. "Here's hoping they both survive until Santa Cruz."

The line inched forward, and a few more people joined them at the back. Eric could see security looking toward the growing numbers and wondering whether they needed to open another scanner. Someone made a call, but no one made a move toward the other side. The agents on duty started moving a little more efficiently, encouraging people to prep for the scanners sooner and gathering the large plastic trays and returning them to the receptacles at the other ends of the conveyers more rapidly.

Eric could feel the tension increase. When it was his and Michael's turns to go through, they had their things ready. Their belts and the contents of

their pockets were inside their bags so that when they reached the stack of
trays, they just placed their bags in them and put them on the rollers. An agent
checked their boarding passes and put their trays through the scanner. Eric
and Michael stepped through the metal detector one after the other without
incident and moved toward the conveyer. It took longer for their bags to
come through, as the agent repeatedly reversed and advanced the conveyer.
Eric and Michael glanced at each other. Eventually, their trays came out of
the machine, but an agent was there to meet them.

"*Est-ce que c'est vos bagages?*" the agent asked.

Eric nodded, not sure of the words but definitely getting the message.

The agent put his hand on the next tray and looked at Michael. "*Et
vous?*" When Michael confirmed, the agent took the trays from the rollers
and stacked them on a counter behind him. "*Attendez ici s'il vous plaît.*" He
turned toward a phone at the end of the counter, picked up the receiver, and
placed it to his ear without dialling any numbers. After a moment, he said
something Eric couldn't hear and hung up.

While Eric and Michael waited, the family behind them was attempting
to prep their belongings to come through the scanners. There seemed to be
some kind of problem. Two of the adults, possibly a married couple, were
arguing about the contents of the woman's bag. The happy excitement phase
appeared over. The man started taking big plastic bottles out of the woman's
luggage and throwing them into large, clear plastic bags hanging from metal
frames next to the scanner, a place to dispose of liquids that weren't allowed
on the plane. The woman was freaking out, nearly to the point of hysterics.
The agent who had made the phone call sighed exasperatedly and went to
help deal with the situation. A moment later, two uniformed guards arrived
and approached Eric and Michael.

"Eric and Michael Bakker?" the first agent asked. He spoke with a heavy
accent. "Can you come with us, please?"

Eric's warning light was on already, and now he felt a shot of adrenaline.
Trying to hide it, he frowned at the agent. "What's this about?" he asked.

"Routine security procedure. A secondary screen." He held out his hand. "Passports, please." A third agent appeared from the hallway beyond security. The woman behind them screeched as something heavy was dropped into the receptacle.

Eric didn't respond right away. A beat passed, his eyes zeroed-in on the agent's. The man's eyes narrowed a fraction, and Eric could see something register in him. In that instant, Eric turned to his left and vaulted over the tray rollers toward their bags. Michael took advantage of the distraction and rushed forward, drove his shoulder into the agent, who had been reaching for something attached to his belt, and propelled him backward into one of the other guards behind. Both sprawled on the floor. Eric grabbed Michael's pack from the top tray and threw it to him, then swung the empty tray hard at the third agent, who ducked to avoid taking it in the face. Eric quickly took his own pack and jumped the conveyer again. Michael had turned ahead of him and was sprinting back toward the corridor. When Eric reached the end of the security counter, he grabbed the tall stack of plastic trays and pulled them down behind him. They clattered to the floor and spread out like they were multiplying. The other agents were either behind counters or had been involved with the Spanish family and couldn't react quickly enough to stop them. Hearing the crashing noise created by the falling trays and seeing the two boys running away, the rest of the passengers, apparently fearing the worst, scattered immediately. Eric locked eyes with Tess as he sprinted past, trying to convey that she should stay away so she wouldn't be implicated, but he nearly collided with a woman running in the corridor and had to look away. He launched himself over a row of seats, narrowly missing a man who was crouched behind them, and headed for the exit.

Outside, a Mercedes sedan was idling next to the curb, a taxi light on the roof and the driver helping his fare unload their bags. Eric and Michael both ran to the driver side. Michael got in front, Eric got in the back, and they sped away, leaving the cab driver cursing at them and waving his fist.

Eric looked back through the rear window. "What now?"

"We get away from the airport," Michael replied. "But we can't keep this car; it's probably LoJacked. We need to ditch it. Quickly."

Michael drove down the ramp from the terminal. Another longer ramp stayed high on the left, creating an overpass. As the road curved beneath the overpass, their path was suddenly blocked by a gate. Michael slammed on the brakes, stopping the car just before it hit the red and white bar. As soon as they stopped, the gate went up. Michael hit the gas again, and the car shot forward. A traffic circle looped away from them, and Michael was faced with a choice. A sign showed right for Terminal 1, Nice, and the cargo terminal, left for Terminal 2, rental car return, the parking garages, and a symbol Eric couldn't interpret fast enough. Instinctively, Michael went right, headed for Nice. They narrowly missed the rear end of a car that went left around the circle. The ramp on their left rapidly descended to their level, and a parking garage emerged beyond it. The concrete barrier separating the lanes ended and was replaced by a tapered island edged with a curb. There was a similar curb on the other side, separating the middle lane from a third road that ran next to the parking garage. This curb ended at a row of white posts that forced traffic toward Terminal 1.

Michael apparently changed his mind. He braked hard, and the Mercedes bucked, its back end swinging to the right as the car aimed at the curb. The first wheel hit, lurching the front end upward. Michael powered the car across the middle lane toward the second curb. The car bounced upward again as it jumped through the gap between the concrete barrier and the white posts. A car in the left lane — the same car they had narrowly missed a few seconds earlier — had to screech to a halt to avoid the collision. A horn blared. Michael continued around the corner, through a stop sign, and into the lane that ran along the side of the parking garage. Streetlights along the top of the wall were on, brightening the road as darkness gathered. The wall was opaque glass — Eric could see the parking levels through it — and there was a gas station opposite. He looked out the rear window again but couldn't see the terminal to tell if guards were coming after them, though they had to be.

Instead of switching to the right lane and following the sign that said "*Sortie,*" Michael stayed in the left lane and followed the signs toward

Terminal 2. "I have an idea," he said. He made two more lefts and slowed down as he entered the parking garage labelled "P6." He took the car up to the second level of the four-level structure and found a spot to leave it.

"Should we wipe it down?" asked Eric.

"Doesn't matter," his brother replied. "They know who we are. Tracking is the issue." He looked around them. "There'll be cameras. We need to move."

They spun over the rails to go down the stairs faster and came out on the street across from the gas station. They turned left and walked hurriedly in the direction of the *Sortie* they'd passed earlier. There was a bus shelter near the corner, hidden from the road by a fence and some bushes. As they approached the shelter, they saw it was a shuttle for the airport.

"Try Seth," Michael suggested.

Eric took out his phone just as a white van pulled up behind them. No one spoke as they climbed in the back next to Lakey and Tess and closed the doors. Sam eased out into the light traffic, slowly heading north away from the airport. After a short distance, he looped around a traffic circle and took a ramp onto a larger highway that turned west. A blue sign above the road indicated they were headed toward Marseille, Toulon, and Cannes. Nice and Monaco were behind them, to the east.

"So I'm guessing you've missed your flight," said Lakey, breaking the silence.

"What did they say to you?" Tess asked.

"They wanted us to give them our passports and go with them for a secondary screen," Eric replied. "I didn't give them a chance to explain why."

"You've been flagged," said Sam. "They would have incarcerated you until someone arrived to question you. It would have taken a long time. You were right to run." He took out his phone and swiped the screen rapidly with his thumb. "You won't be able to travel using your own names anymore." He placed the phone to his ear. Whoever he was calling must have answered right away.

"Carlos," he said, "I need a favour."

5

NEW THREAT

By the time they arrived in Cannes about half an hour later, three key things had happened: first, Sam's contact, Carlos Ruiz Moreno, an Interpol agent from Colombia who was at the Command and Coordination Centre in Lyon, had arranged for them to get out of sight while he worked on travel plans. He was confident he would have something within the hour. Second, Sam revealed that prior to going into hiding in Switzerland, he had been seconded to Interpol's Sub-Directorate for the Trafficking of Human Beings as an undercover specialist from the Royal Canadian Mounted Police. And third, Lakey declared she was hungry.

"But come on! What happened with the plane crash?"

"I can't tell you that," Sam replied. "I mean, I could tell you, but then I'd have to, you know, kill you, and you wouldn't *believe* the paperwork involved in *that*." He rolled his eyes dramatically.

"Oh, man, you're a *spy?*" Lakey looked at Eric then at her brother. "Dude, that's almost as good as vampire hunter."

There were still some traces of purple in the sky as they left the A8 at Exit 41, the white lines on the pavement glowing from the headlights. A sign above the exit mentioned Cannes-Mandelieu, with a picture of an airplane pointing in that direction. The van travelled a short way north on a smaller highway before it looped south, passed through three more traffic circles, and approached the small airport. The last turn took them in front of a hotel with a green awning prominently featuring the word "RESTAURANT." Lakey moaned and rubbed her stomach.

The airport in Cannes was small and featured light business aviation, a couple of flight schools, and several private planes. There was a row of hangars in an area perpendicular to the runway and adjacent terminal, each one large enough for two or three of the small jets or a few of the single-prop planes that sat in orderly, designated spaces on the tarmac or the grass infield outside. As they approached, a man met them, dressed in stained coveralls and a baseball hat that was pulled low over his eyes, and slid a white metal gate open. Sam drove the car through, turned left, and pulled inside the first hangar, H4.

The interior was dark and deserted, no planes or people. The maintenance worker who'd let them through the gate did not follow them into the hangar but pulled the heavy sliding panel doors closed behind them and disappeared. Everyone got out of the van, cautious at first. Sam checked the doors to the adjacent offices and found a small conference room where they could wait. There was a green sign on the wall with 'Siegel' written in yellow block letters. The table was rectangular, and there was a white board on the wall at one end.

"You're probably wondering how we managed this," said Sam.

"The thought had crossed my mind," said Eric.

"The Siegel Group is a big transport and logistics company out of Brussels. They have a presence in nearly every transportation centre in Europe, which makes them useful to Interpol."

"A front?"

"An affiliation. I suspect Carlos will be able to work something out to have you leave from here and go directly to Trondheim."

"Anybody for a takeout order?" asked Lakey. "Sethie and me, we'll make the run." She gestured toward the furniture in the room. "Look, we've got a table and chairs and everything."

"We should wait until we hear back," said Tess.

"No, it's okay," said Sam. "We should all eat. It's hard to tell how long we'll be here, and there might not be a good chance to fuel up once things start moving." He turned to Lakey and held up his hands. "I'll take anything made of meat that I get to eat with *these*. Green things are acceptable but not required."

Seth and Lakey lit up. They paused long enough to get a rough idea of other orders before they scrambled for the door. Sam stopped them just before they made it. "Here, take this. Dinner's on me." He took some money from his pocket and handed it to Seth. "Better to avoid plastic from here on out, Bruno," he added. Eric learned later that this had been his nickname for Seth when he was a kid. "And maybe make something up if somebody asks." Seth nodded and he and his sister left excitedly.

Eric sat down in one of the chairs at the conference table. "So you're a police officer," he said to Sam. Tess sat down across the corner from him.

"Not exactly," Sam replied.

Michael circled to another part of the small room. "And now you're with Interpol."

"No, technically, I'm dead."

"And why is that?" asked Eric. He wasn't exactly suspicious. There was too much trust coming from Tess and too much reassurance in Sam's manner for him to doubt his authenticity. It was the circumstances and how they might affect what he and Michael were doing that made him cautious.

Sam stood behind a chair at the end of the table, his hands resting along the backrest. Tess sat watching him, frequently glancing at Eric, seemingly to gauge his reaction, as though she'd already heard what her father was about to say. "I'm not a copper," he said. "At least not in the typical sense. I'm more of an asset."

"You mean an asset like Jason Bourne is an asset?" asked Eric.

Sam shook his head quickly and looked down. "No, no of course not." Then he shrugged and grinned. "Well, okay, maybe a *little* like that." He pulled the chair out and sat down. "I'm an engineer. I used to work for an oil company that has interests all over the place, but especially in Russia and the Middle East. I was asked to gather information on some bad guys one time, and when it went well, I got picked up by a special program in the RCMP that gave me the training I needed to find out more information on other bad guys. Oil is everything in some parts of the world, and where there's that kind of easy money, there will be human exploitation. I got involved in trafficking when one thing led to another, and I found I had an aptitude and an interest in gathering information that could help police stop people from doing it. So I helped. But like I said, we're talking about big money, which can go a long way. Someone at Interpol gave me up to a crime boss who ran the sex trade in Transnistria in Moldova." Sam looked at Tess. "They came after me and vowed to kill my family, so my death, though unplanned and highly inconvenient, had to be convincing."

"Unplanned?" Eric said.

"There was a plane, I was supposed to be on it, and it crashed. Several important people — some my friends — were killed, mostly French officials and task force operatives returning to Paris and Lyon from Ukraine, where we'd been set up. We'd done some major damage to the trafficking operation. However, several investigators' family members were murdered in retribution around the time of the crash, which was not a coincidence, by the way.

"I don't have Jason Bourne-esque lethality; I'm a watcher and a learner and a reporter. The only thing I could do to protect my family until the mole could be found or the entire Transnistrian human trafficking establishment could be wiped out, would be to be dead. So I'd appreciate it," he waved a finger back and forth between them, "if you could keep this between us."

"Surely Interpol could have gotten you out," said Michael. "Or the Canadian government could have done something in secret to bring you home?"

"Maybe they could and maybe they couldn't, but don't call me 'Shirley,'" Sam replied. Tess groaned, but Michael frowned. "Sorry," Sam clarified, "bad movie reference — you guys probably don't get exposed to much seventies humour." He gestured toward the Siegel sign on the wall. "Human trafficking operations tend to be a lot like transport and logistics companies; they involve big networks, and they have connections everywhere. Except with traffickers, it's much harder to tell where the connections are. I haven't been able to move around much, even within Switzerland, without being worried about getting spotted. I thought about contacting the Canadian government, even started on a trip to the consulate in Bern one time, but until I could be sure the threat wasn't there anymore, I couldn't do it. And because of the leak at Interpol — a group that is also very well connected, as the name suggests — I haven't been able to get any help. Not officially, anyway. Would you bet your family's lives on that?" He shook his head. "Carlos is the only one who knows about me. He's been working hard to take down the traffickers, and he's been trying to find the mole, but he has to be careful, too. If anyone finds out what he's been doing, we're both *goners*." His eyes went wide when he said the last word, and he smiled.

"But now you're out and moving," said Eric.

Sam tilted his head to the side as he looked at Eric, but before he could reply, his phone rang. He answered it, leaning back in his chair as he put it to his ear. "Carlos! What do you have for me?" He listened for a while, offering the occasional "uh-hunh" but otherwise showing little reaction to the information he was receiving. He stood up and wandered out into the hangar.

Tess watched him go, and Eric could see again the extra bit of confidence she'd gained since finding her father.

"Quite a sacrifice he's made," said Eric. He hoped she would take it the way he'd intended.

Tess looked at him and smiled almost sadly. "He said he knew it had to be done, but he was never sure it was the right thing to do." She sighed. "I feel such peace. It's like the last five years have just been erased, and we get to start again."

"What about your mom?"

"We still haven't told her. It's better if she doesn't know until we can get home, but when it happens, it will be the best possible thing. This will cure her."

"Can you even go home?" asked Michael.

"We haven't figured that out yet. There might be other options; we're still working on it."

Sam was on the phone with Moreno for what seemed like a long time. When he returned, his face still didn't reveal anything, but before he could relay what he'd learned, Seth and Lakey came spilling through the doors of the outer offices toward the conference room. They were carrying several bags containing large plastic containers.

"There was a *buffet*!" Lakey exclaimed. "I don't think they normally do takeout with that, but they seemed okay with it when I gave them all my money. You should *see* what we got!"

Sam laughed as he watched the twins unload. "Get started," he said, "but we might have to take it with us." Seth, who had a piece of baguette halfway to his mouth, stopped, but Lakey didn't appear to have heard. "There'll be a plane and a pilot ready in about twenty minutes. Plus, I have some news." Lakey apparently heard that part. She stopped piling pasta on a lid she was using as a plate and looked at Sam. "First, Seth and Lakey, you guys have been flagged just like Eric and Michael, and you will be detained if you show up for your flight tomorrow."

Seth and Lakey looked at each other. "We are so dead," they said, and Eric knew it had nothing to do with airport security or Transnistrian crime bosses.

"Second," Sam continued, "Carlos checked on the state of things in Norway, and he found something. There's been an incident. Sør-Trøndelag police in Trondheim contacted Interpol about two men who were discovered at NTNU, the Norwegian University of Science and Technology. Apparently, they'd broken in and were going through some documents, did some damage, but escaped before they could be apprehended. They have images and were looking for help in identifying them."

Seth set down his baguette and reached for his computer.

"When was this?" asked Michael.

"Day before yesterday."

"What department at the university?" Eric asked.

"Geoscience and Petroleum," Sam replied. "They were going through records and artefacts. Made a mess, but didn't seem to take anything. It wasn't clear what they were after. They might have been interrupted before they could find it."

"Why would Carlos think this would be relevant to us?" Tess asked.

"I'm sure he doesn't know if it is, but it's the only thing that's showing up in the system, so he thought he should pass it along. It might not be in the ballpark, but it sounds like it's at least in the same league as what's going on here."

Eric heard a loud slap from behind him. Everyone turned. Lakey had her hand against her forehead as she looked over Seth's shoulder at the computer screen. "Oh, sweet cheese and crackers," she breathed.

Eric moved toward them. The others followed, and Seth turned the computer to face them. The screen showed a webpage with the Interpol banner at the top. In the centre was a grainy black-and-white photo, a still image taken from a security camera. It showed two men apparently moving through a hallway, one slightly ahead of the other, about to pass beneath the camera's location. It was dark, and it was hard to make out features. Eric leaned closer to look at the first figure, but there was no mistaking the self-assured walk and tailored appearance.

It was Riccardo Azzarà.

6

TRONDHEIM

Eric thought back to what he had assumed were the last moments of Riccardo Azzarà's life. He and Williams had gone into the high-security observation area of Gilroy Stockton's research facility, where Azzarà was the lead scientist. Stockton had Michael on the floor while a guard held a gun to Michael's head. One of the Vidi was there, locked in a cell. Stockton used a device created by Azzarà to incapacitate all of them, including Williams, by acting on the dreylagr inside them. Azzarà had discovered that dreylagr, the special fluid that was used to embalm the dead during the ritual that brought them back to life, not only seemingly sustained that life indefinitely, but was also highly conductive when stimulated in a particular way. Stockton used the device to immobilize the Vidi prisoner, and because he had also given large amounts of dreylagr to Michael as part of Azzarà's experiments, it worked devastatingly well on him, too. When Seth and Lakey cut the power to get them out, the weakened Vidi escaped, but not before eviscerating Stockton. Eric tried to recall what had happened to Azzarà. He'd seen the scientist on the floor against the wall; he wasn't moving. Eric thought he was dead. Clearly, he'd been wrong.

Sam seemed aware of Azzarà; presumably Tess had already filled him in. "Who's the other guy?" he asked.

Eric leaned in again. It was harder to make out the second man, who was slightly farther back and had his head turned. He was smaller than Azzarà and wore a heavy coat and thick scarf.

"He worked for Stockton," said Michael. "He was his assistant or something."

"His name is Davis," said Tess. "He's the one who took us from the security building to the room in the research facility."

Eric remembered him. He'd also been there when Stockton was killed.

"Why would they be in Norway?" asked Seth.

Eric looked at Michael, thinking of their parents. "How could they possibly have known they would be going there?"

"They couldn't," Michael replied. He looked at his watch. "They should have landed ten minutes ago. They think we're in the air. You should call them."

Eric tapped Michael's number. The call went straight to voicemail. He sent a text asking them to call.

There was a noise outside. The hangar door slid open a short distance and stopped. The maintenance worker from earlier stood in the opening. He nodded to Sam and turned away, leaving the door open.

"Well!" said Sam, slapping his thighs and starting to get up. "Grab your things; it's time to go. Somebody find a wheelbarrow for Seth and Lakey's food. There must be one around here somewhere. We'll divvy up on the plane."

Eric glanced at Seth and Lakey then looked at Sam inquiringly. "You're not suggesting we all go to Trondheim."

Sam was helping the twins pack their dinner. "Sure I am! S'n'L can't really stay here now that French police are on their trail, and they can't leave in a normal way without basically holding up a big flashing light telling everyone where they are. This is as convenient a lift as they're going to get." He picked up the bag he had been filling and started toward the hangar door. "As for us," he gestured toward Tess, "I can't let Tess miss out on a chance to go to *Norway*, can I? It's beautiful there. All those fjords. She'll love it. Home of Detective Harry Hole! It'll be awesome."

Fifteen minutes later, they were airborne from a runway that took them straight north. They hadn't had time to gather much information before leaving, and their plane was an older model that didn't have Wi-Fi, so there was nothing to do while they travelled but wait. It didn't take long to finish off the food they'd brought, and then Lakey was out for the rest of trip, snoring like a buzz saw. When Seth confronted her, she denied it at first then blamed the altitude and went back to sleep.

Eric tried to reach his parents whenever he could get a signal, but there was no answer. It was probably because there was no service at the farm where they were planning to meet, but he couldn't be sure. For some reason, not knowing and not being able to do anything about it didn't agitate him. Instead of getting that twitchy feeling like he needed to move, he felt relaxed and calm. He had done everything he could do to this point, and now his job was to sit in an airplane. Tess was back, safe and sound, and everyone had a job to do. It was a good team.

"I think you're getting the hang of this," said Michael. He and Eric had ended up together in the middle section of the plane, with Seth and Lakey at the front and Sam and Tess at the back.

"Which part?" Eric asked. He set his phone on the tray in front of him.

"The part where you let good ideas become good decisions regardless of where they come from."

Eric gave a laugh. It came naturally, and he surprised himself a little. Normally his brother's philosophizing set him off. "Hey, when you're right, you're right."

Michael took a drink from a bottle of water and set it down. He pretended to try to hide a smug expression. "Do you remember that time in Mongolia when Dad had his wallet stolen? The guide ripped us off when he made up that story about some creature."

Eric nodded. "The Äbädä."

"Right! That's what it was called. That thing that was supposed to wear its shoes on the wrong feet. We had to put on all our clothes inside out to keep it from clubbing us to death."

Eric laughed again. "You know Dad. Not one to take the chance, is he? The guy didn't make it up, though. Plenty of mention from North Asia to Turkey."

Michael shrugged, not buying it. "Whatever. Got the job done. Point is, Dad might not know the difference between one of his legends and some shark trying to score."

"I don't know, Mike. I wouldn't worry too much about that — Mom's with him. She's better at this than all of us combined. And Owen's there, too. They seem to work well together."

"What about Angel? If the plan is to get in to the mountain, how do you think she'll handle it? She didn't seem to do so well in the crypt in Montreal."

"I get the feeling Angel is the type that won't let anything stop her from doing what she wants to do, even if it's herself."

"I agree, there, Sigmund," said Michael. "I for one wouldn't want to be on the wrong side when she winds it up. I think I'd prefer the Äbädä."

"I have some insight into her problem, though," said Eric. He picked up his own bottle of water. "I had a conversation with Owen before we arrived in France."

Eric had run into the scientist in the galley early that morning. Eric couldn't sleep and was in search of more baklava, and Owen was trying to stay awake and was looking for more coffee. The scientist seemed to be returning to normal, as far as Eric could tell. He was focused and engaging, and his personality tended to fill the room. The smile Eric was used to seeing in the research team photo, the one taken at the dig in Libya, was showing more often, and Eric could occasionally hear his laughter from other parts of the ship. During the few minutes alone together, Eric had told him about Angel's panic attack at Notre-Dame-de-Bon-Secours.

"He told me why it happened."

Michael raised an eyebrow. "Yeah?"

"You remember what Williams said about how Owen volunteers at the children's hospital next to the yacht club? One time he took a bunch of kids to a cave system outside the city. They have crystals and gemstones and fossils, and they do tours for school groups, that kind of thing. Angel went with them, and one time when Owen was showing some kids one part of the cave, Angel wandered off. She ended up in a network of passages that were too small for adults and got lost. All she had with her was a cheap pen light, and the battery died. She was stuck in there in the dark for hours. She was so messed up, she was nearly catatonic."

"How old was she?"

"Six."

Michael cringed. "That explains a lot."

"Only part of it," Eric continued. "After she was home for a while, she told her parents she'd left with another girl who was a few years older than her. They looked everywhere but couldn't find anyone, and no one had reported anyone missing. Also, no one matched the description she gave. Her shrink told her she'd probably imagined the other girl to justify running away. Apparently he didn't agree with her when she told him he was full of shit."

"That sounds about right," Michael said with a chuckle. "So as a result, she has the obvious problem with being in dark, enclosed spaces, but she also has major trust issues."

"Exactly."

"So walking into the basement of a mountain where the people who live there can see in the dark and with an evil scientist on the loose probably wasn't high on her to-do list today."

"And don't forget the army of resourceful undead killer mummies that could be out there somewhere. And who can also see in the dark."

"Right. Don't forget those," Michael agreed. "Honestly, though, if I had to bet my commission on Angel versus the undead killer mummies, I'd have to think about it for a second."

Eric pressed his lips together. "She had a little trouble with them in Chicago. I wasn't sure she was going to keep it together when we were hauling out of there."

"Maybe. But that was before she knew what she was up against. Now that she has some intel, I suspect the reaction will be a little different."

Eric had to agree. He was sure Angel would come out ahead against anybody in at least one area, more than one area in Eric's case. During their travel, Michael had talked with her about her Wing Chun training, and her success in competition was impressive. Hearing Michael talk about this now, Eric felt he was starting to understand her better, and he knew that anything that could be construed as weakness — such as a phobia of underground places — might have a very different effect than on the average person. He hoped he wasn't in her way when she sorted it out.

Eventually, Michael left his seat next to Eric and went to talk to Seth. A few minutes later, Tess came up and sat beside Eric.

"How are you holding up?" she asked.

Eric smiled weakly. "Another day in paradise."

"Michael's knee seems to be doing all right."

"Yes." Eric glanced in his brother's direction. Michael was leaning across the aisle, talking to Seth in an animated way, his hands gesturing for emphasis. "Better than he was before, actually. He downplays it when I ask, but whatever Azzarà did to him didn't just fix his knee."

"Williams said the dreylagr was powerful. And it would have unexpected effects."

Eric shrugged. "If you'd seen what that Stockton's remote control thing did to him, you'd think he was full of the stuff." He looked toward his brother again. For him to be walking less than two weeks after reconstructive knee surgery would have been incredible, for him to be scaling walls at the Vatican or taking down skilled military types in an inferno in Palermo would have been a miracle, but both had happened.

"Still, it's done some good. Do you think Williams will be okay?" Tess asked.

Eric met her eye. "Honestly, I can't see how anyone could come back from that. I guess we'll see just how powerful dreylagr is."

Tess shifted in her seat so she faced Eric more directly. "What's Ada like?"

"Hard to read, which probably isn't surprising. You know that feeling we had around Williams, like time slowed down and he could wait forever? She's like that times ten. And she's so in tune with everything around her — it's incredible considering what she's been through. She redefines stoic."

"Seth and Lakey told me about it. She was trapped in the rubble of the first Lateran Palace for all those years and was found, only to be locked away beneath a tower at the Vatican? It's hard to imagine what it would be like to be so alone for so long. It's almost like one of those vicious old fairy tales."

"They thought she was an angel," said Eric. "A seraph, actually, the highest rank of angel."

"How could she be kept there for so long? Times have changed so much, someone would have said something about it."

"I'm sure hardly anyone knew. Secrets in a place like that are kept for lots of reasons. Sometimes the reasons change over the centuries, but the secrets stay the same." Eric looked at his hands, running a thumb along a calloused finger. "This cardinal my parents talked about seems to be behind it. Abito. Some secret society thing probably, the responsibility passed on from one particular priest to another." Eric folded his hands together. "I don't think we're done with him, though — Abito. Maybe when this is over we can go back to Rome and get into it with him. I suspect my mother will want to sort a few things out."

"I'm looking forward to meeting her."

"My mother?"

Tess nodded.

Eric looked at his hands again. "I'm sure you two will hit it off immediately," he said. "That's what worries me."

"Worries you?" Tess asked, smiling.

"Yeah," Eric replied with a mild scoff. "You have a lot more in common than anyone else I've brought home. I'm sure I'll be the third wheel ten minutes in."

"Oh." Tess lowered her eyes. The smile faded.

Eric could sense a change and felt he'd messed up again. He searched for something else. "Seth told me what happened in Toronto."

She faced him again, composed. "Let's not talk about that. Did I tell you that I picked up a copy of *D'entre les morts* when I was in Lyon? You were right, it's a great read. Makes me appreciate Hitchcock's *Vertigo* even more."

They continued talking, though this time it was different than it had been when they travelled from Victoria to San Francisco what seemed like years ago. Eric found himself watching her intently while she spoke, occasionally distracted by his internal commentary about her insight and her passion, about the way she looked when she talked about what she'd seen and done since he'd found her in the arbutus tree at Brentwood.

He listened, spoke, gestured, and empathized intently, and it became natural for him. It was like a veil lifting, and he understood. By the time they started their descent into Trondheim, they'd gradually, almost imperceptibly moved closer to each other and had talked in lower voices, their heads almost touching. Eric needed the jolt of the wheels on the tarmac to bring him around.

It was after eleven. The plane landed at Trondheim Airport without incident, and the pilot took them directly into a hangar just southeast of the main terminal. Sam's Interpol contact, Moreno, had a car waiting for them inside the hangar; it was an SUV that could handle all six passengers. Eric noticed a long lever mounted beneath the steering column, with two shafts connecting it to the pedals, and realized they were hand controls. Sam must have asked for them to be included. They already had a destination, and during the few minutes when they were making the transition, Seth and Lakey quickly double-checked their route.

Trondheim Airport was about twenty kilometres east of Trondheim, just across the Nord-Trøndelag county line in the small village of Værnes. It was on the edge of a fjord, with a runway that actually extended out into the water. Their route would take them farther east, away from Trondheim and toward the border with Sweden. But when the twins saw what was just south of the airport on the way to Trondheim, they begged Eric to let them go at least that far. Just across the river Stjørdalselva was the village of Hell.

"Come on, man!" pleaded Lakey. "Don't you want to be able to say you've been to Hell and back? Look!" she added, pointing to a map on Seth's computer. "They have a mall called Hell Kjøpesenter! We need warm clothes and stuff — don't you want to go shopping in Hell?" She whacked her brother in the shoulder. "I bet it's super-cold there, too. I bet it'll be a cold day in Hell tomorrow." Seth nodded in agreement.

Eric didn't seem convinced, so Seth followed seamlessly. "Hey, brah, you remember in *Temple of Doom* when Indy is about to cut the rope bridge he's

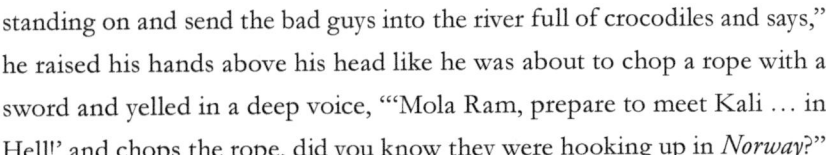

standing on and send the bad guys into the river full of crocodiles and says," he raised his hands above his head like he was about to chop a rope with a sword and yelled in a deep voice, "'Mola Ram, prepare to meet Kali … in Hell!' and chops the rope, did you know they were hooking up in *Norway*?"

Lakey again. "Or in *300* when Gerard Butler says," talking deeper and louder, slightly Scottish, "'Spartans, ready your breakfast and eat hearty, for tonight we dine in Hell!' did you think he meant Norway? We should totally find some place to eat. I really want to dine in Hell. Can we?"

Eric had learned something from their trip to Rome and found himself thinking about how to give them what they wanted, but given the late hour, there was really no other option but to go to the farmhouse to meet the others. The twins accepted this, under the circumstances, but reserved the right to ask again. Eric assured them, smiling, that they would go to Hell eventually.

It was very dark and much colder than it had been in France. The temperature was around freezing, but there wasn't any snow on the ground yet. In the interests of appropriate clothing, Seth checked the weather and found that, despite being sixty-three degrees north, slightly north of Anchorage and Rankin Inlet, extremes were more moderate than upstate New York, with less rain and snow. Everyone had expected to find the ground covered and winter well underway; not so much, but they still needed more clothes than what they had.

Seth sat up front with Sam so he could be close to the SUV's heater. His legs didn't tend to do well with cold. Plus, he was the most highly skilled navigator in the vehicle. They drove along the Stjørdalselva for nearly an hour, past gradually diminishing farmland as the terrain became more uneven. They left the river at a place called Meråker, passed simple block buildings, most of which seemed to be red, and continued upward into forest areas, leaving the farmland behind altogether. They only rarely passed any kind of building, though it was so dark, they couldn't see far from the road. The trees were small and hardy and stood in bunches, with thick undergrowth all around. The pavement ended at a group of buildings set back from the road with a sign out front that said *Velkommen til Grova skisenter.* "'Welcome to the Grova Ski Centre,'" provided Seth, who had already downloaded a Norwegian translator onto his computer. A cross-country skiing club, apparently. "I imagine they have these here like they have churches in Rome."

They continued on the unpaved road under his direction. Sam had to slow down at one point to avoid hitting two animals, large, shaggy brown sheep with white tags on their ears. Their eyes shone brightly when they looked at the truck, reflecting the light from the headlights. A lake emerged on their left. They passed it and came to another. The odd building or small farm sent trace amounts of light toward the road, but otherwise it was complete darkness. The sky above them was thick with stars in great swaths, casting nearly enough light on their own to show them the way. It reminded Eric of any number of trips he'd taken with his parents. India, Mongolia, even Scotland, where they'd been working so far from civilization that it was easy to forget what century you were in.

They arrived at the farm at nearly one in the morning. There was a two-storey red farmhouse set behind some trees on the left side of the road and a long, red barn on the right. They stopped in front of the house, where lights still shone from the lower floor windows. As they wearily got out of the SUV, Angel approached them from the other side of the road, coming from behind the barn. She was wearing a warm coat that was too big for her, and she looked tired and a little stressed, like she'd been waiting for something. Eric knew it wasn't them.

"Everything okay?" he asked. Michael stepped in beside Eric, handed him his pack, and slung his own over his shoulder.

Angel lifted her shoulders and sank her hands deeper into her coat pockets. It wasn't a shrug as much as a way to avoid answering the question. She seemed wound a little tighter than usual, like the coiled spring was starting to hum from the tension. Lakey had assembled Seth's chair, and he dropped into it from the front passenger seat just as Tess and her father came around from the other side of the vehicle. Angel's eyes went past Tess and settled on Sam. They narrowed slightly.

"This is Sam," said Eric. "Tess's dad."

"You must be Angel," said Sam, stepping forward. He must have sized her up quickly, because he didn't offer his hand.

"We weren't expecting all of you," she said.

Lakey nudged Seth. "She missed us. I can tell."

"We had a little trouble at the airport and had to make other arrangements," Eric said.

"Where is everyone?" Michael asked.

Angel shifted in her coat again. "The cabins are on the other side of the barn. There might not be enough space for all of us, though." She turned slightly in the direction she had come from and looked at the ground. The thin gravel road was hard-packed and smooth. "Our fathers are there."

Eric and Michael looked at each other. "And our mother?" Eric asked.

"She went with Ada. They took Williams and went to the Mountain."

7

RETURN TO THE MOUNTAIN

C lara had grown accustomed to moving through the darkness. She'd
learned to respond to changes in direction by feel, though occasionally
she felt jarred by the rough terrain. She had complete faith in Ada's control
of the small utility vehicle; the slight woman had no trouble operating the
machine, despite never having driven anything before. She had a natural
ability, made easier by eyesight that was unaffected by the pitch black. The
only issue was her burned hands, but she seemed to manage. The farmer
they'd borrowed the vehicle from had said it was reliable, even though the
headlights didn't work. Clara had given up trying to use the flashlight he'd
provided and focused on hanging on.

Ada drove more slowly than Clara assumed she would have if she'd been
alone. It had taken plenty of convincing to get a seat in the vehicle, first talking
Ada into letting her come with her, and second, talking Gabe into letting
her go without him. She wouldn't accept any alternative. They'd replaced the
container they'd used to carry Williams with an old stretcher they'd found
in a barn. It was essentially two poles with a sheet of canvas between them,
like the kind you saw in old war movies. Williams was strapped in, and the
stretcher was laid across a cargo area and secured with ratchet straps. Clara
was constantly checking to ensure it was properly fastened.

The trees had been thicker near the farm. They weren't tall, and the
ground around them was firm, but as they wove through, moving steadily
upward, the trees became sparser and the ground harder. There was snow
in places here, areas that were mostly shaded during the day, and it was

bitterly cold this late at night. Clara was grateful for the warm clothing she and Gabriel had brought, and for the windscreen on the otherwise open-air vehicle. They had a compass, but Ada could orient to the mountain in almost every clearing, and as the obstacles became fewer and the land more bare, she was also able to increase speed.

It wasn't until they'd rounded a smaller mountain, headed for the larger peak beyond it, that Clara knew there was a problem. Ada stopped the vehicle on an exposed slope of bare rock.

Clara switched on the flashlight. Ada was looking up and into the distance, but Clara couldn't see what she was looking at.

"What is it?"

Ada didn't respond right away. She continued to stare, shaking her head slightly. "The Mountain is no longer as it was," she said finally. "Something terrible has happened."

Before she could explain, she was driving forward again, faster than before.

Ada glanced in her direction. "There are two peaks above us, one nearer to us, slightly lower, and another just to the left, a little farther away. They are separated by a shallow space between them." Her voice cracked. "This was once one peak, higher than both. It has fallen."

She drove to the left of the first mountain. The ground dipped slightly before rising again. There were no trees at all here. A deep fissure came into view on their left, a wide crack that zig-zagged sharply down from the space between the two peaks. In the short-distance light, it seemed to Clara that it rapidly moved back and forth as it raced along beside them. When they reached the opposite side of the first peak, Ada abruptly stopped the vehicle and got out.

"Please stay with Johannes," she said. "Wait for me here."

As Ada disappeared into the darkness, Clara noticed the ground in that direction was different; the crumbling rock gave way to green, what looked like some kind of grass. The slope continued upward that way, but Clara couldn't tell how far. She switched off the engine, and the quiet settled around her like a blanket. She tried to listen for any sign of what Ada was doing, but all she could hear was her own breathing, accompanied by wisps of vapour in the cold night air.

Clara picked up the radio from the console and got out of the vehicle. There was no cellular signal, even at the farm, so the farmer had given them two-way radios to stay in contact. Clara didn't want to break the silence until she knew what she was dealing with; she didn't want to draw attention to herself, though she was pretty sure whoever might be here would see her long before she saw them. She stepped around to the back of the vehicle and stood next to Williams. He was lying so that she stood to his right, giving her a view of the side that was not affected by the fire. He seemed peaceful, at rest. It had been over twenty-four hours since they'd left the lab in Palermo, but there had been no change in Williams's appearance. He still showed no vital signs, but he also didn't show typical signs of death. It was true that his pupils didn't react to light, but when Clara checked, neither did Ada's. This long afterward, he should have been past the peak of rigor mortis, but the limbs hadn't stiffened. His body was heavier than a typical person's, but his arms and legs were supple and unrestricted.

Clara didn't know enough about Williams's physiology to know what to expect in death, whether actin-myosin cross-bridging still occurred, whether there was any calcium to get into the cytosol to activate the bonding, or whether there was even any cytosol at all. He didn't breathe, so he obviously didn't use ATP to fuel muscles or anything else, so all metabolic functions were out the window. This dreylagr seemed to do it all. Would it preserve the body as well? Was he even dead? She knew that he healed almost immediately from minor injuries; would his body shut down while it worked to repair itself after something like this? Ada seemed to think so. Or maybe it was only hope that guided her.

Shifting the light to the left side of his face, Clara leaned over him and looked at the damage there. The skin was shrunken and blackened in the worst areas, like it was on his arm, leg, and most of his chest, with splotches of mottled dark blue throughout. The edges were more distinctly blue where they transitioned to unaffected areas. There had been no swelling, no redness or fluid drainage, and there had been no noticeable change in his appearance since it had happened. Clara sighed, placed a hand on his chest for a moment, then stepped away.

She checked again in the direction Ada had gone, futilely shining the light that way and listening intently. Hearing and seeing nothing, she switched on the radio, adjusting the volume to a low level.

"You there, Gabe?"

The response came immediately. *I'm here.*

"We're at the mountain. Ada's gone somewhere, I assume inside. There's no sign of anyone."

Are you all right?

"Yes, fine. But something Ada said concerns me. She said the mountain used to be different, that it had collapsed."

I'll talk to Owen, see what we can find out. It would be easier if we had a computer, but we'll come up with something. We're working on a way to get to you; another farm nearby might have another utility vehicle. We're hoping to leave at sunrise, around eight.

"Okay. I should have more information for you by then. Anything from Eric and Michael?"

No, but they're not due for a while yet.

A voice spoke from the darkness. "Clara." It was Ada.

"I have to go," Clara said into the radio.

Be careful, Gabriel said.

Ada stepped closer, her outline visible in the fringe of light from the flashlight. She wasn't alone.

8

GOING TO HELL

Tess had her things laid out on the narrow cot that was her bed, the same way as she had in the RV in Montreal before leaving for Europe, taking stock of what she had and planning for her trip to Hell in the morning. She and her father were taking Seth and Lakey in for supplies, and she was making a list of what she needed. The jacket Joëlle had given her in Orsières had proven useful since arriving in Norway, but she would need more, particularly for the trip to the Mountain.

The two cabins they were using were small — one the same red she'd seen along the roads to get there and the other bare, aging wood — with upper levels made smaller by sloping ceilings. They were simple and practical and probably didn't see a lot of use in winter. Pine panelling covered the thin walls, and the lower level had a full kitchen along one side. Tess and Sam were staying above Seth and Lakey, who were using a daybed next to the kitchen table. The two small steps weren't much of a barrier to Seth, but the bathroom situation proved more challenging. In the end, he was able to rig something up, and as far as Tess knew, he had access to what he needed.

Angel and Owen were staying on the upper level of the other cabin, and Eric, Michael, and their dad were staying on the lower level. Tess didn't think there would be much sleeping, though. Gabriel had been waiting anxiously by the radio for word from Clara, but he hadn't heard anything from her since just after she and Ada had arrived at the Mountain. He and Owen had spent the time drinking coffee and poring over maps and a few geological reports of the area provided by the farmer who was hosting them. Sam was with them now, and his engineering background was proving useful. He and Owen had started talking in a language Tess didn't understand, so she'd left them to it. She hadn't seen Angel since they first arrived.

Tess looked at the clothes she'd brought. There were only enough for a few days: three short-sleeve tops and two long, extra underwear and socks, two pairs of jeans, a thick wool pullover she'd used as a jacket. She'd packed lightly, planning for Montana in October. Now she was in Norway in November and was unprepared. Her father had given her a blessed chance to do laundry before they left Trient in Switzerland and had found her a thin thermal layer people used in the mountains. She might need better shoes and warmer socks and decided to look for some on their supply run.

The door downstairs opened, and Tess could hear someone come in, moving quietly. Tess figured it was her father, trying not to disturb Seth and Lakey, who were already asleep.

"Tess?" A hoarse whisper from the bottom of the stairs. It was Eric.

Tess moved closer and looked down. "Hi," she whispered back.

Eric glanced toward the back of the cabin where Seth and Lakey were. Lakey was once again snoring like a buzz saw, the altitude apparently not a factor. "Can I talk to you for a second?"

"Sure. Come on up."

Eric walked quietly up the stairs. Tess turned back toward her cot, quickly covering her underwear with her pillow, and sat down. As Eric came into view, she gestured to a blue wooden chair at the foot of her dad's cot. "Have a seat," she offered.

"Thanks," Eric said as he sat down. He looked at her for a moment, seeming not to notice her clothes on the cot beside her. She was attentive but patient. Clearly, he had something on his mind. When he spoke, it was measured, almost careful. "I feel like I missed an opportunity on the plane."

Tess waited.

"First, I wanted to thank you for everything you've done to help me. I wouldn't have found Michael or my parents without you." He sat with his elbows on his knees, moving his hands, one over the other, like he was washing them. The words came in a bit of a rush, like he was trying to make sure he covered all the points he wanted to make without forgetting any of them. "I can't imagine what it must have been like, what you did to find your father. You have this incredible way of seeing things that makes me want to see them that way too. I haven't allowed myself to feel anything like this before, but the more I think about it, the more I want to. Feel it, I mean. I've had a lot of hangups lately, and I'm the only one to blame for them. It started long before we moved from San Francisco. This whole thing with my parents has made me see things differently. I find when I'm close to you, everything lines up the way it's supposed to. I guess what I'm trying to say is, if you'd be interested, when this is all over, I'd really like to spend more time with you."

Tess got up and moved to Eric's side of the room. She sat at the end of her father's cot, next to where Eric sat on the chair. She took his hand. "I don't think you missed anything on the plane," she said softly. "Everything you've done up to this point has affected you in ways that have taken you to the next opportunity. Our talk on the plane prepared you for the conversation we're having now. I imagine that's what's happened your whole life. You have skills you don't acknowledge because you don't know any different than what you are. They're things you've learned on your own, like spelunking and playing Buzkashi and everything that goes along with them, and there are things you've learned from the people around you. And I don't mean things like what to do when you meet a revenant. It's more what to do when the people you care about are in danger, how you will react, how far you will push yourself to protect them. There's a reason you're drawn to parkour; it's the same reason you're sitting in a cabin in the middle of Norway. You approach an obstacle with the intention of getting past it, of allowing yourself to use what you have to make it work, to trust. For some, it's easier to trust in yourself than it is to trust in others; second-guessing makes the obstacles more dangerous. There will always be the uncertainty when you're working with other people, what their performance will be, but that uncertainty is really just another obstacle that you run around. You plan, but then you adapt and go with whatever happens. You flow. I've seen you do this, and you do amazing things. And I feel like these are things we can learn from each other."

He looked at her, his eyes unwavering. She grasped his hand the faintest bit more tightly. He started leaning toward her, his eyes still locked on hers. She felt herself move toward him as well, and they met, their lips touching gently at first. She closed her eyes and felt his hand move to her hip. A finger hooked on a loop of her jeans and pulled. She shifted closer to him, put her hand behind his neck, and she was swept away, lost in the kiss.

The sound of a creaking door downstairs somehow reached her, and she pulled back, the spell broken. Eric turned away and looked toward the stairs. They were still trying to compose themselves when Tess's father appeared. He saw the two of them sitting there quietly, looking at him. His eyes widened slightly, as though he realized what he'd done, then right away they narrowed and focused on Eric. Without a word, Sam slowly turned, went back down the stairs and out the door, closing it softly as he left.

Tess stifled a laugh as Eric turned back to face her. He looked worried.

"My dad and I are still trying to catch up after five years," she said. "Remember, he's missed out on all the typical father-of-a-teenage-daughter issues. But don't worry, he's a progressive guy who is as level-headed as they come."

Eric didn't seem that convinced. "I'm sure that's true, but it might be better for my health if we do this in a more ... typical way." He stood up. "It's late. We better get some sleep. Big day tomorrow."

Tess stood up as well. She slipped her arms around his waist and gazed up at him. "You're right. But we'll continue this conversation later."

"Deal." He kissed her again and turned away, his hand lingering in hers as he made for the stairs.

Sam reappeared a respectable time after Eric had left.

"So am I going to have to have a conversation with this kid?" he said. He was trying to be sly, but his voice betrayed a little stress.

Tess tilted her head to the side and laughed. "Maybe. You'll have to brush up. Ask yourself this: What would Spencer Tracy do?"

∞

When Tess woke in the morning, the sun was only hinting it might make an appearance, and the air was so cold, she could almost see her breath. Her dad's cot was empty, and now that she was awake, she could hear clanking and sizzling from downstairs. There was a familiar snorty laugh, and Tess knew Seth and Lakey were up too, enjoying the chef's entertainment.

Tess cleaned up and made her way down. Seth and Lakey were already into muesli while they waited for omelettes. There was bread and cheese and smoked fish, and the kitchen smelled of coffee and ham.

"Morning, sleepyhead!" said Sam. He was wearing an apron and one oven mitt and was multitasking appliances like a symphony conductor. "Last one up gets dish duty." He tossed her a towel and turned back to the stove. "I was just telling Bruno and Betts how much Western Europeans are missing out on the art of the breakfast." He flipped whatever was in the pan. "It's the same here as in Switzerland: cold cuts are a food group and if you don't have the intestinal fortitude to deal with large amounts of cheese, you're not allowed into the country." He picked up a steaming mug. "I must say, though, the coffee is excellent." He drank, made a blissful face as he swallowed, and spoke through his teeth. "Oh, that's goooood." He set it down and returned to the stove. "Had a hard time convincing them of this in Trient, but for me, breakfast isn't breakfast unless there's at least three kinds of fried meat. The English do it right, though; they fry *everything*. Even the bread. It's fantastic."

Needless to say, Seth and Lakey were in heaven before they left for Hell. Sam was discussing the finer points of coffee bliss, adding that he'd heard about a version called *karsk*, invented in Trøndelag, that involved equal parts moonshine, though he barely added a disclaimer about the negative effects of alcohol on young people, particularly before a certain hour of the day.

There was still no appearance from the sun when they left, but the sky was getting brighter. Eric and the others were waiting for the borrowed utility vehicle to arrive from the neighbouring farm and were still planning to leave as soon as it did. They'd given Sam a list of things they needed, but their focus was clearly on getting to the mountain as quickly as possible. It would take Tess, Sam, Seth, and Lakey well over an hour to get to Hell, and Trondheim was another thirty kilometres beyond that.

The second purpose for their trip was to go to the university. Azzarà and Davis had been there for some reason; their job was to find out what that reason was.

They arrived just as the Hell Kjøpesenter opened for the day. They found a store specializing in outdoor sporting goods and apparel, and Seth and Lakey attempted to outdo each other in Helly Hansen. Lakey won, as usual, because she was always the one to take it too far. All the talk was about their next heli-skiing trip, which would happen immediately on returning home. That is, if they survived their next encounter with their mother.

"Hey, why don't we just go straight to the mountain on the way?" said Lakey as they waited for the sales associate to ring them through. "We'll be going right by with the RV anyway. Wiegs'll take us up."

"Wiegs?" asked Sam, amused. "You don't mean Mike Wiegele, the heli-god."

"The one and only." Lakey leaned toward her brother. "He owes us a run, remember, Sethie? When we fixed that bird for him?" She turned back toward the counter, her eyes far away. "Oh, man, I bet the powder's up, too."

"Nice," said Sam. He had that same look Tess was used to seeing on Seth and Lakey. "You know, he took me and some buddies up twenty-something years ago. We did *fourteen runs* that day. Most amazing day ever."

"Shut the front door!" said Seth and Lakey together.

They gathered their things and, with some effort, made their way back to the SUV. Aside from clothes, their purchases included some basic climbing equipment: nylon cord, cams and biners, and because Lakey insisted, an ice axe. "If it's good enough for Lara Croft, it's good enough for me," she'd said. They'd also picked up several headlamps, and they made a quick stop at a nearby hardware store for more flashlights, extra batteries, and a few tools Seth and Lakey hadn't been able to get from the farmer. Seth and Lakey had found an electronics store as well, and they got what they needed to do whatever they needed to do, something about boosting the signal for the comm devices they'd used in montana so they could use them inside the Mountain.

"Wait!" exclaimed Lakey, just as they started moving. "We need breakfast!"

Tess sighed, but not without a trace of humour. "You've already had it."

Lakey faked a high-pitched Scottish accent. "I've had one, yes. What about second breakfast?"

"I don't think she knows about second breakfast, Pip," said Seth.

Lakey continued. Too far, as usual. "What about elevenses? Luncheon? Afternoon tea? Dinner? Supper? She knows about them, right?"

"Easy, Gidge."

"The goal is to dine in Hell, remember?"

"We'll get something on the way back," Tess suggested.

Lakey looked at her reproachfully. "You know that never works. We'll get to Trondheim, do our thing, find something major, and have to rush back to the Mountain all in a state of emergency with no further thought to poor little Lakey's needs."

"Hobbits need to eat," Sam suggested, shrugging.

"Oh, *fine*," Tess gave in with a roll of her eyes. They stopped at a takeout hut on the side of the road, a small blue building with a sign that said "Hell Grill." Seth and Lakey each got Hellburgers, took photos, and seemed content.

The Norwegian University of Science and Technology, Norges teknisk-naturvitenskapelige universitet, or NTNU, was a big school in the middle of Trondheim. Forty thousand students, with an emphasis on engineering and technology, but also with a full slate of humanities, health professions, natural sciences, education, and business. There were several campuses around the city, but the main campus was just south of downtown, on the other side of the river. The Department of Geosciences and Petroleum was just south of that, on the Lerkendal and Valgrinda Campus. The Petroleumsteknisk senter was a five-storey brick building perched on a small hill across the road from the stadium where the Rosenborg Ballklub — a Champions League soccer team — played.

Sam pulled the car into a lower parking lot slightly down the hill from the building. Aside from being set apart from other campus buildings, Tess noticed this one had much the same feel as Kroeber Hall at Berkeley: solid, square, institutional, purposeful. They passed through sliding glass doors into an angled foyer with light-coloured floor and walls. There were seats arranged casually at one end, and people were sitting or coming and going. Everyone seemed young, and they were all shapes and sizes. Most had fair skin and brown or blond hair. They wore greys and blues and blacks, fashionable scarves and leather shoes. No one wore bright colours, and there was no shouting or running. The atmosphere was calm, sedate, almost thoughtful. There was a sense of peace and an intellectual air that Tess picked up on and liked right away.

Sam led them to a directory mounted on the wall and scanned the listings, looking for an official place to start asking questions. A man came from the corridor, did a double-take when he saw them standing together, and started toward them. He had an athletic build, combed brown hair, and short beard and was wearing black pants and navy dress shirt with no jacket or tie. It was as if this was his day job, but the rest of the time he was outside. He smiled as he approached.

"Are you looking for someone?" he asked in clear English. "Need some help?"

"You read my mind," said Sam, turning toward the man and smiling. Full-on British London accent. Tess switched over in her mind as her father continued. "We hadn't planned to turn up today, but we were in the area, so we took a chance. So sorry to drop in like this, but is there someone we could talk to about the university?"

The man smiled again. "How about me?" He held out a hand. "Rune Thorsen. I'm the research coordinator for the Department of Geoscience and Petroleum."

"Trent Thatcher," said Sam. He nodded toward Tess. "This is my daughter Thea and her friends Bruno and Betts."

"How do you do?" asked Tess, nailing the accent. "I hope it's not too much trouble."

"Not at all," Rune replied. "You are in Norway for other reasons? Holiday perhaps?"

"*They* are," Sam said with a sidelong glance at the others. "I'm here on business. They wanted to see the country, so they hid in my luggage."

Rune laughed. "Well, that's one way to see the world." He looked at Tess, Seth, and Lakey. "What are you looking to study?"

Sam responded for them. "Thea is looking for petro — she wants to be a reservoir dog like her dad." He chuckled. "Bruno and Betts here are into exploration tech — surveying with any piece of equipment used for that purpose," he leaned in conspiratorially, "and a few that aren't. Bonus points if it flies, the higher the better."

"If you let me play with drones all day, I will live here forever," said Lakey. She used her British Secret Service accent. Tess cringed a little but hoped for the best.

Rune smiled again. His face seemed programmed for exuberance; he had a positive energy that Tess liked. He turned to her. "If you're into reservoir engineering, we have major projects happening in that area. Reservoir Engineering and Petrophysics is one of the six main research groups within the department. We are a world leader in education in this area."

Tess returned his smile. "That's why I'm here," she said dutifully.

Rune checked his watch. "I have a meeting in about twenty minutes. How about I give you a brief tour, talk about some of our research, and then introduce you to our director. He enjoys meeting prospective students. He can go into more detail about the academic side."

They agreed, thanked him, and followed him on the tour. Sam seemed at ease with the highly technical nature of the conversation, his real-life background serving him well. Some of the talk might have been in Norwegian for all Tess could tell. At one point, they slipped into a lab while a session was going on. The room was brightly lit, with a stone-coloured tile floor and modern white work benches that curved on the ends. There were machines with tubes attached to other machines, and bottles and vials were placed neatly in sectioned containers. There were fume hoods and eye wash stations, and the place smelled like chemicals, but not in a bad way. Tess and the others stood at the back behind a black-and-yellow line on the floor while students who wore protective eyewear, white coats, and purple gloves worked with the equipment. Tess wasn't that interested, but she made herself look like she was. When Rune asked her what she thought, she showed him "impressed" and "excited."

"How much of what you offer is in English?" she asked.

Rune's answer surprised her. "Oh, it's all English," he replied. "But I would encourage you to study Norwegian while you are here! We offer that, too."

When they were back in the corridor, Lakey started to look excited. "Our turn!"

Rune cringed apologetically. "I'm afraid the toys will have to wait until another time. There was an incident in the lab a few days ago, and we can't get in to that area just yet. I can give you some material, though, and show you some photos and videos of our projects. We're using drones to develop methods to search the Arctic as part of ARCEx, the Research Centre for Arctic Petroleum Exploration; it's a big project involving lots of..."

"Aww, man!" Lakey seemed genuinely disappointed.

"Not an accident, surely," said Sam, showing concern.

"A break-in, actually," said Rune. He stepped closer to Sam and lowered his voice. "Two men got in to the lab, did a little damage but didn't take anything. Looks like they were trying to get information. It's the strangest thing. You know yourself how valuable information is on locations of new reservoirs — the money is in astronomical terms — but that's not what they were after."

"No?"

"No. They wanted seismic survey satellite imaging data, that's true, but they were focused on shallow subterranean surveys of *central Norway*. This information was gathered by students as part of basic projects; we have students map remote areas just east of here to become familiar with the processes and equipment. There's nothing there."

"Strange," agreed Sam. "And unfortunate about the lab. We're around for a couple of days — maybe we can come back and see it another time?"

Rune's smile returned. "That would be great. We've had to keep it closed off while we wait for some special investigators. We expect them today, so we hope to have the lab back to us shortly." He gestured toward the elevator. "I'll get my card from my office when we go up to see the director."

Rune took them to the third floor, where he led them to an office marked L314. The door was closed. Rune knocked quietly then leaned inside, spoke briefly to someone, then came out and closed the door. "He'll just be a few minutes, if you'd like to wait. He's actually talking to the investigators right now, so we might have the lab back sooner than later. Let me get my card." He went to an office at the end of the hall.

Sam whispered to Seth. "Let me know when he's coming back." He stepped toward the director's door and put his head close. Tess watched the corridor in the other direction as Sam tried to look inconspicuous. After a minute or two, he stood up, his expression solemn. "We need to go," he said quietly.

Sam ushered everyone toward the elevator. Tess looked back toward the director's office while they waited. The door remained closed. They got into the elevator and started down. Sam took the keys to the SUV and gave them to Seth. "Get the truck, bring it out to the driveway, we'll meet you there. We need to leave quickly without making it look like we're leaving quickly."

They'd parked in a lot at the bottom of a hill from the building. Seth was able to get there faster than anyone else. When the elevator doors opened, he was out to the main doors in just a few pushes and gone before the others made it out of the corridor. When Tess, Sam, and Lakey got outside, Seth had already disappeared. They walked calmly but efficiently down the slope toward the road, and by the time they reached the bottom, Seth was there with the engine running. He'd stacked his chair in pieces in the second row of seats. Lakey climbed in front with her brother. Sam and Tess got in behind them, moving the wheelchair to the back row to make room.

"Drive casual," said Sam. "Like you're Chewie and we're trying to land a stolen Imperial shuttle on Endor."

Seth smirked as he pulled forward. "You got it, Han. Where to?"

Sam thought for a moment. "No, wait. Turn left here." They hadn't left the parking lot yet. "Take a spot over there and park so we can see the entrance to the building and as many of the vehicles in the lot as possible."

Seth drove along the last row of spaces and backed in to one beneath a tree. The main road was behind them. They could see the doors to the building they'd just left, and nearly all the cars parked around it. There was a gravel space up the hill to the right of the building, and they could see some cars there as well.

"Hand me those field glasses, would you, Tess?" said Sam. She took binoculars from one of the shopping bags and gave them to him. He peered toward the building.

"What is it?" Tess asked.

Sam lowered the glasses but continued to watch the doors. "We have two problems," he said. "First, these two guys, Azzarà and Davis, clearly know where the Mountain is. We need to get back there right away to warn everyone."

"Okaaaay," Lakey said. "We're kind of doing the opposite of that at the moment."

"I suspect that has something to do with the second problem," suggested Tess.

"It does. Second, the people meeting with the director were agents. There were at least two of them. One was most certainly from Interpol, male, probably Russian. The other one, a woman, was probably from the FBI. These facts are problematic on their own because: one, I would rather not run into anyone from Interpol, and two, an FBI agent links this back to what happened in the US, which points a big finger at all of you."

Tess immediately thought back to the interrogation at the cabin in the woods on Vancouver Island, and she became worried.

"So why aren't we leaving?" asked Seth.

"Because if they're here so soon after we arrived, they must have already been on your trail, and clearly they've been getting closer. If they're right now getting information on the location of the mountain and they can put it together, then that place is about to get a whole lot more crowded, which is worse than just dealing with Azzarà and Davis."

Seth and Lakey looked at each other, then they both looked at Tess.

"So what does that mean, exactly?" asked Tess.

Sam smiled. "Well, you remember in *Beverly Hills Cop* when Eddie Murphy sneaks up behind the detectives' car and shoves a bunch of bananas in their tailpipe?"

"Oh, yeah!" said Lakey. "They were on a stakeout outside his hotel, and he ordered room service for them to distract them. Hilarious!"

"Right," agreed Seth. "And then when he leaves with his friend to go to the bad guys' place, the detectives' car dies in the middle of the road!"

"So do we get to order takeout?"

"Well," said Sam, "if my hunch is correct, we won't have time." He was still looking toward the building. After a moment, he lowered the binoculars. "There they are," he said. "Everybody just lean down a little. I don't think they can see us, but better to make the car look empty."

Seth and Lakey slowly slid down in their seats. Seth had already turned off the engine. Tess and Sam watched from behind. Two people had come out of the building, a man and a woman, both wearing suits and intent looks on their faces. They scanned the area, tracked the movement of one vehicle that was slowly leaving the parking area, then apparently dismissed it. They watched for another moment then made their way to a sedan parked close to the door.

"Too bad we don't have any bananas," Lakey mused.

Tess tried to make out features but couldn't see well from this distance. She asked to use her father's binoculars, but the two people were in their car before she could get a fix on them. The woman was driving. Tess thought she wasn't tall, though — maybe even a little shorter than average — but she was poised and very confident. The man was big, but it didn't look like he had a cast or anything. Brolov would have needed one after what Williams did to his arm in Montana. It couldn't be the same two people. Tess didn't know whether that was good or bad.

The car drove down the hill toward the road and stopped briefly, giving the agents a chance to scan the area, then turned right.

"Bruno," said Sam, "follow that car."

Seth started the engine, grinning from ear to ear.

"This is so awesome," said Lakey.

9

THE WAY IS SHUT

Eric watched as the SUV's taillights disappeared around the corner into the darkness. He wasn't happy about the arrangement, but he didn't feel the same now as he had when he'd discovered Tess had gone on her own to France. This time, she was only a short drive away, and she wasn't alone. Seth and Lakey were with her, and her father was there. But he still didn't like it.

Eric hadn't fully formed an opinion of Sam Edwards. When he thought about it, though, he didn't have that much information to go on. It was like there were layers to Sam that were only visible if he chose to reveal them, and he could make you see them however he wanted. He also had a way of influencing situations without making it look like that was what he was doing. It didn't make him manipulative, exactly, at least not in the negative sense, just mysterious. It was clear he had skills, though, and he was helping.

A neighbouring farmer arrived at dawn with the utility vehicle. He was a heavy-set man who wore a scowl so naturally that it seemed like his face's resting position. He slowly got out of his truck and lumbered toward the trailer. Eric and the others were gathered at the side of the road, the things they needed packed and ready beside them. Per, the farmer who was their host, met his neighbour at the tailgate of the trailer. They spoke for a few minutes in Norwegian before the other man even made a move to unlock the gate. Eric shifted where he stood but stayed out of the way. The driver of the truck, still scowling and talking to Per, shrugged as he slowly began to release the tailgate. Eric noticed the man was missing the thumb from his left hand. After what felt like forever, the vehicle was off the trailer, the engine idling loudly. Gabriel stepped closer to the two men, said something Eric couldn't hear over the sound of the engine, and passed the farmer some money. The farmer accepted it gruffly, locked the tailgate, and got back in his truck. He left without acknowledging them.

"What's his problem?" asked Michael as everyone gathered their things.

Per smiled awkwardly, like he was embarrassed about his neighbour's behaviour but agreed with his motives. "Jørgen has some concerns about what you plan to do."

Michael raised an eyebrow. "Is he worried about our well-being or his truck?"

Per shrugged noncommittally. "We are placed in a difficult position," he said. "He is concerned about his vehicle, yes, and on a deeper level is concerned about you also, but mostly he is worried for himself and his family."

Eric frowned. He looked at his father inquiringly.

"Eric, the people here don't go near the place where we're going," said Gabriel. "They believe there is unrest there. People from outside who don't heed warnings or don't know about them have been driven away. Anyone who has persisted hasn't come back at all. Jørgen feels," he glanced at Per, "and I suspect Per does as well — that the entities there may retaliate."

"Entities? Like ghosts?"

"The Vættir in this region are plentiful," said Per. "And they are already angry."

Out of the corner of his eye, Eric could see Angel stop short. She looked at her father in alarm. "Did he just say V…"

"Vættir," Owen interrupted. "They're wights. Nature spirits. There are different kinds, and they live in everything. They control the forces of nature, and they help people who consider and respect them, but they can be vicious toward those who don't."

"We have just finished one of the worst growing seasons in many years. It will be a difficult winter. For you to do what you plan might incite the Vættir further." Per looked at the ground. "If they are so angered, they might call forth the dead who dwell in the mountains."

It was Gabriel's turn to look alarmed. He covered it quickly. "I assure you again, Per, we are here to better understand the history of this land, and we have the utmost respect for its inhabitants, past and present, seen and unseen. We will make offerings and request permission to pass, and we will be sure to announce ourselves respectfully wherever we go. We do not wish to threaten or insult anyone." He looked at his watch. "And we should be going. Thank you, Per." He shook the man's hand, but Per did not meet his eye.

The vehicle was a Polaris Ranger Crew, red and black, with a short, muscly front end, two rows of practical bench seats inside a roll cage, and a big dump box in the back. They loaded up quickly, gear in the box, Eric, Angel, and Michael in the rear seat, Gabriel driving, and Owen using the maps to navigate. Seth and Lakey had managed to find a lot of useful information during the crossing from Sicily to France. Ada and Clara had planned to take roughly the same route, following the river west and approaching the mountain from the north side. Ada, who hadn't been involved in the discussion on the ship, choosing instead to stay with Williams, had been confident she knew where she was going.

The sun gradually brightened the sky from behind them as they set out. It was cold, and Eric, who had layered practically everything he'd brought, still shivered in the morning air. They kept the river to their left, guiding them as planned toward the pass between the peaks. Dense clumps of trees made moving in a straight line impossible, and their speed was limited. Gabriel pushed things as best he could, which occasionally resulted in bone-jarring bumps.

Eric leaned forward toward Owen and his father and spoke loudly. "If he was so against us going, why did he help us at all?"

Angel was sitting next to Eric, between him and Michael. "They had a bad year on the farm," she said. She turned to face him. Her eyes had a distant look, as though hardened against something. "They need the money."

Eric was holding part of the roll cage that extended upward behind the driver's seat in front of him. He couldn't see much of what was ahead, so he was frequently thrown off-balance. Space was tight in the back seat, and he occasionally bumped hard into Angel's shoulder.

Eric realized he hadn't spent any time talking to Angel since they'd arrived in Norway. She'd kept her distance from everyone, and though he wasn't sure about the time before he had arrived, she hadn't been involved in much of the conversation afterward.

"That must be tough for them," he said. He paused. "How about you? You doing okay?"

She looked at him again and scowled. "I'm fine."

The Ranger wobbled as it dipped into a low spot, and everyone lurched first to the right and then to the left. Eric and Michael had the roll bars for support, but Angel had nothing to hold on to. She relied on the shoulders of the boys to hold her position. Eric could feel the tension in her muscles, and she was wound so tightly he felt an instinct to protect himself, but he decided to go for it anyway. He glanced at Angel's father. Owen was engrossed in his charts and maps and was talking to Gabriel.

He met her eye and braced himself. "We know what happened to you. About the caves."

Angel sighed so forcefully that it sounded more like a growl. "You have *got* to be kidding me," she said in a low voice. Michael was looking at her sideways, his eyebrows raised.

"You think *now* is the time to get into this?" Angel asked.

"I think it's relevant," Eric replied, careful not to appear tentative. She'd shut him down if he did. "Considering where we're going. Honestly, I don't expect a repeat of what happened in the crypt in Montreal. We were just standing around looking at stuff. If I'm right, purpose gives you focus, and this time, you'll have something specific to do. We don't have to talk about the details, but it's helpful for the rest of us to know what to expect."

"Whatever."

Eric leaned forward to look at his brother. "Just so you know, I know how you feel. Similar thing happened to me once." He sat back, and Angel glared at him, but there wasn't as much venom in it. She didn't cut him off, at least. "We were in Brno in the Czech Republic. My dad had a thing at the time for these monks that like to mummify themselves and keep each other in the basement. One of the things that's led us to where we are today, actually. Anyway, there was a part of the crypt that was smaller and sectioned off, just a handful of mummies in there. They'd set up some portable lights while they were working in the room, something about the walls. Mike thinks it would be fun to lock me in and kill the lights. So here I am, nine years old, stuck in a room full of four-hundred-year-old dead guys, no light, no air circulation, and no sound. At all. It went so silent when the hum from the lights stopped; that's what spooked me the most. Not proud to say, but I lost it, actually tripped over one of the brothers, and ended up with my hand through his chest. Skinned my knee and peed myself before Mom and Dad realized what had happened and got me out. Mom freaked. She lost it for all time. Mike was grounded for about a century."

"So worth it," said Michael.

Angel didn't say anything, but there was a question there somewhere. Eric sensed a very small opening. "I'm not sure it affected me in quite the same way your experience affected you. I had problems after, and I got help, but basically my approach has always been similar to what I've learned and refined through training in parkour."

Angel narrowed her eyes slightly, and Eric could sense the wall going up again. As the UTV passed between two trees, a branch whipped around the roll bar and nearly caught Eric in the face. His hand came up instinctively to shield himself, but he had no emotional reaction at all. Angel noticed this, and she studied him again.

"Let's look at it this way," Eric began again. "Parkour is based on a philosophy of overcoming obstacles through self-improvement. The physical nature of it is one thing, but being strong and fast is a by-product of the process. The goal is to get from where you are to where you want to be, whatever happens to be in your path. Now, apply this approach when the obstacle is a person, and what do you have?"

"A football game," said Michael, smiling.

Eric nodded. "Yes, actually. Thank you, Meathead, for providing an excellent example. If you look at the best running backs ever, they all do this, whether they're aware of it or not. A guy like Marshawn Lynch does it, even though he also runs people over. But you know why Barry Sanders, who was, like, four and a half feet tall, was so good? Because he allowed himself the freedom to react the way he needed to react to overcome a lot of big obstacles that were trying to crush him. Watch tape, you'll see what I mean. But that's not what I was referring to." Eric turned his focus back to Angel. "Any other guesses from our studio audience?"

"You're talking about Wing Chun."

Eric nodded again, seriously this time. "You want to know who one of my all-time favourite parkour role models is? Jackie Chan. I love his stuff. From a pure PK perspective, he's incredible, and he carries it over to his fight scenes. He's the reason I know about it — he's a Wing Chun guy."

"I never really thought about it that way."

"The principles of Wing Chun and parkour are essentially the same, a philosophy of flowing with something and using its energy against it, grab on when it comes close, release it and attack when it tries to pull free. Deflecting, absorbing, instinctively countering. Only a portion of this is physical, but that's where all your focus seems to be. The principles of the form were there already, which is why you got so good so quickly. It's the philosophy that brings you through whatever happens to you, and you need to apply this. Fighting it, attacking first — strength against strength — is what makes it so it never goes away. Parkour principles apply to obstacles both physical and figurative; the same is true for Wing Chun. Use the obstacles. Become the cup." Angel frowned. Eric clarified. "'Flow like water' is an expression that exemplifies parkour, but it's actually a quote from Bruce Lee. He said, 'Be like water making its way through cracks. Do not be assertive, but adjust to the object, and you shall find a way around or through it. If nothing within you stays rigid, outward things will disclose themselves.' Bruce Lee was a Wing Chun guy, too." Eric looked Angel hard in the eye. "Treat your fears like a respected and honourable opponent, like Wu Mei or Ip Man would have done. See what happens."

They lapsed into silence. Angel was still tense and distant, but Eric thought he could sense contemplation, and he didn't want to give her a reason to stop.

While they were talking, the trees gradually became sparser and the ground firmer as the slope continued upward. The river divided and shrank, and they crossed one branch at a narrow point, the Ranger having no trouble with the shallow water.

The trees and undergrowth disappeared altogether, and they were driving over bare rock. Eric could see huge cracks in the surface, several of them, stretching down from the gap between the peaks almost in straight lines, as if something massive had hit the centre and fractured it outward like broken ice. The UTV rolled over the face of the rock, continued upward alongside a particularly prominent fissure, and the other UTV came into view. It had been left next to a large triangle of grass that looked so out of place against the grey of the surrounding rock, Eric had to blink several times to clear his vision. If he'd been in the desert, he'd have thought it was a mirage. The grass tapered up the slope to a point on the side of the mountain, as though it had flowed from a hole in it, spreading out along the space below for about two hundred metres down and ending in a swath about the same distance wide.

Gabriel parked the Ranger next to the smaller UTV. Eric couldn't see anyone around. Michael was first out of the vehicle and went to the other UTV to look it over. When he reached the opposite side, he saw something on the ground, bent down, and picked it up. It was the radio his mother had taken. It had been smashed to pieces.

"Let's search the area," said Eric. "There must be a way inside."

Everyone spread out, looking for an opening. Eric followed the patch of green to its apex higher on the slope, searching the face of the rock at the end. There had to be something there. When he and Michael had found their way through the underground tunnels at the Vatican, the architects had hidden entrances in plain sight. Could it be the same here? He used his hands to follow the edges, not trusting his eyes, but all his hands did was confirm what he was seeing. There was only solid rock.

10

THE POWER OF PERSUASION

Clara followed Ada deeper into the Mountain. The floor and walls were solid stone, but there was very little sound to reverberate other than the rustling of clothing and the fall of soft-soled shoes. The only breathing sounds came from Clara. She had only the weak flashlight to show the way, while the dark figures moved silently around her. There were some ahead of Ada — Clara couldn't tell how many — and two behind, carrying Williams on the stretcher. No one spoke, and Clara distinctly felt the disadvantage of not being able to see in the dark.

They circled as they descended, moving in a large spiral. At one point, an opening appeared on their left. A heavy door was swung wide to reveal a straight, level corridor beyond, but they passed it and continued down. The passage levelled out and turned sharply. Their way was blocked by a massive door made of thick wood and covered with iron. Two of Ada's companions heaved the door open with great effort. Inside, the air became warmer, and a glow edged out the darkness in the distance. Stepping forward, they were in a wide space, a cavern with smooth walls and domed ceiling. The muted light from the far wall revealed four long wooden tables that stretched out evenly in the space, with benches along the sides of each one. As they started down the space between the middle tables, Clara could see a small fire burning in an open hearth. The fireplace was huge and austere, carved into the wall itself and framed with engraved markings. Clara couldn't make out precisely what they were, though she guessed they were the same as those she had seen at the mountain in Libya. Large oil lamps stood on tall pedestals on either side, in the corners of the hall, each burning with three steady flames. There were other lamps spaced evenly along sides of the hall, but only two of these were lit. Extra light came from a few small, battery-powered lanterns scattered on the tables to the left, though what they cast seemed insufficient, like it was swallowed up by the darkness.

Several people were gathered at the ends of the tables to the right, maybe two dozen. They all wore the same clothing as the people who had escorted them in, simple tunics with long sleeves and hems that extended nearly to their thighs and with the same plain material covered their legs. Clara thought it might have been thickly woven linen. Colours varied slightly, but all were earthy tones, though washed out and faded. Everyone was dressed the same way, and Clara could not readily distinguish male from female. All were standing except for one, who sat alone at the table on the far right. There were dark openings in the walls on both sides. More tunnels, Clara assumed. The edges were clean, and the passages looked as finished as corridors in a building.

Two people sat apart from everyone else, at the end of the first table to the left. One sat in a straight wooden chair close to the fire, with his legs stretched out, crossed at the ankles. The other sat on one of the benches, facing everyone else, his hands folded and his elbows resting on the table. Clara couldn't tell who either of these two men were in the dim, flickering light from the fire, and the position of the lanterns didn't help much, but they were clearly not people from the Mountain.

As they approached, the lone figure sitting off to the right stood and stepped forward to greet them. His hair was nearly white, and he moved slowly, as if his joints ached. Ada moved ahead. There was no contact when they met, no warmth. They spoke softly in a language Clara didn't understand. Ada looked at the man with concern. She asked a question. The man shook his head and lowered his eyes for a moment, then he looked intently at Ada and began to speak urgently.

"That's enough," said one of the men sitting to the left. "Have them set the body on the table, please." He stood up from the bench and stepped around the table toward the fireplace. It was Riccardo Azzarà. He had one hand in a pocket of his long coat, which he wore over a cashmere scarf, pressed pants, and leather shoes. He kept his distance but nodded first toward Williams and then the table to Clara's right.

Eric and Michael had told Clara what had happened in Montana, about Azzarà's role in what was done to Michael. He had been responsible for the experimentation on all the subjects at Stockton's research facility, with an emphasis on understanding the properties of dreylagr. The goal was to bring Stockton's wife, who had been maintained in a cryonics tube, back from the dead. Clara knew Azzarà well enough to understand why, and it had nothing to do with helping Stockton. She took a step toward him.

"You…"

"On the table, if you please, Clara," Azzarà interrupted.

Clara stared at him. She could feel heat rising in her chest. Ada said something to the men carrying Williams, and they took him to the table. Clara looked at Ada, who remained next to the man who had greeted her.

"Clara, this is my father," she said. "Viggo." The man nodded toward Clara, a pained expression on his face. Ada gestured toward the others standing off to the side. "And these are what remain of my people." Ada appeared concerned, but she didn't show affection and nothing close to the kind of emotion she'd shown toward Williams.

Clara shifted her focus back toward Azzarà. "What's happening here?"

Ada began speaking softly with her father.

"Research, my dear Dr. Bakker," Azzarà responded as he started toward the table where Williams lay. "We are on the verge of a profound discovery."

Clara's mind was racing. She and Gabriel had been so careful to guard Williams's secret, the gains they'd made in their research enough to satisfy their team while protecting Williams and the others' existence. But even she hadn't known how far the secret actually went. At the moment, however, she was having trouble understanding how this man could possibly be here.

"Discovery of what, Riccardo? What the hell are you doing?"

"You will see soon enough." Azzarà stopped next to the stretcher and looked down at Williams. "I did not think I would be seeing *you* again so soon." He reached out to touch Williams's neck.

"If you value your life," Ada said evenly, "you will withdraw your hand."

Azzarà ignored her. He took Williams by the chin and roughly turned his head to see both sides of the damaged face. Ada reacted almost instantly, but before she could move more than a step, her father reached out and grabbed her wrist. She struggled for a moment then stopped and looked at him in shock. He whispered something to her, and they began to talk again in earnest.

"*Slutt å snakke,*" came a voice from behind them. It was the man seated in the chair by the fire. He spoke haltingly, with emphasis on the pronunciation. Ada and her father stopped abruptly.

Clara turned toward him. He was smaller than Azzarà and wore a thickly insulated winter coat, something suitable for a climbing expedition. He was shivering despite this and his proximity to the fire. He sat with his hands in his pockets, staring at Ada and Viggo with an unreadable expression.

"Who are you?" Clara asked pointedly.

He shifted his focus to her. "It's nice to finally make your acquaintance, Dr. Bakker," he said. He was American. There was respect in his tone, but there was also cynicism. He remained in his chair. "We've been looking for you for a long time. My name is Davis. I've already had the pleasure of meeting your sons, Michael and Eric. I hope to meet your husband soon as well."

"The boys didn't mention you," Clara responded. She glared at him.

Davis gave a chuckle. "I'm not surprised," he said. "I was responsible for managing Gilroy Stockton's business interests while he worked on a personal matter with Dr. Azzarà here." He waved a hand toward his companion. "Now that there are no more business interests — partly thanks to your sons, by the way — I have focused my attention elsewhere, and we have accelerated our progress. Wouldn't you agree, Professor?" Azzarà didn't reply.

"And what do you get out of this, Mr. Davis?" Clara asked.

Davis's face hardened. "I get to feel better," he said, now returning the glare. "I get to use them," he nodded toward the people standing on the other side of the hall, "to right the wrongs done by you and your family, Doctor. I get to take away the future of some for a chance to change the past."

At that moment, Viggo, overcome with rage, left Ada's side and rushed at Davis. Several others from behind him started forward as well. Despite unexpected incredible speed, Viggo had only gone two steps, his arms outstretched, before he instantly went rigid. His momentum carried him crashing into the table. He fell on his back, his arms awkwardly reaching toward the ceiling. His face showed incredible strain. Clara quickly moved to help him and noticed that everyone else — other than Azzarà — was also stricken. Ada was frozen, her arms at her side and her face in a silent scream. A man behind her, the first of the larger group to move forward, fell stiffly to the floor. Clara reached for Viggo's arm. It was like stone. She glanced at Azzarà, who looked on without concern. She flashed back to Davis. He hadn't moved from his seat or changed his expression.

"What is this?" Clara cried. "What's happening?" She moved to Ada and took her face in her hands. Ada's eyes were wide but staring at nothing. Clara could see the fear in them.

"The people here have agreed to cooperate with us," Davis said icily. "Our difficulty has been *communication*. I've only had a few days to learn Norwegian, but the modern version of the language is not as close as we had hoped to the version they use here. We have struggled to reach an understanding." He looked menacingly at Clara. "Of course, we have other ways of getting our point across."

"Stop it!"

"I will see that it stops. But I need some assurances that what we are requesting is both clear and agreed upon. Your friend here will allow us to avoid any further miscommunication." He gestured toward Ada. "She will be our translator."

In an instant, all those affected by the invisible force were released, and everyone collapsed, like puppets whose strings were all cut at the same time. Clara knelt beside Ada. For a few moments, she lay still. When she'd recovered enough of her strength, she went to her father. It took longer for him to come around.

Davis stood up and set his chair near the wall. "Professor?" He was looking at Azzarà.

The scientist shook his head. "No, he's had it. Given the extent of his burns, I do not think he will be of use."

Davis reached for a piece of wood from the floor near the fire. It looked to Clara like a leg from a chair similar to the one he'd been sitting on. He used it to stir the embers and then added it to the flames. The hearth was otherwise clean, like it hadn't been used in a very long time.

He was still looking toward the fire when he addressed Ada. "Miss, would you please ask two others to take the body into the first passage in the right-hand wall. Leave it in the last chamber and return here. I want it out of the way."

Ada didn't move or respond. Davis stood and turned to face her. "I will not ask again."

Viggo, still weakened and dazed, could see that Davis wanted something of Ada. He placed a hand on her arm and urged her with his expression. He whispered something to her, and Ada looked at Davis. Her face was stone. She stood stiffly and spoke to the others, who were gathering themselves, helping each other back to their feet. Ada took Viggo by the hand and pulled him to a sitting position, his back against the bench beside the table. She had four of the People each take a handle of the stretcher and then followed as they took Williams down the passage.

11

A DOOR IN THE DARK

Clara paced inside the small room, one of two connected chambers where she and the others were being held. The night had gone badly. Three escape attempts had been stopped by Davis using this power he had over them. Ada had said that her people thought it was a dark magic, that Azzarà and Davis were demons. It was obvious to Clara that they had somehow managed to control something unique to the People, probably the dreylagr, but she didn't understand how. Davis had punished them mercilessly the last time they tried to get out and included Clara, striking her hard across the face and driving her backward onto a table.

She touched her cheek gingerly. She could feel swelling, and it hurt, but she didn't think anything was broken. The next attempt would have to be different, something they hadn't tried yet.

Since she'd heard what Davis had done, she knew she had to find a way.

When Azzarà and Davis arrived at the Mountain, the first time they subdued the People, Davis killed two of them and dragged their bodies away. The others could only watch, made helpless by a power they didn't understand. Clara thought at first that it was a demonstration. Then it occurred to her it might be for the avelids, the stones inside their chests. Azzarà was continuing what he'd started in Montana.

Ada and Viggo had been in the great hall with Azzarà for more than two hours. Those who were left behind kept their distance from Clara. They were clearly upset and very angry, but they seemed disinclined to try again, and with no way to communicate, Clara soon gave up on them.

She'd tried to appeal to Azzarà, from one scientist to another, and she'd thought she'd reached him at one point. He gave her water and food from his supplies and allowed her privacy and a chamber pot. He also let her keep her flashlight, given that there was no other light in this room. He appeared level-headed and reasonable, and he obviously disapproved of Davis's treatment of her — like his greed hadn't erased all of his humanity — but once he determined she didn't know any more about the chemical composition of dreylagr or how to replicate it, he left her alone.

Davis was different. His motivation obviously wasn't greed. It felt like vengeance. But it was focused, like there was a clear purpose. This man was dangerous.

Before Azzarà had come for her, while in the process of planning their escape attempts, Ada had explained the layout of the living space inside the Mountain. Clara had seen some of it on her way in, but low light had limited her perspective. The Great Hall was the focal point. Two rectangular corridors circled it, one some distance above and the other below: upper and lower circuits. There were chambers along the length of each one. Sloped tunnels led from the side walls of the hall to the corridors, one to each circuit from each side, giving four tunnels. The iron-plated wood door led to the upward spiral, a rising, curved tunnel that linked to the upper circuit — at the door Clara had seen on her way down — and ended at the main entrance. At the opposite end of the hall, openings on either side of the fireplace met behind and connected to the downward spiral, which linked to the lower circuit and continued deep into the mountain to what had historically been the mines and the dwellings of the priests. Ada explained that these areas had collapsed several centuries ago, and the People had not reclaimed them. She wouldn't elaborate, but it was clear from her tone and in the demeanour of the others that a profound event had forced them to abandon their traditional practices. From what Clara had seen, they must have given up nearly everything; there were no signs of productivity or craftsmanship, no indication of study or engagement in anything Clara might consider meaningful. It was nothing like what the research team had found at the Green Mountain in Libya or what Williams had alluded to as their customary way of life. There was a stagnation here that Clara found surprising.

She continued pacing. The room she was in was the first down the sloping tunnel on that side of the hall. The door was visible from there, and Davis had taken a position at a table so he could see the door clearly. One of the problems with being in the lower slope was that even if Clara was able to get out of the room and farther down the tunnel, she could only go deeper into the mountain. To go up to the entrance, she would need to go through the Hall to a tunnel that led to the upper circuit or out the main door to the upward spiral.

Her flashlight flickered. She sat down at the table and turned it off to save the battery, leaving her in complete darkness. She'd done this a few times, knowing there couldn't be much power left.

After several minutes, there was a noise at the door. White light spread across the room as the opening widened. Clara squinted and shielded her eyes until they adjusted. Ada was there, with Davis standing behind her, holding a battery-operated lantern. Ada looked at Clara then called to someone in the adjacent room. One of the People emerged with three others appearing behind her. They watched expressionlessly as the woman approached Ada and Davis. She had pale skin and light brown hair, and her eyes were the colour of smoke. Just before she reached the door, she looked toward Clara, her eyes, suddenly intent, widened slightly as she gave a barely perceptible nod. Clara didn't react but shifted to Davis, who was watching the woman but couldn't see her face from where he stood. The woman lowered her gaze and continued toward the door. Ada stepped back so she could pass, but before she closed the door, Ada looked pointedly at Clara and flashed her eyes to the right in the direction of the descending tunnel, and Clara understood. They were going to try to create another diversion.

When the door closed, she switched on the flashlight. It flickered again and went out. She banged it against the heel of her hand, and it came on again. She looked toward the others in the next room. They were already moving. Two went to the door and listened intently. Clearly, they'd been discussing something but had no way to include Clara in the conversation. Maybe they hadn't given up after all.

Clara went to them. Any movement of the door before had automatically brought the invisible force. They listened without touching it. One of the two gestured to Clara, pointing with a hand and motioning to Clara to go down the passage and around the lower circuit to the other side of the hall. Clara nodded in understanding. She would need to enter the hall again to get from the lower slope to the upper slope, but she would do this on the other side. The second person at the door put a hand on the arm of the first, still listening, then said something to the others. They looked at Clara expectantly.

There was a muffled cry from the hall, and a crash. The one by the door quickly pulled it open just enough, then everyone went instantly rigid. Clara didn't hesitate. She switched off the light, slipped through the narrow opening, pulled the door closed as quietly as she could, and hurried down the passage. She couldn't resist one glance over her shoulder. There was scant light from the hall, but she couldn't see Davis. She turned back, reaching out in front of her in the increasing gloom until she was moving through complete darkness. Her hand came to hard stone, but she didn't react quickly enough to keep from running into the wall. She struck her cheek — the one that hadn't been damaged by Davis — and nearly crumpled to the floor. She could feel a trickle of blood and tried to imagine what Gabriel would think when he saw her. She recovered and felt her way to her left. She was now in the lower circuit. She turned on the flashlight, and the weak beam showed bare stone leading straight away. She followed the corridor to a corner, turned left, and continued. A door appeared on her left, the entrance to the downward spiral, but it was closed. She considered trying it but chose not to waste any time. Gabriel would have been outside for a while now, probably unable to find the entrance to the Mountain. She made another left and knew she was on the other side of the hall above her. Partway along, there was a passage that sloped upward, the mirror image of the one she'd used when she'd left the chamber. She switched off the light, which almost seemed grateful for the reprieve, and began to creep along the wall.

The commotion had settled. Davis had released everyone. The woman who had left the chamber ahead of Clara was sitting on a bench at the table along that side, apparently having just got up from the floor. Clara couldn't see the others but then noticed movement at the end near the large fireplace. She risked a better view. Viggo was still down, and Ada and a few others were attending to him. Davis was furious. He stalked toward the passage with the room where Clara had been, glanced briefly at the closed door, then went back to the woman. He no longer had the lantern he had used when he came to the door earlier, and the hall was darker this far from the fireplace. He continued past the woman to the end of the table Azzarà was using for his interviews, snatched a lamp from the surface, and strode back to the passage.

As soon as his back was to her, Clara crouched low, trying to stay out of sight behind the nearest table, and hurried into the hall. She had thick-soled boots, the pair she often wore when working rough sites. There was hardly any sound when taking steps, but the texture could scrape or scuff debris. She had to be careful she didn't kick something that would rattle across the floor. She skirted the bare wall, entered the other passage, and ran up the slope as fast as she could. She had the light on before she reached the end this time, but it took two strikes with her hand to get it working. From there, she went around to the open door that led to the upward spiral and hurried through. She hadn't made it to the top before the flashlight finally gave out completely, leaving her in total darkness. Blindly, she traced the wall with one hand, holding the other out in front of her, desperately hoping she wouldn't run into anything in her haste.

She reached the end without incident but then faced the challenge of finding the mechanism that opened the door. A lever to reduce the tension, bars to hold it in position, and a crank to shift it. Significant effort would be required. She tried the light again, but it was clear there was nothing more she could ask of it. She scraped her hands on the rock wall before she found the lever. It took everything she had to budge it. Finally, she worked it far enough for the bars to rattle loose. She released them from the back of the door and lowered them to the floor, cutting her palms on the iron when she moved them. She stopped and held her hands tightly, but her thoughts went back to Ada and the others, and she knew as soon as Davis discovered she wasn't there, he would come here looking for her. She started breathing heavily as she searched for the crank. When she found it, she couldn't move it. She used every ounce of strength she had without making it work. Her right hand was slick with blood.

She wasn't panicking, not yet, but her heart was racing. She grabbed one of the bars from the floor, worked it loose in her hands, then braced one end into the rock near the handle of the crank. She leaned on it with everything she had, and it moved a fraction. She repositioned and leaned again. Another fraction. Two more of these, and a crack of light appeared. She did it once more, and then the door started moving on its own. The light that poured in blinded her, and she had to shield her eyes again.

"Gabriel?" she called, unable to see.

"Thank you, my dear Dr. Bakker," said an aged and familiar voice. "We were having a hard time of that ourselves."

Clara rubbed at her eyes, fruitlessly trying to clear the lightning from her vision. Gradually, a form took shape. It was the robed figure of Cardinal Abito.

12

BRINGING A GUN TO A KNIFE FIGHT

Eric walked closely behind his parents as they descended the tunnel inside the Mountain. Michael was next to him, and Angel and Owen were just behind. Gabriel held an arm around Clara's waist as they walked, partly, Eric knew, to give his mother support but mostly to calm her. And himself. Gabriel was furious at the sight of Clara's beaten face — Eric had never seen him so angry — and it took restraint not to storm inside the mountain. If he'd had the freedom, Eric believed he would have done it. However, all of them were kept in a tight group by the six heavily armed officers of the special unit of the Corps of Gendarmes of Vatican City under the command of Captain Falco, a solid, imposing figure in a fitted black bomber jacket and pants and low-cut black hiking boots who walked at the front of the group. He, like the other guards, who were dressed in similar unofficial attire, carried a short-barrel submachine gun and two very bright LED lights, one on his head and the other strapped to his arm. The guns looked intimidating, but Eric found himself distracted by the weapons that hung from their waists; all the men carried *swords*. The type varied slightly from one officer to another, but all had long, narrow blades and metal guards around the hilts. They were old and probably hadn't seen action in a very long time, but Eric figured that wouldn't make them any less effective.

Falco looked like Eric's parents had described him. The cardinal who walked next to him, however, didn't. He wore the cassock, fascia, zucchetto, and cross Eric had envisioned, but he had expected the man to be more stooped and hindered by his age. There was a fierceness to his expression and a pace to his steps that easily kept up with Falco, as though he was determined to do something he had waited a long time for, and something as simple as being old wasn't going to hinder him.

Off to the side, walking by himself in the shadows like a waiting servant, was a monk. He wore only a brown habit, tied at the waist with a knotted rope, and sandals, despite the freezing temperature outside. Eric hadn't heard him say anything since they arrived. Abito hadn't bothered with introductions, but Eric guessed that this was Brother Marcus, the monk who had been guarding Ada while she was in her cell beneath the Tower of Nicholas V at the Vatican.

Falco lit the way while the guards watched everyone closely, paying special attention to Michael. The dark tunnel descended in a large spiral, gradually taking them deep into the mountain. They passed a door that stood open, with a level passage beyond it. One of the guards checked it as the group continued downward. No one spoke, and no one asked Clara for information or directions. Eric looked back through the dancing beams of light at Angel, thinking her anxiety had to be ratcheting up with every step. He caught a glimpse of her face; it was set in stone, her mouth a grim line. He might have been wrong, but she seemed more angry than anxious.

The spiralling tunnel ended at a massive door made of wood and iron. It took four guards to get it open. Inside was a large hall with four long tables arranged side by side, taking up most of the space. Each table had benches running their lengths and large oil lamps standing behind on low pedestals, though only two were burning. There was a fireplace at the opposite end, and two larger oil lamps, each glowing with three steady flames, that stood on high pedestals on either side. That end of the hall was also lit by several portable lanterns that had been placed on the tables, apparently at random. They looked like the kind hikers or back-country campers would use, LED lights with rechargeable batteries. They showed what was immediately around them, but they didn't seem to be doing much to light up the room.

Several people sat or stood together at that end. They looked weary and emotionless as Abito and Falco strode toward them. Eric could hear his mother and father talking quietly but urgently to each other, their heads close together. Clara searched the faces as they approached. Eric looked as well. He couldn't see Azzarà or Davis. "I don't see her," she said. She looked to the right toward an opening that led to another tunnel. Eric couldn't see anyone. "Ada!" she called. She took a step in that direction, but the guard nearest her stepped in her way.

Abito stopped the procession partway into the room, just before they reached the tables. "I wish to speak to the people in control here," he said in a loud voice. He looked around expectantly. No one responded. The cardinal nodded to Falco, who issued brief orders to his men in Italian. Two of them went to each side of the hall and entered tunnels, covering each other with military precision. After a few minutes, during which time Abito made no move to approach the people who were there, the guards who had gone to the tunnel to the right returned. They were carrying the body of John Williams.

The men laid Williams on the table nearest to them. Abito stepped around the end of the table that separated him from Williams and moved closer. He looked down at the half-ruined face and sighed.

"Ah, yes," he said, shaking his head. "So it is as it was meant to be." He turned back toward Gabriel and Clara. "You see, my dear doctors, no one can avoid the path God has chosen for us." He turned away again and called out, "Where is the seraph?"

A man who had been sitting near the fire stood up. He paused a moment until all the eyes of the new arrivals were on him then slowly began to walk up the aisle toward Abito. He'd only taken a few steps when Abito turned to Falco, took the captain's sword with remarkable speed, and raised it above his head as he stood over the exposed throat of Williams lying on the table. The cardinal's voice suddenly filled the hall, speaking in a language Eric didn't recognize. It was almost a chant. A woman's voice split through his words. "*NO!*" It had to be Ada, but Eric couldn't tell where she was. Immediately, everyone flashed into motion. Gabriel rushed at Abito but was knocked aside by Falco before he could reach him. He'd almost made it, as Falco was slow to react, apparently caught off-guard by Abito's actions. Eric grabbed for his mother's arm to pull her back as the gendarmes raised their weapons. She slipped away and moved toward Gabriel. At the same time, the people at the other end of the hall, passive to that point, bolted forward. The first to advance only made it two or three steps before all of them simultaneously went completely rigid and fell to the floor. Michael had lunged at Falco in defense of his father, but he also stiffened and collapsed. A split-second later, Eric felt tightness spread through him, starting in his legs and moving upward, like he was cramping everywhere at once. *Azzarà*, thought Eric. *He has a device.* He braced himself against a nearby table and forced his head to turn toward his brother. Michael was on the floor, his body twisted in one long convulsion. His focus shifted to his parents, who were staring uncomprehendingly at the scene. "Mom!" Eric called. "Get Michael!" They turned, saw him, and rushed over.

Falco and the guards were on alert, pointing their guns at everything, but their faces showed shock and confusion. Marcus had taken a step toward the people who had started in Abito's direction but now stood stock still. Eric couldn't see his face.

Through the initial chaos of that moment, Abito appeared not to have moved. He stood fixed, the sword high above his head, about to bring it down on Williams's neck. Eric thought at first that the cardinal had stopped because he was distracted by what was happening around him. Then he realized that Abito was frozen like the others, locked in position just like Williams had been in Stockton's dungeon in Montana. *He was one of them.*

Owen appeared at Eric's side. "Eric — Jesus, what's the matter? What's happening?"

Eric strained to turn his head toward the big man. "Azzarà," he said through gritted teeth. He looked past Owen toward the huge door to the hall. He couldn't see Angel anywhere. He was still looking in that direction when the device deactivated and everyone affected by it collapsed.

Eric managed to stay on his feet with help from Owen. Azzarà had clearly done something to the device; it was faster-working and more powerful than it had been in Montana. He leaned on the end of the table and scanned the room. Gabriel and Clara were still kneeling with Michael. Marcus had recovered enough to move closer to Abito, who had been saved from a fall to the stone floor by Falco. The captain had lowered him gently and now attended to him. Eric couldn't see where the sword had gone. The other guards were still edgy, their weapons pointing at everyone while they kept their distance.

There was movement in the far corner, to the right. Ada stepped through an opening. She appeared weak. She was followed first by Azzarà and then Davis. As soon as they were visible, the guards trained their weapons on them, flanking out and yelling in Italian.

"Captain, please ask your men to stand down." It was Davis. "Otherwise I will be forced to punish these people again, something I'm sure they will do anything to avoid."

Falco started to stand, but Abito grabbed his arm and used it to lift himself up. He stood erect, the frailty of his previous countenance gone, fury clear in his cold eyes. He spoke to Falco in Italian. The captain stared at the cardinal for a moment in confusion then regained his composure and gestured to his men. They stayed on alert but lowered their guns. They looked nervous.

Ada quickly went to Williams. She placed a hand on his chest and looked fixedly at his face for a moment before shifting her focus to Abito. He stared defiantly back at her. A look of incredulity came over her, and she gasped involuntarily, bringing a hand to her mouth. "*Tomas*," she breathed.

People from the other end of the room, having collected themselves, now stood attentively. Some moved closer to Abito, trying to see him better but keeping a table between them. Eric remembered the story Williams had told them. Tomas had been one of the people from the Green Mountain in Libya. He had left with his wife, Martine, and their son, Tobias, who were later killed by the Vidi. Tomas returned to the mountain with Tobias's body, but they were unable to bring him back, and Tomas, overcome by grief, had left again. It was about a century before the mountain was attacked by the Romans and the Vidi. It had been Tobias's body that had ended up at the lab at Berkeley and had been reclaimed by the Vidi when they killed Dr. Carlson.

Ada put her other hand on Williams's shoulder. She continued to stare at Abito. The people started to gather around her on that side of the table. Azzarà and Davis drifted away in the opposite direction, each with a hand inside one of their pockets and their eyes wary. The guards fanned out around them, all their interest in Eric and the rest of his group gone. The tension was palpable.

Ada said something to Abito. He roared a response and gestured at Williams. The guards tightened their grips on their guns as the tension went even higher. Some of the people behind Ada spoke, though nearly all talk came from Ada herself. Eric tried to read expressions and gestures, but it was difficult to pick up anything. Michael got back to his feet and stood next to his parents. All eyes were on Ada and Abito.

They went back and forth for a very long time, Abito always directing responses at Ada, regardless of who spoke before him. She was calm, almost inquisitive. Abito fluctuated between seething contempt and outright rage. He seemed to collect himself during a particularly long comment, but by the time he finished, he'd ramped himself up to agitation again.

Before Ada could address whatever he had said, Eric saw movement to his right. Without any warning, Azzarà, who had been silent to this point, was abruptly thrust forward into the table in front of him. He groaned as he collided with the edge and sprawled over the top. An instant later, Davis spun sideways and disappeared from Eric's view. He heard a sound that had to be Davis's head hitting the stone floor. Then a figure flew upward from where Davis lay and crashed into Azzarà again, who was still dazed by the previous blow. He was yanked backward by his coat, which slipped off as he fell against the wall and lay still. By the time the guards reacted to what was happening, Angel stood back against the wall, breathing heavily. She had shed her warm coat and was wearing the same black hooded sweatshirt she'd had when Eric first saw her on her father's boat.

It took only a moment for Ada and the others to realize what this meant. Then it was pandemonium.

The People around Ada instantly rushed the gendarmes with lightning speed. The guards, already tight and clearly afraid, opened fire. Michael pulled Gabriel and Clara to the floor and guided them under a table. Eric did the same with Owen, who hadn't needed any encouragement. Eric couldn't tell for sure, but he thought he saw Angel disappear into the passage near her. The submachine guns sprayed bullets everywhere, but none seemed to have any effect on the People. At least two of them came at Abito. Falco, who'd found the sword Abito had taken from him, swung it at the first to approach, cutting the attacker's arm and creating the opening he needed. He pushed Abito along the space between the tables toward the end of the hall with the fireplace. They disappeared through an opening. Eric could see the monk follow through another opening on the other side of the fireplace. Eric looked to his right and saw Ada pull Williams off the table and onto the floor. As the People swarmed the gendarmes, three of the officers who had been closest to Falco realized the ineffectiveness of their guns and ditched them for the swords, letting the guns hang from tethers attached to shoulder harnesses. Beams of white light flashed throughout the hall. Somehow they managed to slip away, and they followed their commander through the same openings. A fourth slashed his way out behind them. The other two were overcome. In seconds, the commotion was over. Two of the People dragged the guards to the other side of the hall to where Azzarà and Davis lay.

Michael, seeing this, stiffly climbed over the table to where Ada sat with Williams. They talked quietly for a moment, then Ada said something to the people who had moved the guards. They replied, and Ada nodded to Michael, who approached and took the guards' weapons and lights. Then the People unceremoniously dragged the four men from the hall.

13

BRINGER OF DEATH

He stepped slowly around the wreckage of the galley. He hated ships. They were necessary and had always been so, but he hated them for the incessant waiting, the deference to imbecilic captains, for their inept navigation and his reliance on them. The last century had changed things, so even the most incompetent crews could find their way, but this hadn't changed his mind. The truth was that what he hated most was the confinement. He was enclosed in a vessel moving slowly toward his destination with no alternative but to continue. Going down did not concern him — anywhere other than the deep sea — it only annoyed and delayed him. And he was not afraid of sinking into the crushing oblivion for any reason other than it would mean the failure of his mission. Long voyages grated, ground his mind inside his skull until he could meet his quarry. Until he could uphold his oath.

He had a keen sense of time, necessary to this end but also giving measure to his tribulations. The ship had been at port for less than an hour. It was dark, which favoured him, and sunrise would not come for another two. Sicily had not welcomed him — islands were not much different from ships — but he had been drawn by the avelid that called him here, and he had to answer.

The woman and three younger men had been dealt with. The captain remained, but he was losing blood. The man sat on the floor, his back against a bulkhead and his eyes glazing. The others stood silently, waiting. All but one, who paced slowly. This one had half the strength, having lost so much dreylagr while captured, but had twice the fire. But all were required for what was to come next. He had not sensed this much movement in many years, so many avelids out in the open. He had gathered all that remained. Something was about to happen.

He stood over the captain and used his foot to push into a gash in the thigh. The captain's eyes sharpened and focused on him. His own eyes showed nothing, only the faintest trace of the bright blue they had once been, but that was many centuries ago.

"Where did you take them?" he asked, his speech raspy and harsh. He hated the sound of his own voice.

The captain's eyes started to glaze again. He kicked him in the leg this time, and the captain moaned in pain.

"Tell me, or I will delay your reunion with your family in the afterlife most painfully."

He took his knife and dug the point into flesh near the captain's shoulder. The captain cried out weakly.

"I will not ask again."

The captain started to slide sideways toward the floor. His killer caught him, held his face under the chin, and forced him to look into his eyes.

When the captain spoke, his voice was congested, thick with blood. "Nice."

Confirmation.

"And where were they going from there?"

The captain's eyes started to close. His killer squeezed, and they opened again.

The word was barely audible.

"Trondheim."

14

9MM CONVERSATION

Tess stayed low in her seat even after Seth pulled the SUV out onto the road. There were two cars between them and the sedan ahead, and there was nothing Tess could see that made her think the agents knew they were there. The road curved slightly and rose up an incline, where it ended at a larger road that ran east to west.

"Watch them, Bruno," said Sam. "If they turn left, they're likely headed for the central police station, in which case we go right and haul ass. If they turn right, then we stay in their blind spot, okay?"

"How did you know they would be coming out so soon?" asked Tess.

"I figured Rune would have talked to the director when he came back with his card and saw we were gone. It wouldn't have been much of a stretch for the agents to think he'd been dealing with us."

The sedan approached the yield sign at the end, paused to allow cars to pass from both directions while Tess held her breath, then turned right. One of the two cars between them went left, removing some of their cover. The other followed the sedan, then it was Seth's turn.

"Give them some room, but keep them in sight," said Sam.

Seth waited as long as he could to give them a head start, then pulled out after them. The sedan picked up speed and began to work its way back and forth between the two lanes, passing other cars when it could do so. The driving wasn't aggressive, just efficient, but it was going to make it harder for Seth to stay inconspicuous.

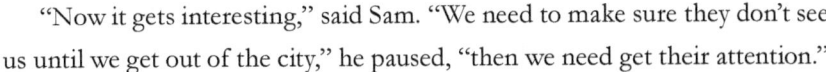

"Now it gets interesting," said Sam. "We need to make sure they don't see us until we get out of the city," he paused, "then we need get their attention."

Lakey slowly turned her head toward him. "Excuse me?"

Sam shrugged. "I need to have a brief … conversation with them."

Lakey nodded contemplatively and began analyzing their route on her phone.

The sedan moved quickly, changing highways as it continued east. Along the sides of the road, organized clusters of homes, often hidden from the highway by fences, gave way to industrial complexes in the outskirts, like most cities, and then to green space. When they reached trees and farmland, the highway narrowed to one lane in each direction, though it still had exits and overpasses. This made following the sedan much easier, but it made arranging a conversation significantly more difficult. The shoulder was narrow and the lanes were divided by a barricade, so there was no opportunity to get closer. At this point, there were four cars between them, with a large gap between the second and third cars. They went through a dark tunnel, and Tess was worried they wouldn't find the sedan again, but when they emerged, it was there, farther ahead but still in sight.

Not long after they came out of the tunnel, the road widened temporarily to two lanes.

"Go, Seth," said Sam.

Seth started toward the left lane, but the car ahead made the same move at a slower pace, blocking them. The road was clear in front of the sedan, and Seth watched helplessly as it changed lanes and picked up speed. The road climbed higher ahead, and an overpass came into view. There was a building above it, and as they got closer, Tess could see "STAV HOTEL" written on the side in white. The sedan pulled back into the right lane, but instead of disappearing into the distance, it took an off-ramp.

"That worked out well," said Lakey as Seth pulled back into the right lane and followed the sedan up the ramp. Lakey turned to look at the structure above the overpass. "Is that a hotel *on top* of the highway?" she asked in awe.

"Hey, Sethie, you suppose because of the trucks rolling underneath their beds, people pay more for the vibrating rooms?"

There was a gas stop at the top of the hill — a yellow Shell station — and Tess could see another one on the other side of the highway. The sedan turned in front of the station, passed the pumps, and stopped sideways in front of the building. The male agent got out of the passenger side and started toward the entrance.

"Go around the back," said Sam.

Seth stayed in the lane to the left and circled behind the station. Two more pumps stood there, intended for big trucks, and there was a large parking lot that separated the station from an entrance to the hotel. There were no trucks at the pumps, and there were very few cars in the lot. Sam asked Seth to loop around a narrow island and park facing the ramp that led back to the highway. "Keep it running," Sam said as he reached for the door handle.

"Wait a second," said Seth. "Tess, pass me the bag with my computer." Tess took the bag from the back seat and handed it to him. He searched through it for a second and came out with a small case. Tess recognized it and knew what Seth had in mind. "Take these," he said. He passed two tiny objects to Sam: an earpiece and a microphone.

Sam knew right away what they were. He laughed and put them expertly in place while Seth booted up his computer.

Check, check, said Sam, his voice coming through the speakers.

"You're good," Seth replied, and Sam nodded, hearing his voice through the earpiece.

Sam got out, went around the truck pumps, and headed for the end of the building. He passed two green dumpsters and disappeared. Tess, Seth, and Lakey turned their focus to the computer. They could hear Sam breathing softly as he moved.

A car door opened and quickly closed.

There was scuffling.

Waitwaitwait! urged Sam. There was a thud, an *oof*, and a sound of clicking metal. *Just want to talk to you!*

Who are you? demanded the woman. American accent. Her voice was solid, authoritative. Not the same as the cabin at all.

I'm a friend of Eric Bakker's.

There was a pause.

Where is he?

Judging from the direction you and your partner are driving, I suspect you already know that. Or think you do, anyway.

Are we wrong?

That depends on why you want him.

And that goes back to my first question, the agent said.

Quid pro quo, Clarice.

Did you just quote Hannibal Lecter?

Seems like one of us fits the right description, Sam retorted.

I hope you don't mean me.

How well do you know your partner?

You think he's Hannibal Lecter?

I think he has motives you might not be aware of.

Okay.

You doubt?

I'm not sure of the reliability of my source.

We'll see what happens when he comes back. Remember, you heard it here first. Now, Sam shifted in his seat, *let's try this: you're tracking leads on a murder in San Francisco, several more in Chicago, an explosion at a research facility in Montana, where several sketchy things were going on, and another in Palermo, where three scientists were killed.*

"And a firefighter," said Seth. "He was shot."

And a firefighter who was shot, said Sam. *You've found all of these are connected to Eric. Plus you haven't been able to find his parents.*

You forgot about the one in Victoria.

Tess jolted upright. Her thoughts immediately went to Brentwood; it was reckless for them to deal with Vojacek and Brolov on campus. It put others there in danger. She thought of her mother. Could they have traced her back to this? "Victoria?"

Did I miss one?

Ray Yamasaki's body was found in a ravine outside Victoria six days ago. We'd like to talk to Eric about that one, too. Apparently he wasn't too happy with the move to Vancouver Island, and word is he held Yamasaki at least partly responsible.

"Oh, no," said Tess. "He was Eric's parents' friend and part of the research team. He helped hide the family when they left San Francisco, set them up at Camosun."

He'll be very upset to hear about that.

Uh-hunh. Who are you?

Another pause.

Until relatively recently, I was working undercover with Interpol.

That so?

Yep.

So you and Salenko have history? Tess could tell the agent didn't believe him.

Sam scoffed. *Not that I'm aware of. Though I'm sure we know some of the same people. What makes you think Eric's in Norway?*

I'm sure you already know that, Doctor Lecter. Just following the evidence.

You ID'd Azzarà from the footage and connected him to the research team. And I'm guessing it was you who tried to have Eric and his brother held at the airport in Nice?

Apparently he made other travel arrangements. That your work, Doctor?

I might still have some official connections that work. On that note, can I ask a professional favour?

You can ask.

Eric didn't do these things. He's been following the evidence, same as you, it's just that he's been closer to the action. There's someone else behind this, and I'm close to finding out who. Give me a little time to sort some things out before you come storming in? Something major is about to happen, and I just want to make sure no one gets caught in the crossfire.

The FBI agent didn't reply. There was silence for a moment.

Oh, boy. Here we go.

Tess could hear the car door open. There was a distant crash that sounded like bottles breaking. Someone was yelling. It sounded like Russian. Seth rolled his window down, and they could hear noises from the other side of the gas station. Two gunshots split the sky, and the sound of glass shattering came both from the computer and from outside. Tess gasped.

Salenko! Stand down! The FBI agent must have been out of the car.

There was grunting, several thuds, and the sound of crumpling metal. More shouts, another loud thud, and then only the sound of heavy breathing.

Stop where you are! FBI shouted. *Get on the ground! Now!*

Remember what I said! Sam replied.

Tess heard footsteps and her father appeared, running around the corner. She opened the back door, and Sam leapt in. Seth yanked on the hand controls, and the SUV shot forward, taking the corner quickly and hurtling toward the onramp. Tess had a brief look at the scene as they went by. The sedan stood with both front doors open; the passenger side window was smashed and glass was all around. The Interpol agent was on the ground near the front of the car, apparently unconscious. The FBI agent was kneeling over him, her gun in her hand. She looked up as the SUV sped past, watching them go.

15

MUSTER

Eric laid the weapons on the table. There wasn't much: several different kinds of swords, some axes and hammers, a few tipped poles that were either long spears or short pikes, and a small stack of thick, round shields. He and Michael had helped gather them from a storage room where they'd obviously been sitting for centuries. It had actually been some kind of workshop, with ancient tools and equipment that probably hadn't been used in about the same amount of time.

After the skirmish, Abito, Falco, and the four gendarmes who had made it out of the hall had disappeared into another spiral tunnel that led deeper into the mountain. According to Ada, this downward spiral was connected to a tunnel that made a loop inside the mountain below the level of the hall; it was the symmetrical opposite of the upward spiral and upper circuit that Eric had seen on the way in. The door between the downward spiral and the lower circuit was secure, so unless Abito and the others were somehow able to force it open, they would need to come back up the spiral to the level of the hall to get out.

The People from the Mountain had fought awkwardly. Considering the way Williams had fought the Vidi in Chicago, Eric had expected them to overcome Falco's men easily, but it hadn't happened that way. It might have been the recent use of the device by Azzarà and Davis, Eric couldn't be sure. Maybe it was just that they were unfamiliar with violence, assuming the Seven Laws that had been so important to the group at the Green Mountain also applied here. But this didn't explain all the old weapons. Regardless, the focus now was on Abito and Falco; there would be a confrontation one way or another, and they had to be ready.

All told, there were twenty-eight People from the Mountain, though two had been hurt by Falco's men. Ada, Clara, Gabriel, Owen, Angel, and Eric increased the numbers, but Michael was the only significant contribution.

Michael had taken a leadership role, despite the communication difficulties. He'd oriented the two People who now had the submachine guns — one had gone with two others to watch the door between the downward spiral and the lower circuit, and another was watching the opening behind the fireplace — and he had arranged to gather the weapons.

Eric had trouble gauging the People's impression of fighting. He'd become used to the emotionlessness of Williams and knew there was more under the surface, but his first impression of the People he met in the Mountain was different. It was like they had no sense of purpose. They were just *there*.

"These things belong in a museum," Michael said, sorting through the weapons.

"No kidding," Eric agreed. He pointed at a sword in Michael's bundle. It was thick and heavy, with a tip that curved into a swirl. "I think that one's made of *bronze*."

Gabriel and Clara were sitting at the end of the table in intense conversation with Ada and Viggo, her father, who sat opposite. A few others stood nearby. Viggo seemed frail, like he actually needed the bench he was using, and Ada had been attentive, as though his condition surprised and concerned her. The others may have been affected as well, but it was hard for Eric to tell. He and Michael left the sorting to the two People who had returned from the storage room with them and started toward their parents.

Eric looked to his left and saw Angel sitting in a chair by the fire. Wood had been added, and the light from it made shadows that shifted across the surface of the table beside her. She hadn't put her coat back on, but she didn't look cold. She sat leaning forward with her elbows on her knees, her head turned slightly toward the flames. On an impulse, he lightly step-vaulted the two tables between them and went over to her. She spoke before he had the opportunity to say anything.

"I'm fine," she said. "Don't worry about me."

"I wasn't worried," Eric replied. "Actually, it's the opposite. This thing heats up, I'm standing next to you."

She smiled. It struck Eric. He couldn't remember seeing her do that before.

"Eric?" Clara called from behind him. She waved him over.

Eric turned back to Angel. "You coming?"

Angel shook her head, still looking at the fire. "Think I'll stay here a bit longer." She worked her intertwined fingers, tightening and relaxing them to manage her tension.

Eric stepped around the table this time and stood next to his mother. Other People from the Mountain stood behind Ada and Viggo, stoic as before. Most of them were so still that if Eric hadn't known better, he might have thought they weren't real. Many of the faces seemed to blend into the darkness of the background. Michael stood among them, his face as grim as the others.

As Eric approached, Michael was telling their parents about the weapons they'd found.

"We'll see if it's enough. They're outnumbered, but they'll be well-trained and they'll have had time to plan." He glanced at the People around him. "Unless we go in first."

Ada shook her head. "We will not instigate the final conflict," she said. "We need to be prepared, but if there is another way, we must remain open to it."

"I would think you'd want to go in sooner rather than later," said Owen. He was standing next to Gabriel. "Consider what else is down there." Owen had a fierceness in his eyes. He was angry. It took a moment, but Eric realized he must have been thinking of Lenny and Evelyn. He wanted Falco.

"What else is down there?" asked Michael.

Clara took a breath before she responded. "After Riccardo and Davis got inside the mountain, they used the device to take control, but they kept them concealed, so it seemed to everyone that they had some god-like power." She took another breath. "As a demonstration and to get everyone to cooperate, they executed two people. By beheading."

Michael ran a hand across his forehead. "Ah, shit." The People around him wouldn't have understood what they'd just heard, but Eric thought they probably wouldn't have reacted anyway. "So after they killed them, they took the bodies down the tunnel."

Clara nodded.

"Why would Azzarà do that?" Eric asked.

"He wouldn't," Gabriel said with conviction. "No way."

"Riccardo wanted the glory, but he's a scientist," Clara said. "He's self-centred and heartless, but he at least had limits. Davis didn't. It was clear from what Riccardo said to me that Davis had been the one to figure out where the Mountain was and how to get in, and it was Davis who was responsible for their treatment of us." She touched her cheek lightly. "Whatever happened to him before he came here, he wasn't motivated by discovery or wealth. This was personal. Riccardo was getting what he wanted, but regardless he told me he didn't dare cross Davis. He was vicious."

"Because of what happened to Stockton in Montana?" suggested Michael. "Revenge?"

Owen shook his head. "That's no reason to come here and start butchering these people." His anger was coming through. "All the talk once Ada was here to translate was about the ritual. They were trying to find out how to do it so they could do it on each other, and they needed two stones."

"You think they killed those two people for their avelids?" Gabriel asked.

"It's obvious, isn't it?" Owen replied testily. "And if the bodies are down the tunnel where Falco went, shouldn't we go get them? I mean, isn't time important here?"

Eric looked at Ada. "And what about Azzarà and Davis? What's been done with them?"

"The fighters have been restrained," Ada replied. "They were following instructions and may not have understood; we will defer their fate until we have concluded with Tomas." She looked solemn. "The scientists have answered for their trespasses."

No one spoke for a moment.

"And how will things be concluded with Tomas?" Owen asked, still edgy.

"I hope through discussion."

"We have time for that?" Owen pressed. He took a new tack. "You're forgetting the reason we came here in the first place. Don't we have to get down there to get what we need to bring John back?" Williams had already been relocated to the first chamber off one of the downward sloping tunnels, as safe a distance as Ada would allow. She'd been reluctant to leave him.

Ada fixed Owen with a look made of metal. "It is not the same with Johannes," she said evenly.

"Owen, *please*," Clara interjected. "We need to be ready either way; I don't think this will drag out very long." She turned to Eric. "Er, I'm concerned about your friends. They could arrive anytime — if they're not here already — and we need to warn them. Can you go to the entrance to watch? Maybe you can pick them up on your radio when they get close enough."

Eric narrowed his eyes then looked at his brother. Michael looked serious and supportive, which was notably out of character. Eric sighed and nodded.

"Good." Clara smiled wearily and turned her head toward the fireplace. "And take Angel with you, okay? I'd feel better if there were two of you, and she could probably use some daylight."

16

NOT THE TIME FOR MONTY PYTHON

It took some time for Tess's heart rate to come down. Seth had taken them away from the scene of the "conversation" quickly, but within a matter of metres, the road had gone down to one lane again and they were forced to slow behind other drivers. Sam had reassured them that moving at a normal pace was better anyway, since speeding would only draw attention.

"Nice work, Bruno," said Sam. "How does the truck feel? All right?"

"It's a little beasty for handling, but there's loads of power," Seth replied.

"Great. Betts, can you get us to the Mountain ASAP? Eric and the others will need an update."

"You mean back to the farm?"

Sam turned to look out the back window. He grimaced in pain and grabbed at his left side before facing forward again. "No, I mean straight to the Mountain. Do not pass go, do not collect two hundred dollars."

"I knew it," Lakey retorted. "Didn't I say we would have some kind of emergency and we'd have to go back all in a panic? I told you this would happen. It's a good thing we went to Hell when we had the chance."

"Dad, are you all right?" asked Tess.

"I'm fine kiddo, no worries." But he grimaced again, and Tess was sure she saw blood on his hand where he'd touched his side.

"No, you're not," she said flatly. "You're hurt." She leaned so she could see. "You've been shot!"

Sam smiled. "'Tis but a scratch," he said loudly with an English accent that sounded a lot like John Cleese. "I've had worse."

Tess ignored him. "Let me see it."

Sam lifted his shirt. There was a gash on the left side of his back, just above his waist where the bullet had ripped through the skin. Blood had run past his belt. Tess forced back a wave of nausea and fear. Lakey saw it as well, a worried look on her face. Sam looked at them both. "See?" he said brightly, still in character. "It's just a flesh wound!"

Lakey snorted. Seth was looking in the rear-view mirror and stifling a laugh.

Tess smiled, in spite of herself. "We need to do something about this," she said. "You need to see a doctor."

"No, I don't!"

"Enough with the Monty Python schtick, please," said Tess, trying to be serious, but her body betrayed her and she let out a laugh. She and her father had done their version of the Black Knight scene in *Monty Python and the Holy Grail* so many times, she was no longer sure how the actual scene went. Her father loved Monty Python; it was *exactly* his kind of humour.

"I am invincible!"

Tess knew her line. "You're a loony," she said dutifully.

"The Black Knight always triumphs!"

In the end, Sam agreed to stop long enough for supplies to dress the wound. They'd seen a pharmacy at the shopping centre in Hell, so they went there. Tess and Lakey went inside with a list Sam had given them: sterile gauze, bandages, vinyl gloves, saline, tape, towels, pain medication, bottled water, and, with emphasis, an Eskimo Pie. For the last item, Lakey got extra for her and Seth. The list also included polyester thread, a medium-gauge needle, and a lighter. Tess had tried to swallow a growing lump in her throat when she gathered these things. She observed that her dad showed an uncanny knowledge of how to treat a gunshot wound.

Seth had kept the engine running. When they were back, he pulled out onto the road again. The wound was in an awkward place for Sam to see it or reach it himself. They'd switched sides so Tess could get at it more easily, and she helped him clean and prep the area, but when it came time for the stitches, she couldn't go through with it. Fortunately — and not surprisingly when Tess thought about it — Lakey had no such qualms. She nearly dropped her ice cream when she climbed in the back, practically shoving Tess aside.

"Are you *kidding*?" she said excitedly. "I've never sewed up a *person* before! This is so cool."

She'd burned herself with the lighter twice before Sam finally got Seth to pull over.

"She's libel to sew her fingers to my ribs if we keep this up."

The road from Hell to the Mountain was smaller than the roads they'd used so far, one lane each way with no controlled access. Seth found a place to stop a short distance past the airport. It was an open space, with a pile of gravel at one end, some truck trailers without rigs, and a couple of maintenance buildings. There was a red-and-white gate that stood open at the entrance, and there was a row of cars near the buildings but no one around. Seth parked out of the way, turning so no one who might come along could see inside the SUV, and Lakey got to work.

Tess couldn't watch. She got out and moved to the front seat next to Seth. Sam talked Lakey through it, fighting the pain but keeping the mood light.

"You're cool if I sew in my initials, right?" Lakey asked.

Tess turned her focus to Seth, who had taken the opportunity to check his phone. He was looking at it so intently, his Eskimo Pie was dripping on the door panel.

"Uh, we have another problem," he said. "Hey, I know you guys are kind of busy back there, but you might want to listen to this. It's from the BBC. *Authorities in Sicily have discovered the bodies of five people on board a merchant ship at port in Palermo,*" Seth read. "*A joint statement from the Port Authority of Palermo and the Italian State Police confirmed the captain and crew of the coastal trading vessel* — sorry, I'm not going to try to pronounce the name — *registered in Egypt, were found murdered Tuesday morning. The ship had arrived from the South of France in the early hours and was scheduled to take on cargo later in the day. Officials say crew on board — one family: the ship's captain, his wife, and their three sons — were the victims of a vicious attack in which their bodies were dismembered. Sources also say there was evidence that the captain, reportedly from Syria, was tortured before he died. No suspects have been identified.*" Seth turned to face them, his face showing concern. "Does this mean what I think it means?"

Lakey had stopped what she was doing to listen. Sam tried to see her work. "That's good, Betts. Switch places with Tess again. We'll need you and Bruno sharp to get us there first. We have to warn them."

Tess started to open her door and stopped. "First?" she asked, though she already knew the answer.

"Yes," her father said stonily. "The Vidi are coming."

17

SAFE DISTANCE

Clara passed a hand across her forehead and wearily rubbed her eyes. She couldn't remember the last time she'd slept, and it was catching up to her. Sparks flew across the inside of her eyelids, and she watched them for a moment, dancing away every time she tried to look at them directly. Their elusiveness seemed fitting. It seemed like everything Clara had been trying to learn or to find lately had been skittering away from her, just out of sight.

She was still sitting at the end of one of the long tables, a bound notebook in front of her, like those she used to record thoughts and observations when working on a project. She always found it easier to think with her hands, like it gave her access to parts of her brain she couldn't reach through thought alone, and she found reviewing the information helped compensate for a memory that might otherwise let her down. She didn't have Gabriel's gift of remembering everything — far from it. This book was a new one with only a few notes so far, scrawled in her efficient shorthand. She'd left it in the vehicle when she and Ada arrived. Gabriel had it with him when Abito and Falco brought him in.

Her thoughts should have been on Abito and Falco and what was likely to happen at any moment, but her writing hand told her she was more interested in the Mountain and its People. Her work in Libya had led her to believe that the people there had been part of a vibrant, creative, and productive — albeit secluded — society. There was evidence of advancement and innovation and a search for knowledge. And that evidence was *archaeological*. Here, she was actually interacting with the very people she might have been studying, but there was no indication of any of these things. Life here wasn't vibrant; it was stagnant. And had been for a long time. Why? What happened here?

Since Eric and Angel had gone up to the mountain entrance, the others had drifted to different parts of the Great Hall. Gabriel and Owen were standing a few metres behind Clara, talking. Michael was going through the weapons and organizing the People into groups to be deployed in various places in preparation for the inevitable fight with Abito. Ada was helping initially, but Michael had managed to come up with a way of communicating that seemed to be working, something she herself had not been able to do. Michael had consistently impressed and surprised her through all of this. She always knew he was capable of more than what he showed, but considering what he'd been through in Montana, what he'd done in Rome and Sicily, and what he was doing here in Norway, he was definitely showing what he was capable of.

"Are you all right?"

Clara turned and looked up. It was Ada. Clara smiled wearily. "Yes, I'm fine."

"You need sleep," Ada said kindly.

Clara sighed. "When this is over. Something tells me it won't be long."

Ada gave her a sympathetic look. After a moment, she said, "Can I ask for your assistance with something?"

"Of course."

"I would like to move Johannes to another location. If there is to be fighting, I want to ensure he is safe until we can tend to him."

Clara nodded and stood. She took a lantern from the table and followed Ada to the opening of the tunnel, where Ada called on two of her people to join them. Together, they entered the chamber where Williams had been placed after the initial skirmish. He looked the same as before, peaceful but lifeless, his face still half in shadow from his injuries. Ada knelt beside him as Clara stood by respectfully. When Ada placed a hand on Williams's chest, his shirt moved slightly, and Clara saw that the edge beneath his shoulder was darker in colour. She frowned and looked closer. Williams still lay on the stretcher that had been used to bring him in to the mountain. It was an old style, essentially two poles joined by canvas. Hooks for attaching to vehicles doubled as stands when placed on the ground, keeping him slightly suspended.

Clara knelt next to Ada and reached a hand beneath Williams's shoulder. "It's wet," she said. "His shirt and the canvas. They're soaked through." She examined her hand. "It's cold."

Ada looked as well. An expression of worry flashed across her face and was gone. She stood and said something to the two others who had accompanied them. They moved to the ends of the stretcher, picked it up, and started for the door.

"What is it?" asked Clara.

Ada shook her head slightly. "We do not have much time."

They took Williams down the tunnel to the lower circuit, turned right, and found another chamber at the end, as far as possible from the downward spiral where Abito had gone. This room was larger than the others and had a heavier door. Benches were arranged in neat rows through the centre, and at one end stood a wide block table in front of high shelves, all of which were empty. Beyond the benches was a short flight of stairs that led to a lower section of the chamber, like the split levels of a house, with the lower section open to the upper. Ada led the people carrying Williams down the steps to the lower level and had them set him down. They did as she asked and left wordlessly, disappearing into the dark toward the door. The place where Williams lay was out of sight from the upper level.

Clara moved toward the stairs. "I'll give you a moment."

Ada stood. "Thank you, Clara, no. We should get back." It might have been a trick of the light, but her normally neutral features seemed to take on a grim, determined look. Clara had a feeling that whatever was supposed to happen, its time had come.

18

LOCK THE DOOR

Eric switched off his light as he approached the mountain entrance. Angel did the same. The door had been left open after they and the others had been taken through by Falco and his men, and now the metal bars used to prop the door from the inside were on the ground. One bar was separate from the others, near the crank mechanism, and Eric could see streaks of blood on it. The opening was incredibly bright, a hot white glow that made it impossible to see anything outside.

Eric stayed close to the wall, edging forward while he let his eyes adjust. Eventually, shapes appeared in the white glow, and the darkness inside the tunnel around him deepened. Squinting and shielding his eyes, he approached the opening.

"Seth?" he said into the mic in his collar. "You there?" He listened for a signal through his earpiece. Nothing.

The door faced east, so the early afternoon sun was behind and to the right, meaning the entrance itself was in the shadow of the peak above, further obscuring it from view from below. Eric stopped as he reached the edge. More shapes resolved as his eyes continued to adjust. He could see the utility vehicles parked near the bottom of the grassy area that somehow covered that section of the mountain. He took another step, and a bright light came into view, like sunlight reflecting off metal or glass. He froze, staring in that direction. Sitting apart from the other vehicles on a smooth and relatively flat area of rock was the papal helicopter.

"Oh, no," said Angel. She'd seen it too. The sleek white craft sat low to the ground, its pointed nose and curved front windows facing toward the Mountain entrance, the same position as when it had landed carrying Cardinal Abito, Brother Marcus, and Falco and his men. The five blades of the rotor were motionless, but the angle of the sun prevented Eric and Angel from seeing inside the cockpit. "We forgot about the pilot."

Eric glanced back down the tunnel and thought of his parents, suspecting they'd forgotten as well. He'd stayed on board when Abito had taken over and brought Eric and the others into the Mountain.

"There's no way he can have radio contact with Falco," Angel said.

"No, but he can contact other people. He might have done it already."

"Exactly. And your friends will be back any minute. What happens when they roll up and surprise him?"

"What are you suggesting?"

There was a clicking noise from somewhere outside, followed by the sound of a door slamming. Eric and Angel looked out together. The pilot was putting on a jacket as he walked next to the helicopter, headed toward the tail section. He bent down, appeared to examine one of the rear wheels for a moment, then stood up and leisurely walked two or three paces away, his eyes looking into the distance to the south. He took a package of cigarettes from a pocket and lit one. Angel turned to Eric. "You realize there is probably no way we will be able to get to him when he's inside the helicopter," she said. "He might not come out again."

"Are you saying what I think you're saying?"

She smiled again, just a little. The main reason for doing this might be to avoid going back into the mountain, but Eric had a feeling there was something else.

Eric held out his hands, thinking one of those bronze swords might not be so bad right now. "We don't have any weapons."

"He's a pilot," Angel replied. "What's he going to do, shoot us with a flare gun?" She stepped closer to the opening, peering down at the pilot, who took a few more steps away from the helicopter. He was nearly blocked from view by a higher part of the mountain slope along the edge of the grassy area, a kind of natural wall. Angel slipped out of the opening in the mountain and started along the wall, crouching low. "Come on," she whispered.

Eric hesitated, eyebrows raised, before hurrying after her. The sun was high, but the shadow next to the wall was enough, and their angle of approach kept them out of sight of the pilot. As the slope flattened out, though, the wall got smaller. They were still ten or twelve metres from him when they ran out of cover. The pilot was gazing out over the landscape, mostly bare rock, cracked and worn smooth. Other mountains stood out in various shapes and sizes, with no sign that any of them had ever been touched by human hands. It was hard to tell what the pilot was thinking, but it seemed like a contemplative moment, maybe even something deeply spiritual. He was the pope's pilot, after all.

Then he flicked his cigarette, unzipped his pants, and started to pee.

Angel looked at Eric, who shrugged. They were about to take advantage of the pilot's preoccupied state when Eric grabbed Angel's wrist to stop her. They backed up a short distance, and he pointed. As the pilot adjusted his jacket, they could see a holster on his right hip. "I don't think that's a flare gun," Eric whispered.

"Distract him," said Angel tersely.

"What?"

"Get his attention. Make him focus on you. What do you think 'distract him' means?"

"You mean get him to shoot me?"

"Preferably not. Hurry up!"

The pilot shivered in the cold as he zipped up his pants and jacket. Eric glanced at the helicopter to his left and made a snap decision. He bolted for it. The thudding of his footsteps made the pilot turn around quickly. He'd been wearing gloves but hadn't put them back on yet. He dropped them when he realized what was happening, and his hand went to his right hip as he advanced toward Eric, yelling in Italian. Eric dove forward, planted his hands on the nose of the helicopter, and did a kong vault over it, landing on the right-hand side with the cabin between him and the pilot. He yanked the lever on the front door and leapt inside, closing it behind him. He looked for a way to lock the door but couldn't see one right away. He figured if this were the pope's helicopter, it was probably bullet-proof, but that would only be helpful if the guy with the gun couldn't open the door. The pilot had his weapon out and now circled to his left toward the front of the helicopter, pointing it directly at Eric. Sitting in the pilot's seat, Eric quickly scanned the instrument panel. He estimated there were approximately a gazillion buttons, knobs, and switches, but at a glance, none looked useful to him. The control lever stood between his knees like a giant joystick, complete with multiple buttons for his thumb and fingers, but he was reasonably sure none of them activated missiles or machine guns. All he could do was stare back as the pilot continued to move toward him.

However, when the pilot stepped past the low wall where Angel was crouching, his back to her and his focus entirely on Eric, as requested, she shot out of the shadows. Eric could only catch a glimpse of her in the background, but then the pilot's outstretched arms suddenly extended straight up, the gun flew from his hands, and he flipped onto his back, where he took about twenty punches to the chest and head in the span of four and a half seconds. Conscious but dazed, he stayed down, shifting slowly from side to side.

Eric was instantly out the door. He grabbed the gun and levelled it at the pilot, making sure he kept a reasonable distance. Angel stepped away to the right but watched the pilot diligently.

The man said something, in Italian again, and groaned.

"Shut up."

"English. Okay," he said as he rolled stiffly. He tried to sit up but fell back again. "English. Got it." He brought a hand to the back of his head and checked his fingers for blood. Shifting to Eric and Angel, he squinted at them, like he was trying to focus, then closed his eyes with a grimace. "You're lucky there are six of you."

"Yeah," said Eric. "Lucky." Then to Angel, "See if there's something on board we can use to tie him up."

Angel nodded and went to the helicopter. She grabbed the handle on the rear side door and slid it open. A moment later, she came back with a roll of duct tape. "This will have to do."

Eric smiled. "Something similar has worked for me before," he replied. "It'll be fine." He visibly sharpened his focus on the pilot. "Up," he ordered.

"Easy to say, cowboy," replied the pilot with only a trace of an accent. Eric insisted with a look down the barrel. "All right, all right." The pilot slowly turned, got to his hands and knees, then to one knee.

"Stop there," said Eric. He moved to his right to make sure Angel wasn't in the line of fire. "Put your hands behind your back and cross your wrists."

He did what he was told, and Angel moved in with the duct tape. She made it halfway around when he suddenly grabbed her wrist, pulled her toward him, and stood. It seemed like he'd intended to put an arm around her neck and hold her in front of him, but it didn't turn out that way. Angel let herself be pulled but changed the direction slightly and pushed farther than he'd intended to go. He let go of her arm, and in the moment he was off-balance, she kicked him in the thigh, buckled his knee, and shoved him to the ground on his stomach.

Angel turned briefly to Eric. "I've got this."

Eric shrugged but kept the gun ready. The pilot was up quickly this time. He came at Angel a little angry, reaching with both hands to grab the front of her jacket. She faced him squarely, looking relaxed. Just before he reached her, she brought her arms up, separated his wrists slightly, and drove the heels of both hands into his chest. Winded, he stepped back then decided to throw a punch. She sidestepped, swept his arm away, and hit him in the side of the head, staying close to him where he moved. When he tried to punch with the other hand, she caught his wrist, and when he tried to break free, she let go and hit him three times in the jaw. Eric didn't even see her hands move. The pilot was stung again, but instead of letting up, he came back kicking at her wildly. Angel, still relaxed and square to him, lifted her knee, absorbed and deflected the kick, and drove her heel into the thigh of his supporting leg. She followed it with a lightning-fast kick to the giblets, and he went down to stay.

Eric gave him a minute then stepped closer. "So does she make herself clear?" he asked. The pilot mumbled something that could have been English or Italian. He got to his knees slowly, put his hands behind his back, and crossed his wrists. Angel taped them together and pulled him to his feet. The sliding door on the helicopter was still open, so they ushered him in and taped him thoroughly to one of the back seats.

Once the pilot was secure, Eric turned his focus back to the instrument panel. Two headsets hung from hooks overhead. He took one down and looked it over, not knowing the first thing about aircraft communications. "Do you suppose these would work to reach Seth and Lakey while they're out of range of the earpieces?" he asked Angel.

She turned back to the pilot. "Maybe we should ask Mr. Hero."

The pilot scoffed. Angel took a step in his direction. "Wait, wait, wait! Okay, maybe, I don't know. What, you want to call someone?"

"How does the radio work?" asked Eric.

"Radio? It's an Aspire 200 satellite communication system with Sky Connect. Broadband anywhere in the world. You and your girlfriend can watch *Teen Wolf* until her dad comes to pick her up."

Eric ignored him. "Internet? I can send someone an email?"

The pilot dropped his chin to his chest and shook his head. Taped to a chair with his arms pinned behind his back, it might not have had the impression he'd intended. He looked up at Eric. "The *pope* flies around in this thing," he said condescendingly. "You probably have God on speed dial."

"The pope flies with *you?*" said Angel disbelievingly.

The pilot scoffed. "No, are you kidding? Those guys are assholes." He made a face. "Let's just say this gig can afford to bring in quality."

"Falco," said Eric dismissively. This was not the pope's pilot, just someone brought in for this job. Eric wondered briefly whether the other men were hires as well. He put on the headset and started flipping switches. "How does it work?"

Before the pilot could make his inevitable sarcastic reply, a broken voice sounded in Eric's ear. He frowned and adjusted the headset, straining to hear. The pilot started to say something, but Eric waved him off impatiently.

...there? D... read?

"Seth?" Eric called loudly. "Can you hear me?" He pushed the headset harder against his head with one hand while moving switches and turning dials with the other, all with no affect.

...ric! We're ... your pos... still out ...tain?

"What? I didn't get that. Say again?"

...on our ... minutes, maybe twenty. If... get inside and lock the door!

Eric suddenly realized that the headset was useless, since the signal was coming through his earpiece. He tossed it aside and pushed a finger to his ear. He glanced through the window at the mountain entrance nearly two hundred metres up the slope then stared at Angel. She didn't have an earpiece. "Why? What is it?"

The Vidi are coming!

19

THE GOD OF VENGEANCE

Eric quickly turned away from Angel, who was staring inquiringly at him. He bent over the pilot seat and looked out the windows, searching the barren grounds for signs of movement. With the helicopter toward the entrance to the Mountain, they were facing roughly west. He looked to his left, south, but couldn't see anything except bare rock. He looked north to the gap between the peaks they'd used when they arrived, but there was no movement there either.

"Seth, are you sure? I don't see anything."

I don't know when ... Palermo yesterday, so it's ... matter of how they ... travelling.

"But how do you know they're coming here?"

Captain Khoury and his family are dead. He was tortured ... had to be them. They knew we were ... and now they know where we went. They were in California a week ago; getting around isn't a problem. And if I'm right, they'll know exactly *where to go. Get inside and stay near the entrance. We have a booster for the comm signal now, so we should be able to get through some of the rock.*

"If you're right? About what?"

"Eric!" Angel was looking to the southeast through one of the vertical rectangular windows on the side of the helicopter. There was rising panic in her voice. "It's them!"

Frick. Go! Seth implored.

Eric looked back to his left, straining to see behind them. A cloth-wrapped figure was coming over the lower slopes of the adjacent mountain, in full view with the brilliant sunshine and moving incredibly fast. As he watched, Eric saw a second emerge behind it, then a third. "Oh, no," he said. "Angel, run."

"Wait!" said the pilot urgently. "What? What is it?" He strained to see out the window nearest to him, his eyes wide.

Angel didn't need any encouragement. She was out the door in a flash. Eric was right behind her. "Don't worry," he called back to the pilot, "they're not after you!"

"What! Who? Jesus, are those … are those *mummies*? Hey, you can't leave me here! Hey!"

Eric didn't take the time to close the door of the helicopter. He bolted up the slope to the mountain entrance. He could hear feet pounding the rocks behind him and knew the Vidi were getting closer. Angel went in just before him. "Get the crank!" he called to her as he raced inside. The transition from full sun to near total darkness meant that neither of them could see anything. Angel fumbled for the handle, found it, but then couldn't move it. She called to Eric and he joined her. Together they tried, but it wouldn't budge. Eric pushed the back of the huge stone slab, trying to get it closed. It felt immoveable.

"Look out!" Angel screamed. She dropped to the floor, and Eric thought she was ducking at first. She grabbed one of the metal rods used to reinforce the door; it was still attached to the floor bracket at one end. She lifted the other end just as the first Vidi flew through the opening. The bar plunged into the centre of its chest and stuck out its back, its arms still reaching toward her. Angel gasped and stepped back.

"Run!" yelled Eric. He grabbed the lantern from the floor where he'd left it, snapped it on, and urged Angel down the passage. The clamour behind them made Eric think the Vidi were pouring into the mountain, but he didn't risk looking. They had to get to the Great Hall; if they could get the main door closed, they might be able to hold them off at the side entrances.

Angel ran slightly ahead as they flew down the spiral. Eric caught up as they came to the door to the upper circuit. "This way!" he called, guiding her through. The door was heavy but nothing like the outer door. The sound of running grew louder in the passage, and just as they slid a metal plate in place to bar the door, a force collided with it so hard, it shook in its frame. Several more collisions followed, but the door held.

"Come on!" Eric turned and sprinted toward the side tunnel that led to the hall. Angel was breathing heavily beside him. "Michael!" Eric yelled into his mic, hoping he was close enough for the signal to reach him. There was no response. They continued along the upper circuit then made the turn into the tunnel that sloped down. Eric kicked hard off the wall as he rounded the corner, keeping as much speed as he could. "Michael!" he called again. Angel stayed with him.

Eric? came Michael's voice in his ear.

"Close the main door to the hall!" Eric shouted. "Close the door!"

Eric heard Michael yelling at someone to get the door closed. There was a struggle and shouting, but Eric couldn't make out words. A moment later, he and Angel flew out of the south side tunnel into the relatively bright open space. Several people were gathered at the end of the hall behind the massive door, a few still working to reinforce it, Michael and Owen among them. Angel continued over to her father, and Eric followed, looking to Michael for confirmation that the door was secure.

"Eric?" called Gabriel. He was next to Viggo and a handful of others at the opposite end. Everyone was standing.

"It's them, they're here," Eric announced, breathing hard. He changed direction and ran toward Gabriel. "They're inside the Mountain."

"Who?" Clara asked. She and Ada stepped out of the downward-sloping tunnel on the north side of the Hall.

"The Vidi," Eric replied. He looked directly at Ada. "The Hunters."

Ada stared. She turned to Viggo and said something to him. His eyes widened.

"Did you get the other door closed?" asked Michael. "The door to the upper tunnel?"

"Yes, but I don't know if it will hold them."

Michael motioned to some of the people to take up positions near the openings to the tunnels that led to the upper circuit. They did as he asked, but when Viggo spoke to them, the tension in the room went up noticeably. Two others left the hall through the opening at the end, apparently to inform the people watching the doors to the downward spiral, but Abito and Falco were otherwise all but forgotten. Silence took over, and all Eric could hear was the blood pounding in his ears.

They didn't have to wait long, but instead of the explosion of shrieking forms Eric had expected, slow footsteps descended the tunnel from the south, the one Eric and Angel had used, until a man appeared in the opening. He was tall and broad, taller than Viggo, wore a modern Western business suit instead of bandages, and his hard-soled shoes clicked on the stone floor. Light-brown hair was neatly parted above eyes so pale there was only the suggestion of colour. He was calm and poised, in complete control. He stepped slowly into the hall, the only figure moving, and stood facing everyone. A moment later, half a dozen shadows gradually took shape in the tunnel opening. The same thing happened on the other side of the hall, so gradually it didn't seem like they were moving at all. The forms were ragged in comparison, tattered strips of cloth wrapped around their bodies. They stopped at the threshold like sentinels.

The man in the suit spoke in a low tone that sounded like rocks tumbling down a mountain. Talk was directed toward Viggo, but again Eric couldn't understand. Tones were civilized, almost cordial, but, scanning the room, Eric could see a change in the People. Their impassive features were taking on a seriousness that might be considered anger. Some shifted on their feet, even fidgeted barely noticeably with their weapons. The reaction was more intense than it had been with Abito, as though this conflict was so much more deeply ingrained. This was a battle the People wanted to fight.

Out of the corner of his eye, Eric saw movement. It was Owen. He had been on his way toward Gabriel when the Vidi arrived and now was the only person to take a step during the conversation. His face showed only fury, his eyes fixed on the Vidi leader.

"Bastard," he said, interrupting. He was walking very slowly. All eyes turned to him, but no one moved. Angel hesitated then started toward him, but Michael, who had been standing next to her, grabbed her wrist and held her back, urgently whispering something that startled her but kept her where she was.

"You bastard," Owen repeated.

The leader held his position but turned a cold, pale face toward Owen, his eyes revealing nothing. "We are all bastards here, Dr. Yancey," he said, the heavy, rumbling voice enough to make Owen stop. "We are nothing more than what we have been created to do."

Owen took another step, less certain, but he was stopped again.

"It is unnecessary to avenge your colleagues, Doctor," said the Vidi leader coolly. "You will soon be joining them."

"You seem sure of yourself," Owen responded, fuming.

"Our success is not relevant." He looked back toward Viggo. "With any outcome, you will not leave this place." He took a few steps to the left, away from everyone else. "Shall I explain to the doctors their fate? Or will you first tell me the fate of Ragnhildr and the others who sent us forth. We have done as she has bade us do, and now the stones have called us home to devastation and ruin and to find only you." He changed to the language of the People, and Eric could no longer follow what he said.

As they talked, Eric did his best to read their body language, which was so much more expressive than he'd seen before. The Vidi leader paced slowly, raising and lowering his voice as he fluctuated between anger, accusations, and ominousness. At one point, Ada showed shock and stared at her father. Viggo looked away. Something he couldn't deny and hadn't told her. The Vidi leader's satisfaction, a laugh, or at least what passed for one.

"Ada, what is it?" asked Clara. "What's he saying?"

"Who are you?" It was Gabriel. He stayed where he was, a few steps from Viggo, but he was looking unflinchingly at the Vidi leader. "What are you called?"

The leader scoffed. "Dr. Bakker, there is no need to know me. There is no discovery here for you to share, no evidence to document for the annals of science." He fixed his stare directly on Gabriel. "There is no future."

"She gave you a name, didn't she?" Gabriel continued. "Ragnhildr. She bestowed it upon you, along with your task."

The leader's expression changed from what might have been mild annoyance to something close to curiosity. He hid it quickly and continued to pace. "Call me what you like. A name will not be as relevant to you as the task."

"Vidarr."

The leader stopped, his focus on Gabriel and his expression now openly angry. As quickly as it appeared, it changed again to a forced amusement. "You rely on stories, Dr. Bakker, tales intended to entertain guests and frighten children." He took a few steps to his left. There were two long tables between him and Gabriel. He would have to go around the table to move any closer. "If you believe the stories, then you know I am one of the few who survive the end of the world. That I will be here long after you are gone."

Gabriel was unfazed. "That isn't true, and you know this. You've come here for another reason. You've been called home for some other purpose than the one you've been fulfilling for the last two thousand years, and you know that something will happen that needs to happen and was always intended to happen.

"You will fail and you will be free."

Absolute silence followed Gabriel's words. Two beats. A third. Then with an uttered growl from the Vidi leader, the room erupted, this time so violently it felt like an explosion.

20

THE KILL BOX

Eric could sense the buildup and knew something was about to let go, but when his father spoke, he still wasn't prepared for what happened next. The Vidi leader, Vidarr, moved like lightning over the end of the first table, rushing straight for Gabriel and pulling a long knife from beneath his jacket. Eric instinctively sprinted the three strides to get in front of his father and turned just in time to see another flash coming from the opening in the wall next to the fireplace. One of the People who had been watching the downward spiral for Abito came out of the passage and collided with Vidarr, sending him sprawling across the table. The impact surprised Vidarr, but it took less time for him to get the upper hand, drive his knife into his attacker's chest, and throw him hard into the wall behind.

Instantly, the Vidi shot into the room from both sides, and the People reacted as quickly, surging forward to meet them. Eric pushed Gabriel back toward the wall as the People ran past. Viggo stayed with them, his fragile-looking frame suddenly taut and ready. He kept Gabriel behind him and urged Eric there too, and Ada led Clara over to them. Screeches of hatred filled the hall, but Eric couldn't tell if it were just the Vidi or if the People were reacting just as fiercely. For all the apparent indifference they'd shown earlier, Eric wouldn't have thought them capable of so much intensity. The Vidi had their savekja, and the People fought with the weapons Eric and Michael had gathered earlier — swords, axes, and hammers they'd picked up when Eric and Angel had first raised the alarm. Those who didn't have one of these drew their savekja as well.

Eric grabbed a sword from the table near him and held it up uncertainly. He looked toward the main door, searching for Michael. He heard a cry from Angel and saw that Owen, instead of drawing back, had grabbed an axe and was moving toward Vidarr, the blade above his head and a wild look on his face. Angel was running after him. A Vidi ran onto a table and leapt at Owen, launching itself at him with ridiculous speed. Angel gave another cry and with amazing speed of her own crashed into the side of the mummy as it moved through the air. The collision sent it spinning off the edge of the table to the floor. It was up even faster, changed direction away from Owen toward Angel, screaming at her. Out of nowhere, Michael was there, swinging a heavy sword down on its outstretched arms, severing both. It slowed but didn't stop, until Owen, who had changed course when he'd heard his daughter, brought the axe down hard on the back of its neck, and its head tumbled to the floor.

Vidarr had recovered and was now backed up by three Vidi, but they were in thick with more than twice as many People. Their numbers were higher and their weapons were better, but they didn't have the skill of the Vidi, and the mummies were making progress.

Owen was visibly shaken by what he'd done, but he held on to his axe. Angel was able to draw him back toward a corner, trying to avoid the fighting. Michael went back in the direction of the main door, helping the People engaged there. The Vidi were divided, half with Vidarr fighting Viggo and Ada at one end and half against the People with Michael. It had the feel of a street fight — not that Eric had ever been in one — except when someone was cut down, they were back up right away to fight someone else, even if they'd lost limbs. Fights were short and violent, and everyone kept switching opponents.

The People coordinated enough to keep Eric and his parents behind them, but the Vidi seemed almost random, attacking whatever was closest, their intensity dialled all the way up regardless of what happened. Two of the People who fell had their chests ripped open and their avelids removed, ensuring they would not get up again. Eric thought about urging his parents through the door on that side of the fireplace, but it only led to the downward spiral, and the last thing they needed was to have the Vidi on one side and Falco's men on the other.

Eric spoke into his mic, hoping his brother could hear him over the fighting. "Michael, can you get the main door open? Maybe Angel and Owen can get out that way."

Not sure that can happen, Eric, his brother replied. *This door doesn't open easily, and the Vidi could go around the other way. And they wouldn't be able to see where they're going.* Michael grunted as he chopped through the thigh of a mummy that was charging someone near him. Eric held his own sword more tightly.

Bodies fell on both sides, but not enough of them were Vidi, and not many of them seemed to stay down. It was only a matter of time. They had to get out of there.

21

LAST OF THE GUESTS TO ARRIVE

Tess watched anxiously over Lakey's shoulder as Seth drove the SUV up the slope into the mountain pass. They'd been able to go faster once they were out of the trees, now that bare rock had replaced the undergrowth. Lakey had navigated them away from the gravel road that led to the hostel, turning right at a fork just after passing between a hayfield and a sheep farm. This smaller dirt road had angled along a narrow river in the direction they wanted, but when they ran out of road, they had to find their way through grass and increasingly sparse woods until the rock showed in the higher levels. Seth drove expertly, working the hand control lever with his left hand and the steering wheel with his right, like the truck was part of him, with Lakey making suggestions while scanning the terrain, using her maps, and watching the compass on the dash. Since making contact with Eric, the urgency had gone up, but Seth seemed to know the fine line between getting there quickly and breaking the truck.

The wide pass took them south of the mountain they wanted. As they started downhill, they turned north and eventually vehicles appeared, the first of which was a white helicopter.

"Seth, stop," said Sam.

Seth was already braking. "What is *that*?" he asked. "Norwegian authorities?"

Sam glanced up at the sun. "Take us out to the right. Slow. Try to avoid reflecting the light."

Seth eased the SUV forward, circling around toward the tail end of the helicopter, which was still some distance away. The sun was behind and above them, brightening the area, but Tess couldn't see anyone outside the vehicles. As they inched closer, she could make out black words along the top of the fuselage, just below the rotor: *"REPUBLICA ITALIANA."*

"Whoa," said Lakey. "Is that the *pope's* helicopter?"

Tess looked at her father. "What could that mean?"

"I think we might get to meet this Falco guy everyone's been talking about," he replied. He reached for the door handle. "Keep going."

Sam slipped out as the SUV continued to move slowly. He circled behind the truck and started toward the helicopter from a different direction.

"So we have the undead mummies *and* the pope's special ops dudes here at the same time? Does anyone feel outnumbered?" Lakey wondered.

"Don't forget that Stockton guy's mad scientist. He could show up anytime, too," Seth added.

"Right."

"How would the Vatican know to come here?" Tess asked.

"Good question," Seth replied.

Tess leaned forward between Seth and Lakey and saw Sam move quickly around to the other side of the helicopter. After a moment, he appeared in front of it and waved. Seth drove behind the helicopter and came alongside, parking in its shadow and facing one of the two peaks of the mountain. Ahead of them, through the windshield, Tess could see a dark opening up the slope — it must have been the entrance — and an inexplicable triangle of grass on the ground below it, like it had spilled out of the door. The green stood out in contrast to the grey stone around it.

The sliding door on this side of the helicopter was open. Tess could see the back of the pilot's seat and some of the control panel. She slid over to the other side of the SUV and got out. Lakey got out on her side and Seth rolled down his window. When she stepped closer, Tess saw a man sitting in a passenger seat in the middle of the cabin. He was shivering in the cold, though obviously trying not to show it. His face was bruised and his lip was split. He was also thoroughly duct-taped to his seat.

"Who's this?" she asked her father.

"I'm the pilot," the pilot replied flatly. "Or don't I look like one?"

"Right now you look like the cargo," said Lakey.

"What happened here?" Sam asked.

"You know, it's been a challenging day, and I've had way more than I bargained for on this gig, so if you would be so kind as to unwind me, I'll give you the highlights. I can no longer feel my hands."

Tess could tell he was spooked, and she knew the type. Being scared dialled up the wise-ass component of his personality. "You saw the mummies."

The pilot turned his head toward her so fast, she thought he'd have whiplash. His eyes went wide for a second before he regained his composure. She could tell he was trying to come up with something sarcastic, but in the end he slumped his shoulders and shook his head slowly, accepting defeat. "You're the one he was talking to. The high-strung guy with the kung fu girlfriend."

"*He* was," Sam replied, pointing a thumb at Seth, who made a peace sign toward the pilot. "So they went inside the mountain?"

The pilot nodded.

"And the mummies did too?"

He nodded again.

"How many?"

"Maybe a dozen."

Tess and Lakey exchanged looks with Seth.

"And how many with Falco?"

The pilot locked eyes with Sam, clearly trying to come up with other options. "Half that."

Sam turned his focus to the control panel. "Betts, can you and Bruno get the radio online?"

"Radio?" said the pilot, recovering again. "What is it with you guys and radios? This isn't a movie. You don't just flip a switch and start saying 'Eagle to Base.'"

Lakey glanced at the panel. "An Aspire 200 with Sky Connect, is it?" she said casually. "That's good." She went to the truck and assembled Seth's wheelchair then opened the cockpit door on that side. Seth got into his chair, moved next to the open door, and lifted himself onto the deck. He took a small roll like a miniature yoga mat from the pack on the back of his chair and spread it on the seat, then he folded his legs so his knees were to one side and hoisted himself up into the pilot's seat. When his legs straightened, they jumped and shook violently for a moment before he settled them into position. While he was doing that, Lakey had gone around to the left side of the helicopter and climbed into the other seat.

"You've got to be kidding me," the pilot said.

Tess picked up a roll of duct tape she found on the floor and pulled the end out about a foot. It made a loud, cracking noise that drew the pilot's attention.

"Okay, okay! No offense, just not what I expected, that's all."

"How much of what you've seen today were you expecting?" Tess asked.

"Point taken."

It didn't take long for Seth and Lakey to get the communications working. At one point, Lakey flipped a switch and said, "Eagle to Base!" glancing back as she said it. It turned out they knew more about how to operate the system than the pilot, since he was basically only useful for flying. Sam gave them the number of his friend at Interpol, Moreno. Seth said there was no answer and no voicemail, just a rapid busy signal, which concerned Sam. He thought a moment and pulled a business card from his pocket. "Try this." He passed the card to Lakey. There was a bloody fingerprint on one corner. Lakey did a double-take and looked inquiringly at him again. Sam nodded.

Lakey started pushing buttons on the console between the pilot seats and listened. "It's ringing," she said and motioned for Sam to take a headset. He took one down from a hook above him, adjusted the mouthpiece, and waited. Tess took a second headset down and put it on as well. The person on the other end had already picked up.

"Hello, Clarice," said Sam.

Doctor Lecter. Didn't think I'd be hearing from you so soon.

"I kind of felt the opposite. I had a feeling it would be very soon. How's Igor?"

Recovering. And arrested. Seems he was a little too motivated to bring you in.

"Let me guess — you found some interesting connections to some bad people in Transnistria."

Something like that. But there's more to this on the Interpol side of things. It goes deeper than my liaison privileges. Or my pay grade. You might want to keep your head down.

"Been doing that for a while now." He glanced at Tess. "Too long. But that's not why I'm calling. If you're still interested in talking to your person of interest, now is the time. And I would recommend the 'storming in' option."

You mean me, Igor's replacement, and local law enforcement?

"I mean how soon before you can convince the Norwegians to send the FSK?"

That much has changed in the last two hours? What do I tell them?

"Two sets of hostiles, numbering around twenty, unknown number of potential hostages. Come ready, but hopefully it won't be just a mop-up job."

"Give me twenty minutes and call me back."

Sam had Seth plot the coordinates relative to the position of their previous meeting, gave the agent the difference so as to avoid openly revealing their position, and signed off. "Here's hoping," he said to the others.

"FSK?" asked Lakey.

"Forsvarets Spesialkommando. Norwegian special ops." Sam grinned at Lakey. "They have an all-female unit, too, Lakes. The Jeger Troop. Full of kick-ass women like you, jumping out of planes, blowing stuff up, shooting bad guys."

"Oh, man, that is so *rickt.*"

"Maybe we can save the career planning for another time," Tess suggested.

"I agree," said the pilot. "Those mummy things could be back any minute, and I would love to have my circulation back before I have to run for my life, so how about we start working to unstick me from this seat?"

Sam ignored him. "Listen, you three stay here. See what you can tap into to find out what they're doing. If FBI tries to get in touch, hopefully I will still be able to hear you through the earpiece, but otherwise help her out as much as you can."

"You're not actually going in there, are you?" Tess asked.

"Just going to have a look." Sam smiled at her. "Your guy might need a hand. I'll be right back."

Lakey groaned. "Oh, I know you didn't just say you'll be right back," she said, exasperated. "Does no one get how that works?"

"Don't worry," Sam said. "If the mummies come out first, just give them shark bait over here while you're getting away." He nodded toward the pilot. "The tape will probably slow them down."

"Oh, great. Thanks a lot," replied the pilot. "But look, if you're going to leave me here, can you at least close the door? It's freezing."

Sam winked at Tess and jumped out. With a knowing look toward the pilot, he slid the door shut and returned to the truck. He rummaged through their supplies, took out a few items, and started up the slope toward the mountain entrance, scanning sideways as he went. He slowed when he reached the dark opening, paused for a moment, then disappeared inside.

Seth had been in the process of connecting his computer to the uplink. Tess whacked him in the shoulder with the back of her hand and gestured toward the computer. He jumped slightly and quickly spoke into the mic. "Comm check!"

I hear you, Sam replied through the speakers on the laptop.

"Booster's working," said Lakey.

Nothing so far. It's very dark, can't hear anything. The tunnel goes down in a spiral.

He took several more steps, the sound of his footfalls muted through the mic.

There's a door here, a strong one. It's been forced open. The tunnel continues down past the door or there's a level passage on the other side. I'm going through ... door and tur...

A few more seconds passed.

Still don't ... Tunnel makes ... can't see far ... passage.

Tess looked imploringly at Lakey. "Can you boost it any more?"

"That's as much as we have, Tess," Lakey replied.

"You're breaking up!" Tess said loudly.

Wait, I hear ... tunnel down ... can't...

"Dad!"

Seth turned up the speaker volume, but they couldn't hear anything else. "Sorry, Tess," he said.

Tess sat very still for a moment. A tightness spread through her that might have been the beginning of panic. Instinctively, she grabbed the handle of the sliding door, pulled it open, and leapt out. She went to the truck, grabbed the first flashlight she could get her hands on, and ran for the mountain entrance.

22

FORSAKEN

Brother Marcus followed His Eminence down the spiral tunnel, his arm braced against the curve of the cold wall as he struggled with what he'd seen. He was some paces behind when they left the Great Hall, and the soldiers had already run past, seemingly without noticing him and with panic on their faces as they tried to rejoin Captain Falco. Marcus was vaguely aware that it was not only a lack of experience with this kind of exertion that kept him from moving more quickly, but also his preoccupation with what he had witnessed. And the trauma it had inflicted.

Nearly every moment since he'd left his cell beneath the Tower of Nicholas V had been traumatic. He recognized the importance of his task, and he could not refuse the request of His Eminence — it did not even occur to him — but he longed for the comfort and familiarity of his chair and his books. And mostly, he longed for *quiet*. He was keenly aware of the presence of other people, felt their proximity even when they said nothing, sensed it like it was noise. The way sound travelled in the open air, the unholy, relentless punishment of the helicopter, the ear-splitting rage of the weapons released here, of all places. He felt his will and ability to do his master's bidding buckling under such an immense, overwhelming barrage.

The tunnel continued, and Brother Marcus followed it. He passed a door that was closed and barred, one that he knew led to the lower circuit, that was if the layout hadn't changed since he had known it. The floor was becoming gradually more broken, with loose blocks of stone in increasing size and number. He heard voices ahead growing louder, and he slowed.

Light shone from around the bend. He emerged carefully, keeping close to the outside wall to maintain as much distance from the others as possible, trying to remain unnoticed but knowing he must attend to His Eminence.

A large pile of debris blocked most of the tunnel, and the soldiers had gathered behind it. Those who could were adjusting some of the stone to become a more effective barrier. Two men had been hurt in some way and were on the ground. Marcus carefully stepped through a low point in the pile and moved farther down the tunnel, separating himself from the others. His Eminence was there, talking heatedly to Captain Falco. They spoke in Italian, which Marcus understood better than English or French, but they spoke so rapidly that he could not gather much from the conversation.

Men were yelling to each other as they tried to secure the barricade, and others cried out in pain. Marcus waited, trying to summon courage to deal with his growing stress. He felt like his head was going to explode. As respectfully as he could, he begged forgiveness for the interruption and in formal Latin requested leave of his master to find solitude for prayer and recovery. It was granted dismissively with a wave of a hand, and Marcus gratefully slipped away, retreating farther down the tunnel amid the debris and ruin, which in itself provided a kind of silent, unmoving chaos that further agitated him.

The monk was too preoccupied with his mental state to properly appreciate where he was or where he went. He ended up in a chamber only when he could go no farther, found a clear spot in the otherwise rock-covered floor, and knelt to pray.

It took some time, though he had long since lost the capacity to appreciate the passage of time or to track its progress. He'd become more aware of it lately, with so much movement and contact with others forced upon him. He could feel it again now as he tried to recover, the cacophony of the last few days, which had blended into a shrill ringing in his ears, gradually decreasing in volume and pitch. He wasn't sure how long it was before he opened his eyes again, willing himself to be fully in the moment, to only perceive and experience that which was right in front of him.

Eventually, he began to take in his surroundings, extending his perceptions outward very slowly. The air was still. He was far enough from the others that he did not hear their movements, and again he was grateful. A large stone sat silent on the floor next to him. It had jagged edges like it had broken off and fallen from the ceiling; it too was silent and still. There were others near the first, all unmoving, all silent, and all likely to remain so. He took a rare breath, felt the depth of peace start to return.

He had only extended outside himself a short distance when his thoughts betrayed him and he remembered the Seraph. The sight of her in the hall had brought the harshest combination of relief and failure. She had stood among these people, had exchanged words with His Eminence, words to which his benefactor had responded bitterly and in anger Marcus had not known. Here was his purpose, exposed and vulnerable, and he'd done nothing. He buried his face in his hands, but it did nothing to change the image in his mind. He opened his eyes searchingly, trying to force it away, when he noticed something he had not seen when he had entered: a body. It lay at the base of the wall farthest from him, feet extending from behind a pile of stone that hid the rest of it from view. The feet were wrapped in cloth in a way he knew well but had never seen before in his lifetime. Panic struck him. *He had defiled a place of Passage.* One of the People had been entrusted to the Mountain, and now Marcus had broken one of the Seven Laws. Instinctively, he crossed himself, stood, and quickly backed away, his eyes locked involuntarily on the wrapped feet. He could not look away. He'd only taken a few steps when he tripped on a rock. Another spike of panic as he fell backward — he thought he saw the feet *move*. But the whole room had gone sideways. He couldn't be sure. Then, instead of landing on cold stone, the ground was soft and shifted beneath him. He turned, and to his horror saw two of the People, lying as though discarded, one's limbs strewn over the other, their bodies thinner than they should be, like they had shrivelled. He tried to see their faces, at the same time afraid to know who they were, but *their heads were missing.* Full panic gripped him, and he fled the chamber.

He rushed up the passage, determined to warn the cardinal and compelled to confess his transgression and beg forgiveness. He hoped His Eminence would hear his confession; there was no one else who could absolve him of this sin. When he reached the barricade, his panic rose again. There was no one there. He stood still a moment, heard movement in the passage leading away from the barricade, and hurried on. A strap broke on his sandal, which came off as he ran. He barely noticed.

"Eminence!" he called.

The men ahead were moving quickly. They were talking to each other hurriedly in Italian. Marcus could not see them as they were just out of sight in the spiralling tunnel. They passed the door to the lower circuit, closed, with no one near it. The sandal broke from his other foot and was lost. He continued running, saw His Eminence and then Falco just ahead.

"Eminence!" he repeated. The cardinal did not stop.

They were nearly at the end of the tunnel when he heard the noise from the hall. It was the sound of violence, intense and too soon to be from Falco's men. He slowed as the opening came into view, then he stopped altogether. Cardinal Abito stood staring into the hall, trembling with fear. Marcus recovered enough to move closer. He followed the cardinal's gaze and again shock took him.

The Hunters were here.

The Great Hall was in chaos. People wielding ancient weapons were locked in battle with cloth-covered demons as several bodies littered the floor around them.

The first two of Falco's men were cut down instantly when they entered the hall. Marcus placed a hand on the cardinal's arm, which felt like stone. Abito flinched and withdrew as though from a spasm. With a shriek that cut through the noise of the battle, the cardinal raced blindly into the hall, ran past the struggling combatants, and disappeared through the opening that led to the upper tunnel and the Mountain entrance beyond, the sound of his screams echoing off the stone walls behind him.

23

UNEXPECTED COMPLICATIONS

Eric stood with his back to his parents in the corner of the hall, pinned there by the fighting around them. The People still outnumbered the Vidi, but the balance was slowly shifting. The Vidi were incredibly fast, attacking almost at random and seemingly undeterred when they failed to get through defenses. Eric looked for any opportunity to get to the opening that led to the upper tunnel, but the circle of protection around them was actually getting smaller.

Despite this, in the few minutes since the fighting had started, it seemed to Eric like the initial intensity had dropped a notch. Eric couldn't believe that either side could maintain such a pace, but he really had no point of reference other than the encounter at Field in Chicago. Still, something wasn't right.

At one point, a Vidi attempted to jump over the People in front of Eric. It fell short, stopped instead by a shield and driven back by a hack to the arm. Another tried to leap off the wall to go around the defenders, but its foot was too low on the surface, and it didn't have enough momentum, landing instead on the floor between the wall and the first table. Its face showed no reaction, but Eric was sure the result was unexpected. A sliver of hope wedged itself somewhere in his mind. The mummy came at Eric anyway, taking advantage of an attack by another nearby to get through. Instinctively, Eric brought up his sword, thrusting toward the figure. It connected in the shoulder, stopping the mummy but pushing Eric back. He quickly pulled the sword behind him and swung low as hard as he could. The blade bit into the Vidi's thigh, buckling the leg momentarily.

The Vidi slashed its savekja, going for Eric's head. The sword in its leg affected its aim, but the blade still made contact with Eric's cheek. Eric ducked, yanked his sword free, and swung again, taking the mummy's hand off at the wrist, then Ada was there. She couldn't effectively hold a weapon with her fire-damaged hands but was able to use a shield strapped to her arm to push the Vidi away, giving one of the others enough time to deliver another strike with a spear, which forced the Vidi to retreat. The spear clattered to the floor at the base of the wall.

The People occasionally seemed to miss steps as well, like something familiar didn't happen the way it should: swinging a hammer that missed, thrusting a sword that only glanced off its target. It might have been rust — any fighting experience would have been centuries earlier — but it had the feel of something else. If Eric had to guess, he'd say it looked like fatigue, but with everything he'd seen so far, he couldn't imagine that being a factor.

The lanterns that had been on tables throughout the hall were knocked around during the fighting, shifting the shadows and exaggerating movement. It was like the walls themselves were involved in the battle. Some of the lanterns were smashed, gradually making the hall darker, as though even the Mountain was losing ground to the Vidi. Clara held one of the lanterns, which gave Eric a chance to see what was close to them, at least. During a fight near the second table, a Vidi was knocked backward onto the table surface, its arms flailing. One of the lanterns flew like a flare across the hall, landing near the opening to the passage that led to the upper tunnel on that side. When it settled, Eric could see a figure in the opening, flat against the wall and watching. Eric's eyes widened. It was Sam.

"Oh, no," said Eric.

"What?" Clara asked, alarmed.

"It's Tess's dad."

I can hear you, Eric, Sam whispered through Eric's earpiece.

Eric looked at Michael. He could see Michael react to Sam's voice.

Where are the others? Michael asked urgently.

Outside, Sam replied.

"You have to get them away from the Mountain," urged Eric. "We're pinned down."

Maybe I can do something about that.

Suddenly, gunshots ripped through the Hall. From Eric's right, two of Falco's men stormed in, firing their weapons. There was a pause as the gunmen took in the scene, which was clearly different from what they had expected. The pause only lasted a moment before they started firing again. The bullets found random targets but had no effect. The gendarmes switched to swords, swinging them like machetes, intense fear on their faces. It was so unexpected to the Vidi that even Vidarr stared unbelievingly for a moment. It took one of the Vidi actually getting struck by a sword before those closest cut the man down. The second was about to fall when an ear-shattering cry split through the noise. Cardinal Abito raced into the hall, screaming, his robes flying behind him. He'd lost his zucchetto, and his arms were waving like he'd completely lost his mind. He ran in blind panic with unexpected speed from the opening beside the fireplace toward Sam and the entrance to the upper tunnel. Falco, a pistol in one hand and a sword in the other, followed closely with fear and uncertainty clear on his face.

The monk, Marcus, entered the hall behind them, running to keep pace but making no sound. The monk's feet flashed upward from beneath his habit as he ran. Eric noticed they were bare. There was no panic in his face, rather a look of confusion and pain. A few paces into the room, he caught sight of Vidarr and suddenly stopped, staring. The confused look changed to recognition then quickly to fear. He continued after Abito, but instead of following the cardinal through the second opening toward the upper circuit, he took the first, disappearing deeper into the Mountain. Eric couldn't tell if it had been deliberate or if he'd gone that way by mistake.

Vidarr said something to the Vidi near him, and three of them instantly ran from the hall, taking the upper tunnel, following Abito and Falco. Eric quickly scanned that side of the room, looking for Sam, and found him crouched to the left of the tunnel entrances. He was exposed, but he stayed low, and it wasn't clear if anyone saw him.

Gunfire erupted again as two more Vatican gendarmes entered the hall. Both were struggling with injuries they'd sustained earlier. They must have been aware of what had happened to the others, but the panic they felt at coming into this situation seemed to be channelled through their weapons. Eric and his parents ducked again in the corner; he assumed Angel and Owen had done the same, though he couldn't see them. The gunfire stopped with the clicking sound of an empty magazine, and the noise was quickly followed by the screams of the guards as they were overcome. Eric stood in time to see Owen, who instead of staying down had sprinted after Falco and disappeared from the hall. Eric tried to see Sam but couldn't find him. Angel tried to follow her father, but the Vidi had refocused on the group at that end of the hall, and she was cut off from the exit. Michael pulled her back as one of the People nearby collided with a mummy that had jumped toward her.

"Eric!" A shrill whisper from right beside him. Inexplicably, Tess was there, holding a flashlight. Eric was so shocked he jumped backward, eyes wide.

"Oh, my God," said Clara. "Tess, how did you get in here?"

Tess pointed toward the openings on their side of the hall. "I came down that tunnel. I was following my dad." She looked around anxiously. "Where is he?"

The fighting had resumed, with the People trying desperately to hold off the Vidi attackers. Eric glanced to the other side of the hall again. "He was here. I think he went back up the tunnel on the other side."

"Watch out!" Tess screamed. She pushed Eric hard and stepped back as a mummy came over the table at them. Clara grabbed Eric's arm and pulled him backward. Tess knelt down, trying to avoid the mummy's outstretched arms, and her hand came to rest on the spear that lay on the floor. In the split second she had, she grabbed it and angled it upward, bracing it against the corner where the wall met the floor. The Vidi was unable to get enough height to clear the tip of the spear, and the shaft plunged into its abdomen. It hung suspended there for a moment before falling to the side, still reaching out for Tess. Ada stepped in with her shield to push it back, grabbing the spear under her arm to keep the mummy from getting to its feet. Eric quickly passed behind Ada to Tess and drew her back into the corner behind Viggo and the others. The Vidi struggled until it freed itself and withdrew, the spear still sticking out of its body.

Eric turned quickly to Tess. "Are you all right?"

"I think so."

Her sleeve was torn, and the material looked wet. "You're hurt!"

Clara was beside her immediately. She helped Tess out of her jacket, quickly ripped the rest of the sleeve, and looked at the wound. "It's not deep," she said, taking the sleeve and tying it around Tess's arm. "Eric, we have to get you out of here. Tell Michael we need to leave."

Before Eric could say anything, there was a loud crash from just a few metres away, near the fireplace. Eric looked up in time to see one of the Vidi go down, apparently driven back by one of the People. A table had been shoved hard enough to shift it, and a bench had collapsed on one end, sending the mummy spinning sideways and out of Eric's view. An instant later, there was a bright light and a bone-chilling shriek from that direction. The Vidi was back on its feet, but its entire arm was on fire. It shrieked again as it tried to wipe away the flames, but the fire only spread to the other arm. Everyone nearby, Vidi and People alike, leapt away and kept their distance, their entire focus on the burning form. The rest of the Vidi absently separated themselves from the People, gathering instinctively around Vidarr. Eric looked to his left and saw that the fighting had stopped at that end of the hall as well, and the mummies were drifting toward the others, their blank eyes staring with what seemed like fear.

Tess pulled Eric in the opposite direction, moving quickly along the wall. Gabriel and Clara slipped away, following Eric and Tess toward the tunnel entrance, and Michael and Angel met them there. Up to that point, the balance had been slipping steadily toward the Vidi. Now, Eric felt things were worse instead of better.

"Why would it burn like that?" Angel asked.

Eric looked back. The burning figure, nearly engulfed now, had started toward Vidarr and the others almost pleadingly. Eric could see that there was no fear or compassion in Vidarr's expression; there was only fury. As the mummy dropped to its knees, succumbing to the flames, the leader's focus shifted to the group of People opposite, and Eric knew things were going to be worse.

His mother must have been thinking the same thing. "Gabe, we can't leave them here like this."

Gabriel looked from Clara to Ada, who stood among the People, as stoic and determined as the others, with the shield still strapped to her arm. There were six Vidi left, not counting the three that had gone after Abito and Falco. The People had nearly twice that but had taken a lot more losses. Sensing them, Ada looked in their direction, and seeing their expressions, made her way over.

"My friends, thank you for all you have done. You must go. But," she glanced at the People, who were bracing themselves for the attack that was about to hit them, "please take Johannes with you. Give him the only chance he now has."

Clara placed a hand on Ada's arm and turned to Eric, her eyes wet. "Go with the girls. Seth and Lakey might need help. Michael will stay with us so we can get out. We'll be right behind you."

It didn't feel right, but with no time to discuss it, Eric reluctantly agreed. Michael, who had already shown himself to be up for it, stayed in the hall to wait for his parents' return while Gabriel and Clara followed Ada into the lower tunnel. Eric took his sword, joined Angel and Tess, and started up the other tunnel, headed out of the Mountain.

When they reached the broken door from the upper circuit to the spiral tunnel, Eric stopped. Tess and Angel continued past him a few steps then turned and looked expectantly at him.

"Eric?" Tess asked, concerned. "What is it?"

"I have to go back," he replied. "I can't leave them down there."

Angel took two more steps toward the door and peered through it before turning back to face him. "I can't do that, Eric. My dad is out there." She paused a moment. "And I need to get out of this mountain."

"I'm not asking you to go with me. Find your dad and Tess's too. Meet up with Seth and Lakey. Try to find a way to call for help."

"Expose them?"

"I only see one way this ends, and I don't think the Seven Laws are going to matter anymore."

Angel looked at him for a moment and finally nodded. Tess, her composure impressive but no longer surprising, threw her arms around his neck. "I'm not fond of this pattern," she said. "Be careful, Runnerboy." She stepped away.

Eric was about to leave when Angel stopped him. "Wait," she said. "Take this." She held out a small metal object. Eric recognized it as a device like the one Stockton had used in Montana, the stimulator that immobilized anyone with dreylagr in their system.

"Jesus. You had this?"

"Honestly, I'd forgotten about it. But I think somehow I'd ruled it out; you saw what it did to Michael."

Eric knew very well what it had done to Michael, and if it came to it, he wasn't sure if he could use it either. He put it in his pocket, waited until Angel and Tess had disappeared through the door to the spiral tunnel, and ran back toward the hall.

24

NOBODY DOES IT BETTER

Seth sat in the pilot seat of the helicopter, which had involved an epic transfer from his chair through the front door. The seat was firmer than his butt bones would like, so he didn't want to stay there too long, but he couldn't pass up the chance to get an up-close look at the nerve centre of this beast. He'd been familiarizing himself with the instruments, getting a sense of what it would be like to fly it, and decided he would make it a priority when he got home. He could talk Mike Wiegele into it the next time they went up to Blue River to ski. The Popecopter was sophisticated, but it worked on the same principle as all helos. Collective pitch lever next to the seat, basically the throttle, and cyclic pitch lever in front to control direction. He scowled at the antitorque pedals on the floor and mentally devised a method to operate them with his left elbow. He'd have something to try next time Wiegs took them up.

"WHAT?" exclaimed Lakey. "There's no way that can be right. You're cheating. I know you're cheating." Seth looked over his shoulder. She was sitting in the seat directly behind him, facing the rear, while the pilot sat facing forward in the second middle seat, behind the copilot's spot on the left side of the cabin. Lakey had found a deck of cards somewhere and had a game spread out on the seat between them. Seth wasn't even sure what they were playing, but he figured Lakey didn't know any of the rules. Regardless, it was the third time she'd accused him of cheating, which Seth considered unlikely, since the pilot was still wrapped in duct tape.

The pilot raised his eyebrows and swung his head around in a circle. "Seriously?" he replied, exasperated. He moved his shoulders a few times to show his arms were still securely fastened. "How, exactly?"

"You two behave yourselves, or I'm turning this thing around right now and going home," said Seth.

"She started it," the pilot replied.

His name was Antonio, and he was brought up in Brooklyn by Italian parents who thought it was important for him to have his traditionally compulsory military service. These things seemed to explain the attitude, but then again, Lakey did have this effect on people.

Seth looked up toward the mountain entrance again. There'd been no movement there since Tess had gone inside, but Seth wasn't sure if that was good or bad. He took the headset down from the hook on the ceiling. It was time to check in with Mr. E's new friend, and he wanted to hear somebody other than the two durps in the back seat.

Yes?

"Miss Clarice?" said Seth tentatively.

Who is this?

Seth wasn't sure what would show up on call display with this setup. He figured "Popemobile Air" was unlikely.

"I'm, uh, with Dr. Lecter. He said to check in."

Seth could hear a trace of amusement. *And where is the good doctor?*

"Well, you know, the room service here isn't really up to his standards."

What's your status? Any change?

Seth glanced behind him. Lakey and Antonio were arguing over another alleged card-playing infraction. "Other than possibly increasing the number of hostages by two — the doctor being one of them — the only thing would be a potential double-homicide of the two jokers behind me." He turned his head and covered the mic with his hand. "Would you two shut it!" He faced forward again and lowered his hand. "I hope you're coming soon."

Yes, well, we've hit a bit of a snag. The Norwegians aren't buying. Seems some unidentified foreign guy telling them about a hostage situation in the middle of nowhere has them a little concerned about the verifiability of the supplied information. Have you got any proof, anything I can use? When do you expect the doctor to come back?

Seth looked toward the mountain entrance again. "I wish I knew."

Then, movement. Seth's eyes widened. A figure suddenly appeared out of the black opening like it had just passed through a portal from another dimension. It was an older man, running surprisingly fast, his movement made more dramatic by flowing crimson robes that trailed behind him. Even from a distance, Seth could see the wild look in his eyes and panic on his face.

"What the…" said Seth slowly. He called over his shoulder. "Uh, guys, you might want to see this."

What is it?

Lakey leaned in beside Seth so she could see through the front window. The first figure was followed through the portal by a second, this one dressed in fitted black jacket and pants and black boots. He was carrying a sword; Seth squinted at it, trying to confirm this. It was definitely a sword. His face showed more effects of the effort of running than the priest.

"I think this guy wants his helicopter back."

Helicopter?

"Here we go," said Lakey. "Wait — is that a *sword*?"

"That's right," said Antonio smugly. "It's payback time. We'll see how you like being duct-taped to a chair."

"Yes, that sword looks really pointy."

"Il Comandante is not your problem. It's the cardinal you want to worry about."

"He looks a little on the hysterical side to me."

This had to be Abito, the cardinal who was behind the abductions. "Pretty spry for an old guy," said Seth. Abito was running straight for them, with Falco close behind.

"What do we do?" Lakey asked.

"Lock the doors, Gidge!" Seth replied. He anxiously looked out the side window at his wheelchair. There was no way for him to protect it.

"What, like with a button?" She searched the side panels looking for a way. "Got it; we're good," she said from behind him. "Sethie, your chair!"

"I know, I know!"

The cardinal reached the helicopter first. He shoved the wheelchair aside so it toppled away between the helicopter and the SUV and grabbed for the sliding door on Seth's side, pulling so hard Seth felt the helicopter shift. The priest screamed something in Italian and banged his hands on the window. Falco circled around to the other side and tried the door next to Antonio. The captain yelled at the pilot, who shrugged his shoulders roughly to show he was bound, yelling back and gesturing to Seth and Lakey.

Lakey had shifted to the middle seat and was still fixed on the cardinal, who suddenly stopped pounding and screaming. "Oh, my God," Lakey exclaimed. "Seth, look!" She pointed past him to the mountain entrance. Seth turned to see three mummies racing down the slope toward them.

Antonio broke off from yelling at Falco. "What is *that*?" He gave a kind of stifled cry. "*No, no, no, no, no! Il Comandante!*" He continued to implore Falco in Italian through the window. The captain reached inside his jacket and drew out a pistol. He stepped back, pointing it the helicopter and yelling. Suddenly, an engine roared to life to Seth's right. He turned in time to see the SUV lurch forward and peel away. It turned sharply in front of the helicopter and raced toward the bare rock to the south. Seth had a good look at Abito as he went by, hands locked on the wheel, the panic clearer than ever on his face. Falco took a few tentative steps toward the vehicle as it accelerated away from him, then glanced to his right at the approaching Vidi before holstering his gun and sprinting behind the helicopter. He gripped the sword tightly as he ran, apparently headed for one of the other vehicles parked some distance away. Two of the Vidi broke off and ran after the SUV. Seth wasn't sure exactly where they went, because his focus was entirely on the third one, which was running straight at him.

"Get it started, Sethie!" said Lakey. "Slice 'em!"

"No time!"

When the mummy was only a few metres away, it launched itself into the air and landed on the nose of the helicopter. All three people inside yelped at once, though Seth could only really hear Antonio. The Vidi drew a hand back and swung hard at the window in front of Seth's face, but the windshield held. It snarled in apparent annoyance then immediately jumped down to its right. It stood outside Antonio's window, hands braced on either side of the pane as it stared in at the pilot. Antonio stared back for a beat then started thrashing in his seat. Lakey quickly moved to the opposite side of the cabin. Seth desperately searched the cockpit for something he could use. He remembered the manual and the inventory information he'd read earlier. He reached down and searched blindly beneath his seat until he came up with a box about the size of a travel med kit. Opening it, he took out a small orange device shaped like a wide-mouthed pistol. He turned his head in time to see the mummy lean back and make one powerful thrust with its head directly at the centre of the window. The polycarbonate split enough for it to get its hands between the edges and start to pull. Seth loaded the flare gun as fast as he could, repeatedly glancing back. Antonio was still thrashing as the window flew outward with the force of an explosion. Bandaged arms reached in through the opening and grabbed the pilot's shoulders. Seth took aim, hesitated only long enough to make the shot count, and pulled the trigger. The recoil pushed him back toward the door as a flash surged from the end of the gun. The flare hit the mummy under the left arm, forcing it back. Almost instantly, the glow from the flare erupted into flames. The Vidi fell backward away from the helicopter, the fire quickly spreading to cover its entire body. Seth looked at the gun in his hand then back at the growing blaze, slightly confused.

"Should that work like that?" asked Lakey from behind him.

Seth shrugged. The Vidi was running now, the flames reminding Seth of the cardinal's flowing robes, and disappeared.

"Seth!" It was Sam. He was running down from the mountain entrance. When Seth turned, he saw Owen running down the slope to the right. The two men must have come out together, and Owen must have caught sight of Falco, who had one of the utility vehicles moving and was heading north, away from the mountain. Owen was carrying something that Seth could have sworn was an axe. "Are you all right?" Sam called.

Seth opened his door and leaned out. "We're fine!"

"Speak for yourself!" said Antonio testily.

"The cardinal went that way in the truck," Seth called loudly, pointing south. "Two mummies went after him. Falco was alone, but he has a gun — go with Dr. Yancey! Use the mic!"

Sam nodded and sprinted toward Owen, who had almost reached the other UTV. In a moment, they were gone. Seth turned to his computer to confirm contact with Sam. "What happened?" Seth asked.

The Vidi and the People are fighting, Sam replied. *The Bakkers and Angel are caught in the middle. The Vidi had a leader, someone organizing them, but it's still chaos. We have to get the FSK in here. Did you talk to Clarice?*

"Clarice? Oh, shiz! Hang on a minute." Seth scrambled for the headset, which had come off when the mummy attacked the helicopter. He snatched it up and slapped it on his head. "Hello? Hello? Miss Clarice?"

I'm here! What was all of that?

"I shot a mummy with a flare gun."

You shot a mummy. With a flare gun.

"Yes. It caught on fire and ran away."

Silence.

Is the doctor there?

"He was, but he's gone again. I have him on two-way."

Seth? called Sam. *Is she there?*

"Yes, she's here."

Is she sending the FSK?

"Are you sending the FSK?"

What I've just heard should be enough to convince them. Sit tight and be careful. We're coming.

"Thanks," replied Seth. "Mr. E, she says they're coming."

Good. Can you put Tess on?

"Tess? She isn't here. You didn't see her? She went in right after you did."

She did WHAT? Owen, stop!

There was screeching, crashing, and cursing, and Seth figured the UTV was on its way back. A few tense moments passed. Seth watched the Mountain entrance closely, occasionally glancing to his right to look for the UTV.

Then, movement at the entrance. "Wait! I see her; she just came out!" Tess and Angel were coming down the hill toward the helicopter. "Angel's with her."

Sam passed this on to Owen. *Thank Christ*, Seth could hear Owen say.

Seth, said Sam, *when they are on board, you figure out a way to get that bird in the air. Get to a safe distance and stay in touch through the radio.*

"Uh, okay, there are several things wrong with that plan."

Not from where I sit. I would have expected you and Lakey to have built your own helicopter by now.

Seth glanced back at Lakey. She had her hands clasped in front of her chin, biting her knuckles and trying to contain her excitement while nodding vigorously. "Just get back here as soon as you can," he said to Sam.

Tess and Angel arrived at the side door, and Lakey slid it open. Tess sat in the first middle seat, and Angel went to the third row in the back. Tess had a rip in the sleeve of her jacket that wasn't there before.

"What happened to him?" Angel asked, gesturing at the pilot. His face was streaked and wet, and his clothes were torn where the Vidi had clawed at him. He'd started to shiver slightly, though sitting next to the hole in the fuselage where the window used to be likely wasn't the only reason.

"This is Shark Bait, I mean Antonio," said Lakey. "He's one of the bad guys. And he cheats at cards. A mummy tried to eat him, but Sethie pulled a James Bond and shot it with a flare gun."

"Right!" Seth said. "The boat chase in *From Russia With Love*." He waved the orange pistol. "Eric would have been impressed."

"Where's my dad?" asked Tess. "Did you see him?"

"Just talking to him now," Seth replied. "He went after Falco with Angel's dad."

"Can I talk to him?"

Seth passed the computer to Tess and looked at Lakey. "You better get up here, Gidge. I'm going to need your help."

25

THE LIGHT AND THE DARK

Eric ran back down the sloping tunnel to the hall. Hearing the now-familiar sounds of clashing weapons as he approached, he gripped the hilt of his sword and put his back to the wall before looking inside.

"Michael?" he whispered. His brother should have been in the next tunnel, close enough to pick up the signal through his earpiece. There was no response.

Eric tried anxiously to look into the hall without being seen. He'd only been gone a few minutes, but he could see three more People were down. As another one fell, Michael had had enough. His huge frame stepped into the hall, blocking Eric's view.

Stay here, he said through his mic. He didn't even glance in Eric's direction.

As Michael strode forward, the atmosphere in the hall changed. Vidarr saw him coming, but instead of stepping out to meet him, he stood impassively as two mummies pulled back from the fighting and went at Michael.

"Oh, no," Eric said softly.

Michael changed course long enough to grab a shield from a table, and with shield in one hand and sword in the other, advanced straight toward the oncoming Vidi. He sprinted the last few steps, put all his weight behind the shield and crushed it into the first mummy's chest. The collision echoed around the hall.

The second mummy had picked up a sword and now swung it wildly. The blade crashed into Michael's shield, splitting the heavy wood in two.

Michael staggered backward. The Vidi pulled the sword back and swung again in a sweeping arc. Michael ducked and moved to his left, tossing away what was left of the shield. He rolled over the surface of a table, landed on his feet, and backed up to widen the gap between them. The first Vidi circled around, watching, as the other went after Michael, jumping over the table and raising the sword again. Michael blocked it, the clash of swords rang out, and he followed with a front kick that drove the mummy back. They met again, Michael swinging first this time, low, but he missed, the blade instead smashing an urn that had stood on a pedestal next to the wall, one of the oil lamps. It shattered, spilling the oil. Michael swung again but slipped and lost his balance. The Vidi took advantage, thrusting the sword toward Michael. It came away bloody, and Michael clutched at his side. As he recovered, his sword came down on the next lamp, which was lit, igniting the oil that covered the blade. Flames spread along its length. At the sight of the burning sword, both Vidi jumped back, keeping their distance but still circling. Eric thought he heard a growl from one of them.

Michael was down on one knee; Eric couldn't tell how badly he was injured. He glanced over at the other side of the hall and saw the rest of the Vidi relentlessly pushing the last of the People. Vidarr, who had become engaged in fighting the People directly while still coordinating the attack, now stood watching. Michael stood up slowly, his eyes fixed on the Vidi leader. He raised the sword and pointed it at him, but the flames had already started to diminish, and before he could start forward, the two Vidi had begun to close in.

"Michael!" Eric called. He ran without thinking.

As the first Vidi leapt toward him, Michael dodged and swung, and the mummy abruptly changed direction, writhing. The second started in just as the first made contact, about to blindside him, but Eric was there in time; he caught it from behind and powered it past Michael into the wall, smashing it into the stone as hard as he could. The Vidi twisted away, reaching for him. Eric thrust upward with the short sword, connecting with the mummy's shoulder as it spun toward him. The sword embedded between bones and was wrenched from Eric's hand. Before the Vidi could reach him, Eric dove sideways to the floor and rolled across his shoulders to his feet again. The mummy came after him, but then Michael was there, swinging his sword and severing its arm. Immediately, the Vidi grabbed the hilt of the sword still buried in its shoulder, wrenched it out, and went after Michael, furiously swinging the blade.

The two battled each other, moving from the side of the hall into the centre. Eric looked to his right and saw that more People had fallen. There were now only four People left against Vidarr and two Vidi. Viggo was among the People, but all of them were moving more slowly. They looked weary from the fight, which didn't make sense to Eric. The Vidi seemed slower than before as well but still showed more speed than their opponents. Eric glanced at the tunnel leading down to the lower circuit, but there was no sign of his parents.

Eric backed up, looking for another weapon. Then he had an idea. He took the bandages from the severed arm, found the shaft of a broken hammer and wrapped the bandages around it, then soaked the bandages in oil from the shattered urn. Quickly, he moved to the burning oil lamp and ignited the makeshift torch. As he turned, he saw the mummy Michael had slashed was up again, a wide gash across its belly, and it charged at Michael. Eric lunged forward and thrust the torch into the Vidi's midsection. It went up like it was made of rocket fuel. Everyone in the room stopped, like before, as the mummy was consumed. Eric could feel Vidarr's stare bore into him.

The impact with the Vidi had pulled the bandages from the end of the hammer handle, so all Eric had left was a piece of wood. A snarl came from the one-armed Vidi as it leapt onto a table near him. Eric thought he could see something close to hatred in the white eyes of the mummy as it lunged. With incredible speed, Michael changed direction and went low, swinging his left arm at the mummy's legs and tripping it, then he planted his foot on the table, pushed hard, and followed the mummy toward the floor. Before the Vidi could recover, Michael chopped its head off at the shoulders. The expression of hatred was frozen on the blank eyes as the head rolled across the floor.

The kill hadn't gone unnoticed by Vidarr. Michael, not wasting any time, moved over to Eric and herded him back toward the tunnel opening. Viggo and the last two People were retreating in that direction as well. Vidarr pushed the Vidi forward. None of the oil lamps were burning on this side of the hall, so there was no way to make another torch. Michael urged Eric into the tunnel and followed, with Viggo close behind. Eric saw one of the remaining two People stop short, cringing, like something had hit from behind. Turning slowly showed an axe buried between shoulder blades. The closest Vidi was there instantly to finish the job. The last of the People, reacting instinctively to help, was quickly overcome by the other mummies. The struggle gave Viggo, a look of pain clear on his face, time to urge Eric and Michael on. Ada's father was now the only thing between Vidarr and the remaining Vidi and Eric and his family, and their retreat was taking them deeper into a mountain that was quickly becoming a tomb.

Eric's steps became more cautious the farther he went down the tunnel. He hadn't had time to get a lantern, and the light from the hall was fading rapidly.

"Keep going," said Michael.

Eric held his arms out instinctively. His hand brushed the wall beside him, but he couldn't see it. A few more steps and he no longer felt Michael's presence. He stopped. He could still feel the downward slope of the tunnel beneath his feet. A strong hand on his shoulder pushed him roughly forward, guided him around the corner, and planted his back against the wall.

"Stay here," Michael told him.

Eric looked in the direction of his brother's voice but couldn't see him. There was scuffling, a clash of metal on stone, a thud. Eric pressed his palms against the smooth stone behind him. His eyes were as wide as he could make them, but it made no difference. He'd never felt so helpless.

"Viggo!" Michael shouted. Another clash. Eric stayed against the wall but turned toward the sounds, inching forward. He felt something shift in his pocket. The device. He took it out and held it in his hand. There was a scurrying sound close by, something moving quickly within the lower tunnel. It was close, but he couldn't tell how close.

"Mike…" Eric said softly and pushed the button.

26

THE MOUNTAIN BREATHES

Clara and Gabriel hurried to keep up with Ada as she moved ahead of them down the tunnel. Gabriel carried a lantern, but Ada walked on the edge of the light, the way ahead shrouded in shadow. Over the last few days, Clara had become close to Ada and trusted her completely. Though leaving her here was painful, she couldn't bear the thought of anything happening to her family if they didn't take this opportunity to get out. The least she could do was honour Ada's request and take Williams with them, despite Clara's falling hopes that anything could be done for him, especially away from the Mountain. Either way, Clara was determined to get help and come back. She just hoped Ada could hold out long enough.

They came to the right turn at the bottom of the slope, and Ada disappeared for a moment. Clara quickened her pace to make the turn and saw her, slightly farther ahead, before she disappeared again, this time into the chamber where they'd left Williams earlier. They followed past the rows of benches to the steps that led to the lower level, and Clara hurried down. Gabriel stayed above, holding the lantern up so she could see. Ada was kneeling next to Williams, and it seemed like everything was as it had been before, except when Clara knelt down, she noticed the stone floor was now very wet. She thought of the other chamber where Williams had been, about how the stretcher and Williams's clothes had become damp before they'd moved him. There was so much more of it now. Clara reached out to touch Williams's arm. His shirt was soaked and cold. She brought her hand up to her nose but couldn't detect any smell; if it was water, she couldn't tell where it possibly could have come from. She looked up at Gabriel inquisitively. Gabriel started toward the steps, still holding the lantern high, but then suddenly stopped, his eyes wide and fixed on Williams. Clara turned back toward him in time to see his arm bend as he raised his hand in the air.

27

HOW HARD CAN IT BE?

Seth went over the controls again while Lakey went around to the copilot seat. It suddenly seemed like the console was twice as big, with about a thousand more buttons and switches than there had been a few minutes ago. He kept glancing up at the mountain entrance, expecting mummies to come pouring out at any second. Lakey had grabbed Seth's wheelchair — thankfully, Abito hadn't run over it with the SUV, and it seemed okay — and loaded it in the back row of the cabin. There was no way Seth was leaving it behind, wherever they ended up.

Lakey heaved the door open and leapt in. The gap between the pilot seats and the first row of passenger seats was high and narrow, basically a window too small to crawl through, so she'd had to go around. "What do we do?" she asked.

"There must be a manual around here somewhere. Find it."

"What, like *Helicopter Flying for Dummies*? Really?"

"Just look for it, Gidge!"

She found a small white booklet stuck in a slot next to the centre console, laminated and coil-bound. She flipped it open. "It's in Italian!"

"What about him?" asked Tess. Seth looked back. She was looking at the pilot, who still sat with his eyes wide, apparently unaware of anything happening around him.

Angel waved a hand in front of the pilot's face. He didn't seem to notice. "He's useless."

"I think I have it," said Lakey. "There's a title and a list: *Controllo preliminare, Controllo di sic...ur...ezza.* What's that?"

"Preliminare? The preflight checklist," Seth guessed, looking at the entrance again. There was no telling how much time they had. "Skip it — just go to the startup!"

"Okay, okay!" Lakey riffled through the pages. "Um, all right, I think I have it. It says, *'Avvio normale del motore.'* There's a couple of paragraphs here that say, *'Nota.'"* She flipped the page again. "I hope they're not important," she added casually. "Here we go: *inter...rut...tore* ENG 1 FUEL - ON. 'ENG 1 FUEL' and 'ON' are all in capitals."

"That's good — must refer to what's on the panels." Seth searched the centre console. "Just skip anything that doesn't refer to a switch or a lever." Fortunately, all the labels were in English. He found the FUEL 1 and FUEL 2 levers near the top, directly above the fuel pump switches. They had flat, red triangles on the ends of the handles that made them stand out. He reached for the first one.

Lakey was flipping ahead in the manual. "Cheese and crackers, this is a long list. And there's more than one." She stopped. "Wait! There's a *'rapido'* version! The list is almost all caps. Awesome. Let's do this."

"Go!"

"ENG 1 FUEL first, then FUEL PUMP 1 - ON."

"Saw those already," said Seth. He flipped the switch for the fuel pump, and a green light came on above it. He could hear noises start coming from somewhere. "Got it."

"ENG 2 FUEL and FUEL PUMP 2 - ON."

Another lever switch and another green light. More noise. "Next?"

"ENG 1 MODE - FLT and ENG 2 MODE - FLT."

Dials just below the pump switches. Seth moved the first one to "FLT" and was reaching for the second when Lakey stopped him.

"One at a time, bro. We do ENG 1 first, then ENG 2." She referred to the instructions again. "Next to ENG 2 MODE, it says, 'FLT *quando* Number 1 *motore* NG *supera il* 25%. Something has to get to 25% before we flip Number 2."

Seth checked the displays on the front console. Numbers were changing and lines were moving like gauges on the screen. He didn't know what he was looking for. He looked at Lakey, shrugged, held up crossed fingers, and turned the second dial. More numbers and lines. The helicopter definitely did not explode.

"There aren't any more capital letters for a while," said Lakey. "I think we're supposed to start the engines now?" She said it like a question.

Seth looked up. He remembered Mike Wiegele using big levers to get the blades moving on the heli-skiing runs back home. Two long levers with large, round handles like wheels on a Tonka truck extended down from the roof and pointed toward the rear, one with a "1" on the side, and the other with a "2." Labels near the base read OFF, IDLE, FLIGHT, and MAX along an arc. He moved both levers to the FLIGHT position. The word "START" was printed at the base of each, wrapped around a button. He pushed the button on the first lever and held it for a few seconds as a loud noise came from all around them, drowning out everything else. The rotor started moving above them, slowly at first, then faster until he couldn't see the individual blades. Numbers on the display were changing rapidly again. The noise reached a certain pitch then stayed consistent. He pushed the button on the second lever, and the noise grew louder again. Seth took the headset down from its hook above him, and Lakey did the same.

"Check, check," said Seth. He heard his own voice crackle through the headphones.

Roger wilco niner, Lakey crackled in reply.

"What else you got?"

Lakey flipped nonchalantly through the pages then snapped the book closed. *The rest is checks and stuff,* she said, stowing the book where she'd found it. *Stick time, Sethie.*

Seth looked behind him into the cabin. Tess and Angel were sitting in the front seats, facing the rear, belts on, and were taking headsets down from hooks on the ceiling.

"Comm check," said Seth. "You good?"

Tess nodded.

So how much flight time you have? Angel asked.

Seth had turned back to the controls, so Lakey answered for him. *Well, between the flight simulators and drones, over ten thousand hours, easy.*

And actual?

We'll let you know when we're done.

Oh, God.

Seth pulled slightly upward on the collective lever with his left hand. It was positioned along the side of his seat, much like the parking brake in a car. He felt the resistance he knew was built into the mechanism to prevent inadvertent movement. The noise from the rotors became a little louder, and the helicopter started to shift. He held the cyclic with his right hand, leaving it in its starting position as they began to rise. A familiar rush went through him as he felt the power of the engines through the structure of the machine. He was surprised at how smooth and tight it was, considering there were five enormous knives spinning around very fast above him. He knew they were made of composite wrapped in fibreglass and graphite tape instead of metal but figured they could still dice like a Slap Chop. Maybe better.

Oh, yeah! yelled Lakey.

They rose a couple of metres and drifted slightly to the right. Seth compensated with the cyclic, and the helicopter held its position. He looked at Lakey. She nodded eagerly. Seth pulled hard on the collective, and they started upward, slowly at first then faster and faster. They were above the peak in front of them quickly, and a moment later, they could see parts of what must have been Trondheim in the distance. The sky was clear and bright, and, thankfully, empty.

Not too high, Seth, said Angel. *Shark Bait has no window.*

"Right." Seth eased the collective back to level and shifted his focus to the ground.

Whoa, said Lakey. *Check it out.*

She was looking down to her left. Seth tried to see but couldn't. "Turn us that way, Lakes," he said.

Pedals?

"Yep."

Lakey planted her left foot and pushed. The helicopter turned as it hovered, and a black object came into view. It stood out against the grey stone, and Seth recognized it as the SUV. The front end was in a crevice, one of the rear wheels was off the ground, and both back doors were open. There was no other sign of the cardinal.

I don't see them, said Tess. Seth glanced back at her. She was looking in the opposite direction to the SUV.

"Spin us around again," Seth said to Lakey. "Let's go have a look."

28

LAST RESORT

The effect of pushing the button was nearly instantaneous. The noises in the dark stopped. The now-familiar tightness began to spread through Eric's body, starting in his legs and moving upward. He could hear Michael start to breathe through incredible strain, and he nearly let go of the button involuntarily but forced himself to hold on. His muscles continued to flex, and he was suddenly worried he might not be able to release the button again when he needed to. He pushed a hand against the wall to steady himself and took a laboured step forward. Then another. Fighting hard, he worked his way around the corner into the sloping tunnel. A dim glow from the other end of the passage gave his eyes something to work with, and he could see the barest outline of the figures in front of him. Only one was standing, the farthest away from him. It had to be Vidarr. He stood, feet apart, arms slightly outward, fists clenched and back arched, his face upward, the strain obvious and silencing.

Eric willed his feet to move, though it was getting harder and harder to do. His initial thought was to get back to the hall, to get light and a weapon, but he had no idea if he could use them. And not only would Michael not last much longer with the device activated, he would be in no condition to fight when Eric released the button. Eric was filled with indecision; he didn't know what to do.

He reached out a hand, searching for his brother in the darkness, and found him bent like an archer's bow, no longer able to breathe. Every muscle in his body was pulling him apart.

"I'm sorry, Mike," said Eric. "I'm sorry."

Eric could barely move. His hand held the device firmly, and he was no longer sure it would obey him and let go. He stared at it, using everything he had, trying to lift his thumb. He looked back at Vidarr, unsure of how the Vidi would be affected when the power of the device was lifted. The mummy in Montana had eviscerated Stockton and fled, and that with most of its dreylagr gone. As he watched, something changed in Vidarr's stance. Eric tried to focus as his own head started to shake. The tension was there in the mummy's figure, but it was like the strain was gone, like he was no longer fighting it. He looked back at his immovable thumb. He couldn't hear Michael anymore; he couldn't wait any longer. It had to be now.

Eric pried the device from his grip and threw it into the darkness. Immediately, the electric current that had been coursing through him was gone, leaving his muscles spasming as they tried to relax. He quickly turned back to Vidarr, taking two shaky steps backward as he did so, but instead of rushing toward him, the mummy fell, dropping to lay among the other Vidi. None of them were moving.

Eric looked desperately for Michael and found him a few feet away, down and hardly moving but conscious.

"Can you hear me?" He kneeled stiffly beside his brother. "Are you all right?"

"What's happening?" Michael asked weakly.

Eric looked around, trying to see enough in the dark to come up with an answer. "I don't know. I don't understand."

"Where's Viggo? He was down. Over there." Michael pointed. Eric could see shapes there, but he couldn't tell who they were.

"Was he hurt?"

"He was knocked down just before you pushed the button. I don't think he was hurt. Not yet." Michael started to turn, trying to get onto his hands and knees. Eric did what he could to help, putting a hand under his brother's arm, but it didn't feel like he made much of a difference. Michael stood and staggered toward one of the figures on the ground. He roughly moved one aside and focused on another. It must have been Viggo. He looked down at the old man, held his shoulder, then irrationally felt for a pulse. "He isn't cut. I don't understand."

"I'm going back to the hall for lanterns," said Eric. "Be ready."

Eric limped up the sloping tunnel to the Great Hall, stepping around the two People who had been taken down by the Vidi when they started their retreat. He approached the hall warily, even though he knew it would be empty, but he wasn't prepared for the absolute stillness he found. It was like being in a house after a storm when the power had been knocked out. The fire in the hearth had burned low, and the oil lamps that were still lit burned with steady, unmoving flames. He didn't linger. He grabbed two of the portable lanterns and a short sword and turned back to the tunnel.

The light he carried brought up the scene: one Vidi down was separate from the others, evidently taken out by Michael before the device. The other two were next to the wall. Michael had apparently moved them away from Viggo. They must have been on him when he pushed the button. Vidarr hadn't moved from where he'd fallen, but Eric stepped carefully around him.

"I don't understand," said Michael.

"Can you walk?" Eric asked. "We need to find Mom and Dad. Ada will know what to do. We need to get out of here before they wake up."

Michael looked up at his brother. His eyes shone bright blue in the lantern light. "I don't think that's going to happen, little brother."

"Yes, it will. We can do it if we hurry. Come on."

"No, I mean I don't think they're going to wake up."

29

BIRD'S-EYE VIEW

The nose of the helicopter dipped slightly as Seth pushed the cyclic lever in the direction Sam and Owen had gone. It didn't take long to find them — there were no trees here, so they were surrounded mostly by bare rock — but he couldn't see Falco.

The terrain looked different from this height, smoother and more undulating, and he had more appreciation for the steep slope. Owen's utility vehicle bounced violently as it raced across the hard surface. It was a yellow Can-Am Defender, a two-seater with a dump box, and must have been what Ada and Clara had used to get to the Mountain.

"Anyone see the other one?" Seth asked.

It's a red Polaris Ranger, said Angel.

No one did. Seth pulled his headset off long enough to put his earphones in and put it back on again. "Lakes, see if you can tie us in to the onboard." He looked down at the yellow speck below them. It was weaving back and forth seemingly at random. "Mr. E, can you hear me?"

Barely, Sam replied. *There's a lot of noise.*

"We're just above you."

Ha! Told ya.

Seth smiled. "I take it from Dr. Yancey's driving that you don't have a visual?"

We figured this called for a serpentine overground strategy. Either that, or we're going against the wind and Owen thinks he's in his boat. Help us out?

"Give me a minute."

Seth flew on ahead, opting for a straight line but scanning in all directions.

There! said Angel, pointing. A small dark dot was shifting over the grey stone in the distance to their left.

Falco had stayed higher on the mountain until he'd gone partway around it, possibly trying to hide from view but likely just trying to get to the west side as quickly as possible. He was making for a stand of trees some distance away. Seth moved in closer.

"Got him," he said. He checked his compass. "Maybe a kilometre away, almost due west. You might have to stretch that to go around the base of the mountain. Once he hits undergrowth, he'll have to slow down, though."

Sam relayed the information to Owen. The yellow speck turned west and picked up speed, taking a direct route this time. *Keep an eye on him,* said Sam.

"On it."

Falco was driving fast and obviously wasn't that good at it, since he was having trouble keeping all four wheels on the ground at the same time. The slope wasn't as steep at that elevation, but gravity can be a bitch when it wants to be.

The Polaris was about the same size but not nearly as rugged as Betty. Of course, it also hadn't had the benefit of Seth and Lakey's touch, but Seth figured if they had a few days they could do something with it: aluminum doors to keep the roost out of the cabin on the low ground, F-22 bumpers to brace the chassis, Assault turret-style radius rods and tie-rods to handle these crevices and get the sprung weight down, and definitely some 30" Motovators on M31 Lok2 beadlock wheels...

Stop it, Seth, Lakey said.

"What?"

I know you were refitting the Ranger in your head. Save it, brah, we'll get it later! You're flying a helicopter, man!

"Right! Sorry." Seth gave his head a shake and refocused.

Falco was still moving wildly over the rock. He swerved to miss a gap, still hit some of it, and actually caught some air.

How is this guy still going? Lakey asked in wonder.

They watched as the red UTV somehow made it to the flats, picking a line that seemed to flow directly from the centre of the mountain. Looking at it from this angle, Seth could see the west side of the mountain was two separate peaks with a deep depression in the middle, the bottom of which Falco had found and was now following toward the trees. A huge jagged line ran out from the edge of the depression and curved north into the distance.

Check it out, said Lakey. *It looks like someone whacked the mountain with a giant hammer.*

It did look like that. The jagged line clearly was not a river; it was a massive crack in the rock, like something really big had struck it really hard.

Hey, do you remember that coconut I tried to open that time in Maui? Lakey said reflectively.

"I do," answered Seth. "And I still don't think a 9-iron has the best design for that purpose."

You're probably right. Should've gone with the pitching wedge. The ground here looks kind of like that, doesn't it?

"Watch out ahead," Seth said into his headphone mic. "You'll be coming to a span. Not sure of the grade change, but Evel Knievel down there made it interesting."

You still have him? Sam asked.

"Yeah, he's in and out of trees but still booking it. This will not end well for him."

Despite Falco's recklessness, Sam and Owen were gaining. Angel's dad was pushing it even harder than the comandante, with only slightly better results, but the smaller Defender had its advantages over the Ranger, and Owen had a spotter. He pulled up before he hit the gap, enough to get across it, then picked up speed again.

After a few more close calls, they banked along the edge of a slope and just crested a low rise when a small flash blew upward from the front of the Defender like a cloud of dust. Owen swerved abruptly to the right but kept moving.

It's Falco! Tess exclaimed.

Everyone had been watching Sam and Owen. Seth shifted focus to the Ranger. Falco must have caught a glimpse of the Defender behind him; he'd stopped in a clearing and pulled his sidearm. The trees were scrubby and sparse and didn't do much to block his view. As Seth watched, Falco fired three more shots. Seth couldn't hear them, but there was no mistaking the recoil of the weapon. Owen weaved a little but didn't slow down at all. If anything, he gained more speed. Sam had one hand on the roll bar in front of him and the other on the back edge of the roof, trying to keep from flying out of the cab. Falco fired several more times, and there was the occasional flash where a bullet made contact, but the Defender kept coming. Falco eventually gave up or ran out of ammo, Seth couldn't tell which. He tossed the weapon into a compartment near the steering wheel and started the Ranger moving again, the roost flying behind him as he ripped up the sparse underbrush. With no gunfire to deter him, Owen straightened out his line and floored it.

Seth glanced back at Angel. "I see where you get it," he said.

Angel didn't take her eyes off the scene below. *Get him,* she whispered.

Falco must have sensed his chances were slipping. He increased speed even more, and the vehicle tossed violently as the increasing vegetation made the ground harder to see. He hadn't made it very far when he hit a ledge and bounced in the air, whipped partway through a Man-with-the-Golden-Gun corkscrew, and landed on his lid. The roll cage worked, but there wasn't enough momentum to get upright again. Seth circled above with Lakey's help on the pedals, trying to get a look inside the cab.

I see him, said Tess. *He's there!* She pointed toward the far side of the overturned UTV. Falco had crawled out and now staggered a few steps to get his bearings. His black bomber jacket was torn at the shoulder, and he was limping. Seth couldn't see the gun, but Falco did have the sword he'd carried out of the mountain. He hobbled away in the direction he'd been driving.

Definitely shaken, not stirred, Lakey observed.

"He's on foot," said Seth. "Continuing west. Take it easy as you get closer; there's a bump coming up."

Seth guided them through the launch zone and around the downed Ranger. In a few moments, they were on him.

Stay where you are! yelled Sam. It was so authoritative that Seth stopped flying and sat rigid in his seat for a second.

Seth, can you take us closer? Tess asked.

Seth took them lower and angled off so Tess and Angel could see clearly through the windows on the right side. Owen bore down on Falco like he meant to run him over with the Defender. Falco heard them and jumped aside at the last second, dropping the sword. He was on the driver side of the vehicle, rolling quickly as he tried to get back to his feet.

Uh-oh, said Sam.

Owen didn't bother to stop the UTV; he grabbed his axe and leapt out while it was still moving. He went straight toward Falco and raised the weapon. Sam was out of the passenger side a moment later and running around the Defender to try to catch up. *Owen, wait!*

Before the big scientist could swing down — a chop that would likely split Falco like firewood — the captain got hold of the sword and rolled on his back, holding it up to defend himself. Owen seemed undeterred, lifting the blade higher as he came into range.

Owen, stop! Jesus, your daughter is watching!

Owen faltered slightly. He wavered for only the briefest of moments, glancing up toward the helicopter, and Falco saw his opportunity. Still lying on his back, he brought the sword down and swung it around hard at the scientist's leg.

NO! Angel screamed.

When Owen looked up, Seth could see his face for the first time since he'd come out of the mountain. It was from a distance, but in that instant, his countenance changed from a look of mindless rage to something like wonder. Almost involuntarily, he took a small step backward. It was just enough. The weight of the blade missed, the tip only catching the front of his shin. Owen looked unflinchingly down at Falco, but instead of bringing the axe down, he kicked hard at Falco's wrist before the captain could bring the sword back at him again. The captain's wrist was pinned to his stomach by Owen's foot. Falco dropped the sword, gasping for breath, and Owen leaned over, holding the axe close to the man's throat. Neither of them moved. Owen was saying something to him when Sam stepped in. Sam coaxed Owen off and had Falco roll over, which he did gingerly, and put his hands behind his head.

Still have that roll of duct tape, Bruno?

Seth smiled. "Sure do!" He and Lakey circled around to a better position, and he had Angel toss the tape out the broken window.

Tell Shark Bait he's about to have some company. See what you can find out on the other side of the mountain, okay?

"You got it. Abito didn't get far; his driving is worse than Falco's. We'll go find him, but keep an eye out for his mummy buddies."

Seth pulled on the collective to gain altitude and took the Popecopter up and around the south side of the mountain. Everyone scanned the ground for the SUV. They found it in the same place they'd seen it before and in the same condition: nose down, rear end up, doors open.

He has to be around here somewhere, said Angel.

Not sure about that, Lakey said. *The way he was moving down the mountain, he could be anywhere by now. Must have had some kind of divine intervention.*

What's that? Tess asked. She was looking out her window, southwest of their position. Lakey turned the helicopter slightly as they hovered. Tucked in beside a couple of small, haggard-looking trees and partially covered with what little brush there was available was another UTV. It was black, with a large, flat bed in the back and tether straps lying loosely across it. The back end was pointing toward the mountain, and the front had branches and moss over it, like someone was trying to conceal it. Seth took them in closer. When they cleared the low trees, they could see three figures lying on the ground close together. One of them was dressed like a cardinal.

"Uh, Mr. E?"

Yeah, Bruno. Have something?

"You might say that. When you get around to this side, head over to our position. There's something you have to see."

30

TWILIGHT OF THE GODS

C lara remained perfectly still as Williams's hand came to rest on Ada's arm. She put her hand on his and looked at him fondly. His eyes fluttered open and locked on her immediately. He whispered her name. She put a hand to his cheek and held it, speaking softly in a language Clara didn't understand. Clara glanced up at Gabriel and quietly drew back toward the stairs. In a moment, she was next to him, leaning in with her head on his shoulder as they watched from a respectful distance two people separated until now by fifteen hundred years of steadfast belief and searching by one, of hope by the other.

They stayed a while, entranced, Clara didn't know how long, until she felt Gabriel turn and look toward the entrance to the chamber. It was so unfair that Williams and Ada couldn't take all the time they wanted, Clara thought, but if they could get out of the Mountain, then perhaps that's exactly what they could do.

She looked at Gabriel, who held her gaze. "Ada was right," she said. "She knew this would happen."

"I don't think this is what she had in mind," Gabriel responded. "But what *did* happen?"

She turned back toward the couple below them. "I'm not sure. But I did notice something. When we moved him earlier, the back of his entire body was wet. The stretcher too. And just now it was even more. He was soaked. What could it be?"

"The fluid inside him was draining out?"

Clara shook her head. "It didn't look that way. He didn't seem desiccated, and he'd have to be if he'd lost that much. If anything, he seemed less so, like the burns were less severe. It was like he was drawing it in from outside himself."

"Or it was given to him," said Gabriel thoughtfully.

Clara looked inquiringly at her husband.

"There's something about this place," Gabriel said. "There's an energy here. Can you feel it? It's different from the Green Mountain in Libya. Completely different."

"But that mountain collapsed, remember? It was destroyed in an earthquake."

"So was this one. And I don't think that's a coincidence."

"What do you mean?"

"We've been to lots of places that have layers of history or centuries of continuous use, and we've seen enough to know there are forces at work on levels we can't see directly. That temple in Bihar in southwest India or the ruins of the castle north of Wick in Scotland — or the Yarrows Broch itself, for that matter — not to mention San Marco in Rome and the Lateran Basilica, but it's always been about a presence, a life force *inhabiting* the space and affecting people in it. This is different. It's like the space itself has influence. Strong influence. Whatever it is, it's sustained these people, even when they are away from it."

"Animism as reality, you mean. The Mountain is alive? These people are more sophisticated than that, and there's no idolatry here."

Gabriel shrugged. "The difference between physics and spirituality or having a soul is in the system's level of complexity and the observer's capacity for comprehension. Something weird happens, we come up with an explanation as best we can. Sometimes a complex system has a simple explanation."

"This has something to do with the ritual, the Passage?"

Gabriel nodded. "In each of them, the avelid must be the vessel and the dreylagr the conductor, but the Mountain is the source. The ritual didn't work for the People in Libya, because whatever this power is, that mountain didn't have it."

"Or they just didn't have dreylagr. They used what they could find within the mountain, remember? It might have been nothing more than water."

"That's the same thing, isn't it? About the difference between the mountains? Having that power, I mean."

"What about the earthquakes?"

"A reset, maybe. A way to protect the People. From others or from themselves. It happened there because of the Romans and the Vidi, and it happened here because of civil war."

"If one place has power and the other doesn't, how did it happen at both places?"

"It must have been the reach of one toward the other. The strength to follow the People. Thor's hammer — our project's namesake, after all. I don't know. Either way, whatever I'm sensing is something more than just the presence of these people. It's like the Mountain is *doing* something, playing an active part in what's going on. Whether that's good or bad, I can't say." He looked back toward the door again. "Given some time, we might figure it out, but now we need to go."

Clara looked back toward Ada and Williams. They were still talking softly. Ada leaned over Williams, and they embraced. Ada's shoulders shook slightly, like she was crying, then stopped. Williams's damaged hand rested on her back consolingly.

"You're right," Clara said, starting toward the stairs. Gabriel followed, holding up the light as Clara descended. "I'm so sorry, Ada. We need to get going. Are you ready?"

Ada didn't reply. She stayed over Williams, maintaining their embrace. Clara approached awkwardly, feeling like an intruder. She reached out to place a hand on Ada's shoulder and on contact caught her breath. There was such stillness in Ada that Clara knew immediately that something terrible had happened. Withdrawing sharply, she inadvertently brushed Williams's arm, which slid from Ada's back and fell lifeless to his side. In her professional career, Clara had come to know death, the stillness and the emptiness. Despite all that had happened in recent days, Clara knew without question. Ada and Williams were gone.

31

TRADING ONE PROBLEM FOR ANOTHER

Eric and Michael moved down the corridor of the lower circuit, Eric still carrying the lantern and the sword. Michael, who was labouring, kept falling behind, but Eric wasn't sure where they were going. When he checked a chamber they came to, it gave Michael a chance to catch up.

"Which one is it?" Eric asked. He was getting exasperated, and his leg still hurt.

"Try the next one," said Michael, still breathing fairly heavily. "They're not far."

The door to the last room on the left before the next corner was heavier than the others, old wood worn smooth from centuries of hands pushing it open, like Eric did now. There was a faint glow from inside, the only room so far to have this, and he knew he had the right one. His guard went up, though, not sure what he would find.

There were several benches arranged in rows in the middle of the room in front of a wide table with shelves behind. The table and the shelves were empty. The light was coming from below the far wall. Eric approached cautiously until he saw his parents with Williams and Ada. He took a couple of steps and stopped. His mother was kneeling next to Ada, who seemed to be embracing Williams as he lay on the stretcher. Neither one appeared to be moving, and his mother was crying softly. His father stood next to her, holding the light.

"What happened?" Eric asked.

They turned like they hadn't known he was there, but they weren't startled. Michael stepped in behind him. "Oh, no. Them, too?"

Their mother moved to the stairs and came toward them, embracing them both. "It's over," she said. "They're gone."

Eric looked at her in confusion. "But what happened?" he repeated.

She shook her head. "I don't know."

"The others — is it the same?" asked Gabriel. He seemed like he already knew the answer.

"Yes," Michael replied. "Viggo was the only one left. But it's Vidarr and the Vidi, too."

"What do we do?" asked Eric.

Clara shook her head solemnly. "I'm sorry, sweetheart."

"I don't understand."

"Whatever the power was that sustained these people, it's gone now," said Gabriel. "The Mountain is silent. There's nothing more we can do for them."

Eric wasn't sure what to believe. He looked down at Williams. He thought of the airport in Oakland when he'd first seen him, how hard he tried to lose him on the trains, only to come back from Berkeley and find him with Tess waiting for him. The flights back to Victoria, the long drive to Montana, and the longer drive to Chicago. Williams had saved his life in all three places, had put himself directly between Eric and what would have ended him solely because he made a promise. And then he made the biggest sacrifice of all to save Eric and Michael's parents from the fire in Palermo. It wasn't right; there had to be something they could do.

"How does the ritual work?"

Clara looked at him, tilted her head, and smiled weakly. A few weeks ago, Eric's first reaction would have been to take this as patronizing and condescending. Now he saw an overwhelming sense of obligation to her purpose as a scientist, empathy for these people she knew she couldn't do enough to help, and a fondness for him. In that moment, Eric saw his mother differently, felt his world expand, and he understood. He walked over to her and embraced her warmly.

"I'm sorry, Mom," he said. He felt her relax and begin to cry.

After a moment, Eric stepped back, and his mother wiped her eyes.

"You're right," she said. She looked at Gabriel. "We need to try."

"Clara…"

"They have their avelids," she said. "And the bodies are intact, so the bandages really aren't necessary."

"But the dreylagr."

She looked down at Williams. "What if the moisture really was dreylagr? If we'd left him long enough, it might have had time to work."

Gabriel shook his head. "You may be right, but the dreylagr isn't the source of the power, it's only the medium. Williams was weak, obviously, but nothing happened to Ada. She already had the dreylagr she needed. No, there's something else missing, and I don't think it's something we can control."

"We're only assuming the same thing has happened to Abito and the Vidi who went after him," said Michael. "And we still have Falco to deal with. Owen and Sam and the others might need our help."

They decided to leave Williams and Ada together in the chamber and return to the Great Hall. Viggo and Vidarr were where Eric and Michael had left them, and as they passed, Michael explained to his parents what had happened there. The hall was also as Eric had last seen it. The fire was reduced to embers, but the oil lamps were enough to cast a glow over the scene, and a few random lanterns still added light in some areas. There were bodies lying throughout the hall, especially near the place where Eric and his parents had been cornered. There were also the four gendarmes who had tried to escape with Falco and Abito, their bodies standing out from the others because of the black clothes and the blood that had darkened in pools around them.

Clara checked each of them carefully and found one was actually still alive, though his pulse was faint and he'd lost a lot of blood. Immediately, she went into action. She had Gabriel and Eric move him to a table so she could assess him and they could try to stop the bleeding. While they worked, Michael took a submachine gun and left the hall to go find the others.

It took some time, but they managed to use strips of clothing to bind the gendarme's cuts. There were lots of them, but none had hit any major arteries. He was still unconscious, and Clara felt he would likely stay that way until he could be properly treated or he died. She asked Eric to go find Michael; they would need to get help in there as soon as possible.

Eric had taken another submachine gun, drawing a concerned look from Clara, and was about to leave when they heard a noise from a tunnel that led to the upper circuit. Eric heard footsteps then voices, and the sound of something sliding on metal. Light danced out of the opening like someone walking with a flashlight. Eric lowered the weapon as Owen stepped into the hall, carrying an axe in one hand and the flashlight in the other. Angel was next to him. Seth and Lakey came after, the sliding metal sound coming from Seth's handrims as he slowed his descent down the slope. Tess, Sam, and Michael came last. Everyone seemed okay and in good spirits. Tess came toward Eric, and he met her halfway. She threw her arms around his neck, and he hugged her warmly.

"Whoa," said Lakey. "It's like *Resident Evil 6* in here."

Clara went to Owen and hugged him around his broad shoulders. "You okay?" she asked, stepping back.

"Fine," he replied. "Little nick on my shin, but it's nothing."

Michael was carrying a large med kit that he took to Clara. She returned to the gendarme on the table.

"Falco get away?" asked Gabriel.

"Nope."

"What'd you do with him?" Eric asked.

Owen smiled. "He's keeping your pilot friend company on the helicopter. Left them talking about the highly effective adhesive properties of duct tape."

"It's okay," said Lakey. "I already warned him that if they decide to play cards, he should watch out because Antonio cheats."

"What about Abito?" asked Gabriel.

"Not so lucky," Sam answered. "We found him with two Vidi. He'd made it a fair distance from the Mountain entrance before they caught him. There were signs of a struggle; it looked like they were about to rip him apart — literally tear him in half — when something stopped them. They just dropped. Strangest thing." He seemed to reconsider his wording.

"Well, maybe not the strangest, considering." He glanced around the hall. "Michael says the same thing happened here? Happy about the outcome, of course, but have to say, a little surprised. Things were looking bleak the last time I checked."

"In the end, yes," Eric replied. "It was us and Viggo against Vidarr and two Vidi. We were down the tunnel where there wasn't any light." He looked at his brother. "*I* couldn't see anything, anyway."

Michael scoffed. "Hey, I could see just fine. I had everything under control until you zapped all of us."

"You pushed the button?" asked Angel, staring wide-eyed at Eric.

Eric shrugged. "I figured if there were a 'last resort' situation, that was it."

Clara was using supplies from the med kit to improve on what they'd done with the gendarme. "I want to gather everyone," she said, glancing around the hall. "They deserve more dignity than this. And I want to move Viggo next to Ada."

Everyone agreed, and they began moving the bodies from where they'd fallen to tables throughout the hall. People and Vidi were gathered at random and placed respectfully side by side. Clara insisted on having People and Vidi together, that they were one people and should be reunited, even if the circumstances didn't allow more than a symbolic gesture.

"Is everyone else accounted for?" Clara asked.

"The monk," said Michael.

Clara looked toward the tunnel where Marcus had disappeared.

"I'll take that one," said Eric.

"I'll go with you," Tess offered.

She took a lantern, and they started up the tunnel. She was wearing the same jacket she'd had in Pincher Creek on their way to Montana, and Eric was reminded of their walk the night they arrived there. So much had changed in such a short amount of time, and though he didn't doubt his feelings, he still didn't trust his instincts about hers.

"What happens now?" Tess asked.

"What?" he replied, unsure if she were thinking of Pincher Creek, too.

Tess gestured around her. "With all of this. Up to now, it was so important to keep the secret; is that still true? What will your parents do?"

"My first thought is that they'll camp here for the next six months until they know everything there is to know. But I'm not sure what they'll do with it. I suspect they will honour Williams and Ada, but keeping everything quiet might not be possible anymore. Or even necessary."

They checked the chambers along the sloping tunnel but didn't find anything. They had a decision to make when they reached the lower circuit: right or left. They chose right and continued searching.

"What do you suppose he was thinking when he left the hall?" Tess asked.

"I'm not sure. I find it hard to tell what any of these people are thinking. *Were* thinking, I guess. I found them hard to read. But he definitely registered something when he saw Vidarr and the Vidi, and not just because he and Abito hadn't expected them. I feel like the monk knew who Vidarr was, and it terrified him."

"They'd met before."

Eric shrugged. "Something must have happened. He might have been attacked — like Tomas before he became Abito — maybe lost someone close to him in the same way, too. Marcus might have gone to the Church because of Abito, or it might have been a coincidence and they found each other there. He could have known Vidarr by reputation and relied on the Church to hide him."

"Or they may have been here at the Mountain at the same time in the past," Tess suggested. "They could have known each other from the beginning."

"Maybe. I guess we'll never know."

The last chamber on the left before the tunnel turned and continued around the circuit was bigger than the others, similar to the chamber where Eric had last seen Williams and Ada on the opposite side of the mountain. This room had several long tables instead of just benches, and all around the walls were rows and rows of shelves set up in identical alcoves and filled, floor to ceiling, with books. They took many forms, were made with different materials, but all were ancient and looked like they hadn't been disturbed in centuries. Eric stepped closer, but before he could look at anything, Tess called to him.

"He's here."

She was standing near the edge overlooking the lower section at the back of the room. Eric joined her and saw the monk Marcus collapsed on his side, his hands still clasped together in front of him. He had obviously fallen over while on his knees in prayer and would have been unaware not only of the fate of everyone in the Mountain but of his own as well.

Tess went down the steps, walked directly to Marcus's side, and knelt, placing an unwavering hand on the monk's face. After a moment, she looked up at Eric and nodded in confirmation. She stood. "Should we try to move him?"

Eric shook his head. "Let's go back and tell the others. We'll need a better way to carry him."

Tess glanced back respectfully and rejoined Eric on the upper level. She held the lantern up as they walked toward the door. "I suspect this library will be helpful in your parents' research," she said.

They retraced their steps in the lower circuit, headed back toward the sloping tunnel that led to the hall. As they made their way up the incline, they heard raised voices. Eric couldn't make out the first one he heard, and he didn't recognize it. His mother's voice came through clearly, though.

"But we were here!" She was irate. "We saw what happened, and we can tell you about it!"

A male voice, trace of an accent, probably Norwegian. "You still should not have moved them. But regardless, you must leave with us immediately so we can secure the area. Leave everything behind."

Tess turned out her lantern as she and Eric crept forward, trying to see without being seen. There was more light in the hall, bright LEDs that moved and shifted, strong enough to permeate the space.

"This is bullshit," said Owen angrily. Eric didn't know where he was. From the tunnel entrance, they could only see a narrow section in the middle of the room. Owen seemed to be to the left, toward the fireplace. There were several people in view, officers or soldiers, dressed in body armour and helmets and carrying the lights that brightened the room. They carried automatic weapons clipped to the fronts of their vests; they weren't pointed at anyone, but fingers were very close to triggers, and the stillness from earlier had been replaced by an intensity Eric could feel.

There was a woman standing near the end of the tables, at the far right of Eric's field of view. She was looking where Owen must have been, her face calm and her hands in the pockets of her long coat. Her dark hair fell back over her collar, and a scarf hung loosely around her shoulders. She was professional, authoritative, and unfazed by the bodies lying around her. One of the response team members, likely the leader and the one who had been arguing with Clara, stood just in front of her to one side.

"That's the woman my dad talked to in Trondheim," Tess said quietly. "The FBI agent."

"Dr. Yancey, everyone here wants the same thing," said the agent. "No one anywhere has more interest in this place than all of you do, and with all you've seen and everything you know, your help will be crucial in understanding this. We are way behind you here, and we have a lot of questions." She gestured toward the military presence. "If we can just step out for a minute, let these guys do their thing, you can bring us up to speed, then we can start taking the next steps together. Okay?"

"Well, you see," Clara responded, "that's part of the problem. If these guys move in, there's a good chance crucial information could be lost. What happened here today has been devastating — and heartbreaking — but we can't have a bunch of trigger-happy flyboys stomping all over what's left."

"The flyboys are only here to make sure everything is safe for the forensics team to come in. They have to follow their procedures, for everyone's safety. Let's go out. You must be exhausted. We have food and water with us. You look like you could use it."

Eric thought he heard Lakey's voice, but only for an instant before another voice came from behind them, gruff and forceful. It was a blunt command in Norwegian. Eric stood and turned to meet two bright lights that suddenly shone in his face. He couldn't see past them, but he assumed there were also weapons pointing at him. "Hands!" Eric and Tess raised their arms, shielding their eyes as they did so. They were ordered to turn and walk into the hall.

As they stepped into the brightened space, Eric could see everyone gathered at the ends of the middle tables, near the stone hearth. Clara and Gabriel stood next to Owen. Michael was just behind them, closer to the wall. Sam and Angel were with Seth and Lakey in front of the fireplace itself, the space now cold and dark. Everyone was looking at Eric and Tess, but the FBI agent paid particular attention to Eric. She watched him closely as he entered, and her expression changed subtly. It might have been satisfaction, but Eric thought it looked more like intrigue.

"Mr. Bakker," the agent said. "It's nice to finally meet you."

"Steady, Clarice," said Sam.

The agent held up a thin-gloved hand defensively. "Don't worry, Doctor. We have plenty of time to get acquainted. Now, how about we start by chatting over a bite to eat?"

32

RUNNING OUT OF OPTIONS

It was a shock to step back out into the daylight. The afternoon was nearly over, but even the low sun forced Eric to squint and shade his eyes as he transitioned from the darkness of the Mountain. The FBI agent led the way, with Sam walking next to her. The Norwegian FSK was considerably more imposing than the gendarmes, decked out in their gear and acting like the unstoppable force in search of an immoveable object, but despite the firepower and the scrap brewing with his parents, instead of jacking his anxiety, Eric felt safe for the first time in two weeks. As a result, all the aches and pains he'd accumulated over the last several days and hadn't noticed seemed to fight for his attention at once. His right lower leg was especially insistent.

The FBI agent's name was not Clarice. It was Special Agent Sally Brown. Or at least she said it was. Eric was pretty sure that wasn't it, either. He started down the grassy part of the slope outside the mountain entrance anyway, feeling the weight of his body increase with each step. When his eyes adjusted, he saw the place where they'd left the helicopter was now crowded with several others, including a massive twin turbine that made the pope's AgustaWestland AW139 look like a *Transformers* action figure.

"Whooooa," said Lakey. She looked seriously at her brother. "Hey Sethie, maybe we can get Angel to duct-tape the pilot for us. And it's my turn."

There were at least a dozen people moving in and around the aircraft, all wearing coveralls with hoods hanging behind their shoulders. They were gathering crates and bags of equipment and piling it, getting ready to move. A half dozen EMTs were there as well, ready and waiting. Two others had already gone into the mountain to help the wounded gendarme, who was hanging on, and there was still the other two gendarmes who had been locked up by the People after the first skirmish. More FSK operatives were scattered around the area, focused especially on the pope's helicopter. Eric thought he could still see Falco and the pilot in the seats where they'd left them, though he wasn't sure if the duct tape was still in play.

Before the group reached the first vehicle, Agent Brown turned to face everyone. "Supplies are on the Chinook," she said. "There should be enough space for everyone to be comfortable. We can talk more once we're onboard."

The group started to move again, but Clara remained where she was, her eyes shifting over the busy scene. They settled on the UTVs parked together to one side. Agent Brown stopped and watched her patiently.

"Can I make a suggestion?" Clara asked.

"Of course," the agent replied.

"The kids have done enough today. I'd like them to return to the hostel where they can rest. They don't need to be here anymore. We can talk here while we're waiting to continue the investigation, then if you need to speak to them afterward, they won't be far away."

Agent Brown made a gee-whiz-I-wish-I-could face that Clara wasn't buying. "You'll have our cooperation. Once you've heard everything, you'll understand why they deserve a break."

"Actually," said Agent Brown evenly, eyes levelling on Eric but still addressing Clara. "Your story is number two on the must-read list."

There was more back-and-forth, but Agent Brown eventually relented. Eric, Michael, Tess, Angel, Seth, and Lakey took the UTVs and drove back to the farm. It was dark when they arrived, but they didn't lose much time thanks to Seth and Lakey's navigation skills. Per met them with some anticipation, though he was genuinely more concerned for them than for the vehicles. He did seem especially interested in any encounters with the Vættir, and his concern had deepened when he'd seen a fleet of military helicopters fly very quickly in the same direction his guests had gone. Eric felt bad about not telling him more, but he knew that wouldn't sit well with Agent Brown. He had to explain the damage to Jørgen's UTV, though, and in the end he discreetly blamed it on Seth and left Per to figure out how. He didn't mention the helicopter.

They stayed together as a group in one of the cabins, gratefully accepting supplies from Per that largely went to Seth and Lakey but satisfied everyone regardless. There was very little conversation, at least initially. Once the food took hold, things started to loosen up.

"Dude, you should have *seen* that snipe Sethie made with the flare gun," Lakey said, leaning back to give her stomach more room. She looked at her brother. "The mummy went up like that time I used the acetylene torch to flambé those *huaraches* in Baja, remember, brah?"

Seth nodded. "I do. I remember the firefighters down there weren't all that understanding. Very responsive, though." He looked at Michael. "Totally worth it to have the Gidge *sans* eyebrows. You should have seen it. Hysterical." He picked up his glass. "Still, I don't get it. Not that I'm complaining or anything, but why would the mummy light up like that?"

"One of the Vidi in the hall went out the same way," said Eric.

"What, like something in the bandages?"

"I think it's the dreylagr; it's flammable."

"So that stuff not only helps dead people run around and be wicked strong, it's also basically lighter fluid?" Lakey asked.

Eric shrugged. "That's my guess. Williams and Ada were hurt in the fire at the lab in Palermo. If we hadn't made it to them when we did, it could have been a lot worse."

"And there's the fire at the Lateran Palace when Ada and the others were held there," said Angel.

"I still can't believe you hit that button," said Lakey, shaking her head. "Aznuts, brah."

Tess looked at Michael. "Any lingering effects?"

Michael was standing near the counter. He reached for the coffee pot to refill his mug. "No, nothing. I'm good." Turning back, he lifted the mug. "And if my little sister thinks this gives her some kind of advantage from now on, she's mistaken." He sipped and smiled.

"You still have that remote?" asked Lakey. "I'd love to have a closer look at it."

Eric's eyebrows went up. He'd completely forgotten about it. "I can't remember what I did with it. I must have dropped it in the passage."

"What about your knee?" Seth asked Michael. "I still can't get over what you're doing on it, considering it was rebuilt a couple of weeks ago. You bitten by a radioactive spider at the lab at Berkeley?"

Michael laughed. "Sort of. All I need is the red and blue tights and some snarky one-liners."

"When they gave you the dreylagr in Montana, it didn't just heal your knee, though, did it?" said Angel.

Michael shrugged and sipped again but didn't reply. He'd also shown no effects from the cut made by the Vidi during the battle. Eric couldn't see it, though, and decided not to mention it.

∞

About two hours later, Eric heard a faint thumping outside that gradually grew louder until it drowned out every other sound. The noise changed as the helicopter set down on a level spot near the cabins and began to power down. Eric watched from the doorway as his father climbed out, followed by his mother, Owen, Sam, and the FBI agent. She looked the same as she had at the Mountain, though this time she carried a small black attaché case. A man dressed in the military gear of the FSK climbed out last and secured the door. They stayed bent over as they quickly moved toward Eric. The helicopter continued to power down. Eric couldn't tell if there were more FSK operatives onboard.

The new arrivals stepped into the small cabin. Eric and the others moved farther in to give them space, and the room filled quickly.

"Everyone all right?" Clara asked. She looked more haggard than Eric could recall ever having seen her before. Her clothes were stained and over-worn, her hair was struggling to recover from the helicopter ride, and the dark bruises stood out on her pale face. Her strength was obvious, but everything she'd been through was taking its toll.

"What's going on?" asked Michael.

"I'll explain everything," Clara replied, "but first, Eric, if you and Tess could go with Tess's dad, Agent Brown has some questions for you. The other cabin would probably be a good place."

Eric looked at his mother for a moment, then he and Tess followed Sam outside. The second cabin was where Gabriel and Owen had done their planning prior to going to the Mountain, so the table was still covered with papers, maps, and books. Eric left everything as it was, and he and Tess sat on one side of the table, with the daybed behind them. Agent Brown took a chair opposite, removing her coat and draping it over the back before she sat down. Sam took a chair, spun it around, and sat on it backward, arms folded across the top of the back a short distance away.

"Did you get something to eat?" asked the agent as she removed her gloves, pulling each finger until they came off in her hand. It was colder in this cabin than it had been in the other, but she didn't seem bothered by it.

Tess nodded, but Eric didn't respond. He could tell Tess was slightly wired. She must have felt better with her father there than she would have otherwise, but she seemed more inquisitive than worried. Eric wasn't nervous, but part of him would have preferred it — the tired part. Normally, he would have been ticked off in this situation, irritated by a conversation with someone who wanted something from him and wasn't going to ask for it directly. He hated it when people asked him questions they already knew the answers to. Nervousness and irritability would have made him sharper, less exhausted.

"Before we start, you should know that the forensics team found something in the mountain," the agent said as she placed her gloves on the table.

"Did they?" Eric replied, though he honestly wasn't that interested.

Agent Brown nodded. "Down the spiral tunnel below the level of the main hall. Two bodies — people similar to others who appeared to be living there."

"We know about that. Davis killed them."

The agent acknowledged with another slight nod. "Did you know about the third one?"

Eric turned his head slightly and narrowed his eyes. "A third?"

"Yes," said the agent, her expression neutral, almost pleasant. "This one seems to have been dead for a while; forensics isn't sure how long because it appears to have spent some time in cryostasis, but I have a pretty good idea. The victim is male, around seventy, died from massive blood loss, evidently. The body was wrapped head-to-toe in cloth strips. Like a mummy."

Eric and Tess exchanged looks. Eric glanced at Sam, who gazed back, his expression similar to the agent's.

"Do you know who it was?" Eric asked.

"We've made a positive ID," the agent replied. "One Gilroy Stockton, owner of Stockton Pharmaceuticals out of San Francisco, missing since last week when an explosion and fire destroyed his research facility in Montana."

Eric let out a long breath. He looked at Tess again, who stared back, incredulous. *Stockton.* It made sense. Here was the reason Azzarà and Davis had come to the Mountain; not for their own immortality, but to bring Stockton back from the dead. Clearly, they'd worked together so they could both get what they wanted: fame and fortune for Azzarà, retribution for Davis.

Agent Brown's expression remained neutral as she made space on the table, opened the attaché, and placed a black portfolio in front of her. "I need to ask you some questions," she began, opening the portfolio to show a typed page on white paper with the FBI seal at the top. "Why don't we recount the events of the last two weeks; I can tell you what I know, you can fill in the gaps, and I can let you know what I'm thinking. Sound okay?"

He felt his interest fade again, replaced by the fatigue. "Sure," he replied.

Agent Brown turned the top page in the portfolio. "Here's what I know, and your parents have confirmed most of it: On October 25th, Dr. Edmund Carlson was found dead on campus at UC Berkeley, and we have someone who looks a lot like you leaving the scene literally with blood on his hands. Apparently, this person was able to elude campus security by jumping from the roof of the building. Both the person and the building had close ties to your parents. Also, Homeland Security has the two of you coming into the country the day before, and a cab driver puts you at your old house in San Francisco. Tracking backward has your parents booked on a flight from Victoria, Canada, to Chicago in the early morning on October 23rd — they check in but don't board. Less than two hours *after* Dr. Carlson's murder, we have you on a flight from Oakland to LA and on to Victoria via Calgary."

Eric watched the agent impassively.

"Couple days later, you're crossing the border from Alberta into Montana, same day Ray Yamasaki's body is found in a ravine outside Victoria and a big fire destroys the research facility in Montana. A little digging shows there is a connection between Stockton and your mother through his late wife, who was found in the basement in a cryonics tube." The agent looked up from her notes. "The timing puts you in both places. With me so far?"

Eric nodded. She was gradually becoming more suggestive in her tone, but it didn't make him any more nervous. He was calm, and his legs were quiet.

"Oh, and we have another body in Montana, a big time ex-military type, Olaf 'The Butcher' Meszaros. This one makes me pause, I'll admit, thinking he should be out of your league, but hearing about leaping tall buildings with a single bound, among other things, I'm not prepared to rule it out at this point. Plus, he was stabbed to death just like Carlson, and two of his henchmen were tracked back to Victoria in the previous days when you were there — no bodies this time, but it's early yet.

"Next we have multiple stabbing deaths similar to the others at the Field Museum in Chicago, where your parents were headed when they were abducted, and you show up on security footage there too. It's concerning, because things seem to be escalating. Then you cross the border at Detroit, just before I get up to real time, but it also gets more complicated because now I have to get Interpol involved. You catch a flight out of Montreal to Rome, then another to Palermo, just as another fire starts in another lab, this one featuring the deaths of three more of your parents' colleagues, and there you are again. But again you disappear. So you see where I'm going with this; Berkeley, Montana, Chicago, Palermo, all facilities involving your parents or their team, all visited by you within a short time, and all with bodies left behind. Next you show up in France, and I'm closer now, so I arrange to have you picked up at the airport in Cannes, but you run again. Who does that? Guilty people do that, Eric; that's what guilty people do. Fortunately, your parents also popped up on the grid taking a flight from Nice to Trondheim, and Interpol had a report of a break-in at the university." She gestured toward Sam. "Enter the doctor here and our long-awaited gathering." She closed the portfolio and sat back in her seat, looking hard at Eric. "So, have I missed anything?"

Eric placed an arm on the table, watching his finger as he traced a line in the pattern of the vinyl tablecloth before responding. Clearly, she knew more than she had said. She watched him patiently as he began to speak. When he was finished, everything he'd told her was the truth. He could tell from her reaction that she believed him, though he suspected she also knew that he hadn't told her everything.

As he spoke, Eric came to understand why his parents had allowed him to talk to Agent Brown without them there. It was a sign of trust, and through their absence, he felt closer to them than he ever had.

33

HOME

E ric sat at a table in the dining hall, his mind tired but at ease as he looked at the screen on his phone. He'd received another text from Tess before he'd sat down; she was on her way.

It was a grey Monday morning, and the atmosphere at Brentwood College School was subdued, though when Eric thought about it, it didn't seem much different from other Monday mornings. The room was gradually filling with other students, some laughing and smiling, others bleary-eyed and weary-looking after the weekend, likely for different reasons than Eric.

He'd arrived very late the night before, having flown in on his own from Trondheim, changing planes in Oslo, Reykjavík, and Vancouver. It wasn't raining, thankfully, and he was able to take his dad's motorcycle — the 1964 BSA A65 Thunderbolt he and Tess had left in an abandoned barn near the airport just over two weeks earlier — and drive to Brentwood. Getting up this morning had been easier than expected, which was good considering he had lots of missed time to make up at school.

He looked around the room again. He was used to eating alone here, had preferred it actually, and no one made any attempts to join him. He could tell a few people were curious about where he'd been for the last two weeks. The lady at the counter, cheerful as always, had said how nice it was to see him back in the hall. Eric found himself smiling and chatting for a few minutes, even holding up the line briefly while he did it. Her name was Rosemary. The two girls from the morning when he'd received Michael's video message were back, heads together and laughing as they glanced his way. Eric smiled and gave them a wave. They blushed furiously and turned away, still laughing, though now in disbelief.

Eric had just finished eating when Tess arrived. She spotted him and came over, not bothering with the food line. Eric knew she'd already had breakfast with her father, who took the meal as seriously as Seth and Lakey did. She'd spent the weekend with her mother, working through what was sure to be some major changes, though it was still too early to tell how it was going to go. The deadbeat second husband had left, which was a start, but it was going to take some time. Eric figured there had to be a lot of issues to address when coming back from the dead.

"Morning," she said, hanging her jacket on the back of a chair and sitting down opposite him. "How was the flight?"

"It was great. I'd never been to Iceland before," he replied. "I think I'll have to go back."

Tess didn't hesitate. "Count me in," she said.

Eric and Tess hadn't had much time to talk since the interview with Agent Brown six days earlier. She and Sam had flown back with Seth and Lakey early the following morning, arriving in Montreal that evening and bolting for the West Coast in the twins' RV. The mission they chose to accept: get home to Mill Bay before their parents returned from Hawaii. Sam knew he was taking a chance going back with them, that he would be exposed to the people he was hiding from, but they *had* to go, and he wasn't going to let them go on their own. Having a couple of extra drivers was his excuse, and it ended up making all the difference for Seth and Lakey. They were home for twenty minutes before their parents came through the door.

Eric had stayed with his parents during the initial stages of the investigation at the Mountain. He didn't have any cell coverage or Internet most of the time in Norway, so he was looking forward to getting up to speed.

The sky brightened outside, drawing Eric's attention. The two-storey windows at that end of the room let in the light, and the atmosphere changed. The chatter in the room seemed to include more laughter all of a sudden. As if it were a cue, the door opened, and Seth and Lakey came in. Like

Tess and Eric and everyone else in the hall, they were wearing their school uniforms, but unlike Tess, they headed straight for the breakfast line. When they finally made their way over, their red plastic trays were crowded with enough supplies for another mountain expedition.

Tess got up and moved to Eric's side of the table to give them room. "Didn't you guys have breakfast at home already?" she asked, though Eric was sure she already knew the answer.

Lakey frowned at her disapprovingly. "Yes, of course," she said, setting down her tray. "This is second breakfast. How does no one get how this works?" She took one chair and deftly spun it around to the end of the table, out of the way, before sitting down in another.

"Twenty minutes and it could have been prison rations for both of you," Eric said, grinning.

"You have no idea," said Seth, wheeling up to the empty space next to Lakey, his tray on his knees.

Eric laughed.

"No, seriously, brah. The twenty minutes didn't save us. They knew exactly where we were the whole time."

"You're kidding."

"Nope," Lakey said, piling scrambled egg onto a piece of toast. "We still haven't figured it out. Let's not talk about the details, but we've been given house arrest for now — home and school and that's it — pending sentencing." She folded the toast into her mouth. "Won't be pretty, though," she mumbled.

Eric nodded solemnly, covering up another laugh by pretending to cough.

"What's happening with *your* parents?" Tess asked Eric, mercifully changing the subject.

Eric pushed his tray slightly farther away and leaned back in his chair. "They had a lot of trouble getting access to the mountain. The Norwegians refused to let them go back after the forensics team went in, but they've worked something out now."

"Poor Willy," said Lakey. "I still can't believe he was able to wake up like that. Do your parents know what happened?"

"It had something to do with the dreylagr. He'd been absorbing it from the mountain somehow, and it was enough to bring him around. It was like being there was enough to bring him back, no rituals required. If he'd had more time, it might have done more for him, but in the end, everyone ran out of time. Mom and Dad haven't been in the mountain long enough to find out why, but they're looking."

"So they don't know why everyone collapsed the way they did?" Tess asked.

Eric shook his head. "Dad thinks that whatever power the Mountain had, it stopped working. The People and Vidi were clearly affected by something during the fighting. Neither side seemed to be moving the way they expected. He thinks it has something to do with the avelids, the stone spheres inside their chests."

"Oh, I know what that's like," Lakey said casually. "You remember that time, Sethie, when the drone had a mind of its own for a few minutes then dropped dead in the middle of that field? A cow peed on it. It was awful."

Eric raised an eyebrow expectantly. "And that's the same how?"

"Battery failure," Lakey replied, spearing a sausage.

"Yeah, your failure to charge the battery," Seth clarified.

"Still, it seems like the same thing here," Lakey persisted. "Maybe these avelids were batteries, and they just ran out of juice."

Tess turned back to Eric. "Did your parents find out any more about what happened to the People after John and Ada left all those years ago? How they ended up the way they did? It seems like things had changed a lot."

Eric glanced around the room. The dining hall was filling up, and the noise level was increasing. The rectangular mahogany tables set up end-to-end reminded him of the Great Hall inside the Mountain, with matching wooden chairs instead of benches. He pictured the People sitting together like the students here and wondered how long it had been since they had talked and laughed like this.

"Mom said Ada explained some of it. She and John and some others left because they could see where things were headed. The People were becoming divided on how to follow the Seven Laws. Everyone believed they needed to keep their existence a secret, but there were some who insisted they stay hidden, while there were others who felt it was important to interact with the outside world to grow and evolve and they could do it without revealing who they were. It got to the point where some of them killed outsiders who came too close to the Mountain, which caused major problems between the two sides. Ada knew the conflict would get violent, so they got out. She had a huge falling-out with her father, and they didn't speak again until she went back with us. They'd been right about the violence; the People fought for years, killing and resurrecting each other until the Mountain was crushed in an earthquake and one side of the conflict was taken out. The People we saw were all that were left. Viggo and the others were on the side in favour of interacting with the outside world, but they were so affected by the conflict that they completely withdrew afterward. It was like they'd lost everything."

"How did the Vidi and this Vidarr guy fit in?" Seth asked. "John didn't seem to know what they were about."

"Abito told Ada something about that when they talked in the hall," Eric explained. "The Vidi evolved, basically, as foot soldiers. They'd been resurrected so many times, they weren't capable of thinking for themselves anymore; they just followed orders. At some point, this Ragnhildr, who was the head of the side that wanted everyone hidden, sent Vidarr and the Vidi out to hunt down those who had left the Mountain and eliminate them so they couldn't reveal their existence. They had no other instructions, and when the Mountain collapsed and Ragnhildr and her followers didn't survive, there was no one to call them off. That is, if anyone left even knew they were out there. Apparently, Cardinal Abito — who was Tomas from the Green Mountain in Libya — was terrified of the Vidi, and of Vidarr in particular, probably because of what they'd done to his wife and son. He embedded himself in the Catholic Church to hide from them, and seeing them in the Mountain must have triggered him, so he lost it."

"So Tomas was responsible for Ada's imprisonment, right?" Tess asked. "How did he convince the Vatican to keep her there?"

"Actually, we heard from Sallah on that point," said Eric. "He was at the Vatican trying to find out more about Abito. He said the cardinal and Brother Marcus were the only people who knew she was there. He was sure of it. They'd been able to hide her completely."

"How is that possible?" Tess persisted.

Eric shrugged. "The guy was persuasive. Not only did he manipulate the Romans — and somehow the Vidi, too — into attacking the Green Mountain fifteen hundred years ago, but do you remember when Ada told us about all the other members of her people that were locked up with her at the Lateran Palace? The people who died in the fire there? That was him, Cardinal Abito, a.k.a. Tomas. The roundup actually involved the sacking of Constantinople during the Fourth Crusade, no less. And according to Michael, who had talked to the pilot before he was carted away, Abito completely fooled Falco; he had him bring in freelance soldiers instead of using his gendarmes and paid them extra to take orders from him directly without Falco knowing."

"But why would Tomas do that to his own people?"

"Ada seemed to think that at first it was for revenge, but then as time went on, it changed into something else. She thought he had some kind of spiritual awakening, like he thought God spoke to him. He started gathering People up as a twisted way to protect them, to deliver them into God's hands, and whatever happened to them after that was God's will."

"And setting fire to the lab in Palermo with the research team inside?" Seth prompted.

"Dad thinks Abito saw fire as a test," Eric explained. "If God spared them, they were worthy of protection. He might have had the idea after the fire at Lateran, who knows. As for Palermo, it wouldn't surprise me if the mercs overstepped their mandate, though. They didn't seem like the type to spare people, regardless of what God might think."

Someone must have said something funny, because several people laughed loudly over by the food tray return area. The tide of students had changed, and now people were headed out of the dining hall instead of into it.

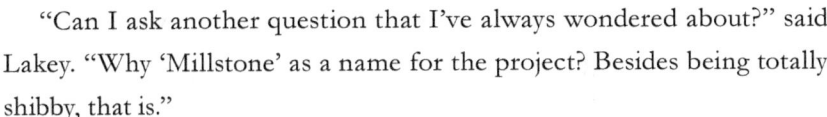

"Can I ask another question that I've always wondered about?" said Lakey. "Why 'Millstone' as a name for the project? Besides being totally shibby, that is."

"I asked my dad about that," Eric replied. "It's a reference to Mjölnir."

"Thor's hammer?" Seth asked. "Like in *The Avengers*?"

"That's the one. The hammer had the power of resurrection, as well as the ability to level mountains; plus, the avelids are covered with markings that might have evolved into runes. The team knew they were from that part of the world, so it seemed like a reasonable connection. The god Odin, Thor's father, is credited with giving humanity the gift of the runic alphabet. Maybe he wrote them down on stone balls for us. Making this kind of connection and coming up with these names is typical Dad."

"I never get tired of hearing you talk about this stuff, man," Lakey said. "If you ever decide to become a twenty-first-century Indiana Jones and you need a techie sidekick to help find old stuff and fight mummies, you know who to call." She finished off her apple juice, flipped the glass with a flourish, and slammed it triumphantly down on the tray.

"You mean Angel?" Tess asked with a smile.

"Yeah!" Lakey replied, unfazed. "That would be awesome, wouldn't it? She'd have to be there! Seth's been talking to her; she and her dad were back in Chicago a few days ago. I'm sure he could get her to…"

"Hey, how's Michael?" Seth interjected.

Eric glanced at Tess and smirked. "He's good," he replied. "We left Trondheim at the same time. He's back in San Francisco now." He pointed at Seth like he'd just remembered something. "And actually, he asked if you guys could do him a favour."

"He wants us to bring him a board he can use at the Wharf when we go to Santa Cruz?" Lakey asked. "That's going to be an awesome trip, brah, provided we're not locked in our parents' basement." She turned to her brother. "We still have that soft-top, don't we, Sethie?"

"He probably will, but that isn't it," Eric said. "There's this nurse — he met her in Montana. He's hoping you can track her down."

"Probably wants to apologize for blowing up her previous place of employment," Lakey guessed, reaching for her last strip of bacon.

"Something like that. Her name's Keira."

"No problem," Seth said.

The twins had no trouble finishing off their second breakfast, and it was time to head to class, though no one was in a hurry to get moving. In the end, Tess was predictably the responsible one who got them back on track, and they started toward the tray return area.

"Dude, how about this," Lakey suggested as they walked. "I need to work on my rails, and I know an awesome place to do it. You know that sweet move you were showing me? The Italian Job? I want to get that down in case we go back to Rome. What say we go do that instead?"

Five Months Later

Eric followed Tess down the steep, winding trail, the path worn bare by years of foot traffic that had exposed stones and tree roots and showed the way through the forest. The spring morning air was crisp, but the sun helped when it hit them. They were dressed warmly enough, with layers they could add or remove, packs to carry them in, and hiking shoes that could handle the terrain. The steepest parts of the trail had makeshift stairs, some made of wood with a rail on one side, some made only of stone slabs arranged in the ground like crooked teeth. Occasionally, Eric would thief vault a rail or precision a rock, lightly moving from surface to surface as they climbed steadily downward.

Rocks and tree trunks were moss-covered in the shadowy places, and green leaves had begun to appear in places that saw more sun. The rough surfaces and steep descent gave lots of opportunities for climbing and jumping, and Eric did a few simple transitions, pushing off one and lightly landing on another. He restrained from more aggressive moves but didn't stop himself from visualizing them with almost the same effect.

Tess's phone chimed, and she stopped to take it out of her small pack. "It's Dad," she said, reading the text. "He's going to be tied up with the investigators for another day and won't be able to come until the day after tomorrow." She typed a brief response then looked up at Eric as she put the phone back. "He'll meet us in Geneva."

They continued walking. "Does that mean whatever he's doing at Interpol is going well or that it's not going well?" Eric asked.

Tess shrugged. "He figured this would happen. He'd put them off for so long, he thought it would be unlikely that they'd let him leave once he arrived." She tightened her shoulder straps. One of the conditions Sam had insisted on when he agreed to come back to Interpol to help with their investigation — which had included taking out the Transnistrians behind the plane crash and the mole inside their own organization — was that they provide three extra flights. "He won't miss meeting us, though. It's not in him to go back on a promise."

"He won't miss out on meeting Sophia Loren, you mean," said Eric, smiling.

"That's if Seth and Lakey can track her down again," Tess replied. "We'll get our 'chance' meeting one way or another." She placed a hand along a tree trunk as she followed the trail that looped around it down the slope. "Did you hear from your parents this morning?"

Eric pushed off the opposite side of the tree with his foot and landed noiselessly on the path beside her. "Just that text from Michael," he replied. "The time difference makes it hard to connect in real time, and Mom and Dad aren't big on texting."

"You said there was a photo, right?"

She hadn't seen it yet. Eric stopped, took his phone from his own pack, and pulled up the text. There were three photos, actually, and he opened them so she could see. The first was a snap of Michael and Keira, heads together, making faces at the camera. Keira was wearing scrubs and her UCSF Medical Centre ID badge, probably on her way to the hospital for her shift. Michael was in fatigues, likely on his way to class or PT. One more year before he went for active duty, and he couldn't wait. He was excelling in his ROTC program at USF and loving it, having completely embraced the school. Eric wasn't surprised that Michael had continued to downplay the major effects of the dreylagr in his system, but there was no denying the benefits.

The second was a wide-angle shot of Gabriel and Clara, standing with other faculty and administration from UC Berkeley at the commemoration at Kroeber Hall. At the centre of the image was an embossed metal plaque mounted to a wall in the anthropology department. Eric couldn't make out the inscription, but there was a large framed photo just above the plaque featuring the smiling portrait of Dr. Edmund Carlson. Eric already knew that the new wing that had been added a few years earlier had been re-dedicated to Dr. Carlson, and the main lab was now named after Leonard Shipley.

The third photo in Michael's text was another image of Gabriel, taken apparently without him knowing as he worked at the desk in his office, the same office where Eric and Tess had met with Dr. Carlson just before he died. The office was much the way Eric remembered it, with the desk at the far end so Gabriel's back was to the camera and with framed photos covering the wall to one side. The photo Dr. Carlson had given Eric had been replaced by an enlarged version and featured a small plate beneath, likely describing the scene and giving the names of the people in it. Eric now looked at the image from an angle — Michael's perspective from the office doorway — but he knew it very well: the picture of the research team taken at the Green Mountain in Libya shortly after their discovery there. Owen was flashing the same bright smile Eric had come to know since Norway. Gabriel and Clara were there, covered with dust and happy, their arms around the others. Sallah, the reserved Egyptian archaeologist, was even smiling. Everyone looked so happy. Francesco Azzarà, one arm raised in celebration, killed by the Vidi and placed in his lab in Palermo by Falco's men. Evelyn Spencer, an arm around her friend and mentor Clara, killed in the explosion and fire at Francesco's lab. Lenny Shipley, kneeling in front of everyone, with the legionnaire's hat he always wore, beaten by Falco's men and killed in the same fire. Ray Yamasaki, crouching slightly to make room for the others, a smile as big as Owen's, killed accidentally by Falco's men when they tried to apprehend him near his home in Victoria. And Edmund Carlson, standing like the proud father of the family, killed by the Vidi on campus at Berkeley.

"That place suits him," said Tess. "Your father."

"It does, doesn't it," Eric replied. He looked at the photo again. His father was bent over some papers as he worked. Eric recognized a specimen box from the lab on one end of the desk. The lid was open, and an avelid sat on a low pedestal in front of it. Eric knew that Gabriel had smuggled it out of the Mountain in Seth's pack before the forensics team had gone in, and he'd spent the last several months studying it. Since discovering that the avelids had emitted some kind of radiation that acted on the dreylagr when stimulated by the brain — a method that was amplified and sustained by the device Azzarà had created — Gabriel had turned his focus to the origins of the stones. The radiation had been decaying exponentially and had dropped below a threshold of effectiveness in those last moments at the Mountain. Basically, the batteries had run out of juice, just like Lakey said. The timing wasn't lost on Gabriel, who still felt that the spirit of the Mountain had pulled the plug to end the conflict between the People and the Vidi — that Thor had seen enough. The mineral composition of the stones was not one previously known to be on Earth, so Gabriel was working with the Astro Department, among others, to look elsewhere.

Clara had been working with the written information discovered in the Mountain, focusing on how the People had become what they were in the first place. She hadn't had an opportunity to talk with Ada about this, and she would need a lot of time to translate the records — assuming this was even possible — but she had the few volumes that Ada had carried with her from the Vatican, books she had already translated to Latin. One of them made reference to their origins: miners had discovered the stones, and after an accident where several people were killed in a cave-in, they were buried inside the mountain, each with an avelid as a symbolic gesture. The stones settled into the crushed bodies, the dreylagr had soaked into them from reservoirs found at those depths, and the people walked out about a week later. The process eventually evolved into the ritual, and their entire society became centred around the Mountain.

Eric darkened the screen and put the phone back in his bag. "They're both where they belong."

"We'll see them after exams," she added as they continued on the trail.

Eric had no regrets about staying at Brentwood when his parents went back to California. None whatsoever. He'd come to see the campus as a place of his own, a place where *he* belonged. But he and Tess were already planning a trip to San Francisco, and he was looking forward to it.

Tess was also planning to go look at the theatre program at the University of San Francisco. Eric hadn't been familiar with it, but she'd told him that the performing arts programs at USF had a big emphasis on activism and social justice, and she was excited to check it out. It was a unique program that seemed to suit her. Tess had been encouraging Eric to think about his own options before they started their last year at Brentwood, though the only pressure she applied was to *do* the actual thinking, not what to think. When he did think about it, there might actually be something for him at one of these schools he knew so well.

They came to a bend in the path next to a bench with a large boulder behind it. The rock had a post on top, with orange road signs that showed they were going the right way. The twisted roots on the path were eventually replaced by a boardwalk with a rail on one side and the ravine wall on the other. The slope was impossibly steep here otherwise, and Eric could hear the sound of running water grow louder as they walked. Old leaves from the previous autumn still gathered along the edges of the walkway. The wood was old and weathered, and some of the boards had fared better than others over the years, so Eric was careful to notice anything that wasn't stable enough to pull or to climb on. They found the water, a multilevel waterfall that appeared intermittently through gaps in the rock before finally vanishing somewhere below them. A network of stairs allowed them to follow it until they also passed beneath the rock, leading them into the grotto.

Eric had heard Tess tell the story many times about where she had been going when she found her father. Of all the places she'd seen while travelling, it was the place she hadn't seen that she talked about the most. The opportunity to go while her father was in Lyon was worth a few more missed days of school, and it was worth it to Eric to see her face when they arrived. They were deep in the Gorges Mystérieuses in Tête-Noire, outside Trient in Switzerland, and it was time to visit the nymphs.

EPILOGUE

Arrival to Earth

The pilot knew she was in trouble before the ship reached the planet. Main power was failing, and the integrity of the vessel would only be maintained as long as there was enough energy to channel through the hull nodes, the lattice of spheres that solidified the fluid into a flexible shell. If they lost power, the hull would be breached and the atmospheric pressure inside the vessel — necessary for the pilot and her passengers to maintain their forms — would be lost to the vacuum of space. They would expand helplessly in all directions until they ceased to be entities at all.

The hull nodes, each distinguished by the engraved markings that identified its origin and also increased its surface area, emitted radiation that acted on the fluid around them, organizing and stabilizing it in the required patterns. The nodes also had a precise expiry; they would retain their charge for the time it took the planet below to orbit its star fifteen thousand times, by the pilot's calculations, before they were no longer effective. However, without the main power supply and central controls, they could not interact with each other to form the ship.

The pilot checked the ship's status again. Power levels were approaching critical. She had no choice. She willed the vessel forward, entering the atmosphere at an angle to limit stress on the hull node connections. Whatever power was left would be needed for deceleration. She knew the atmospheric pressure on this planet was far below what her kind preferred, but it was more than most other bodies in this solar system and certainly more than empty space. The second planet had more pressure, but the conditions were too harsh — high temperature and wind velocity — for their particle cloud forms. Pressure, atmospheric stability, and solar radiation were the key factors in sustaining the charged connectivity of their cellular components. Basically, air pressure kept their forms from flying apart, and sunlight gave them energy. There was another, more suitable place, a moon around the ringed sixth planet, but it was not reasonable to expect the ship to make it that far. What this planet lacked in pressure, it made up in proximity to its star. It was this or nothing.

The hull handled the heat from the increasing drag through the atmosphere, and the compressive strength was good enough that the ship didn't implode, but it still shook violently. As the surface rotated below her, the pilot observed large ice sheets that extended from the poles. Readings had shown that a significant portion of the planet's surface was covered with liquid water, which, if they were to land in it, would make it nearly impossible to move, and their telekinetic abilities would be limited, though their telepathic communication range might actually be enhanced. The pilot had targeted a landmass near the equator, but as they descended, the ship's power gave out, leaving her with no way to manoeuvre or slow down. Auxiliary power would be enough to hold the hull nodes together for a few moments, but that was all. The ship overshot its target, continued toward the polar ice and precariously close to one of the largest bodies of water, and hit the ground with tremendous force. The ship remained intact through the initial impact as it bore deep into the surface, vaporizing ice and scattering rock and dust into the air. It was not until the aux power failed that the ship broke up, the hull nodes scattered, and the shell liquified. Immediately, the pilot and passengers, protected to that point, expanded rapidly in the low-pressure atmosphere.

The others were all aware of what was happening, since they'd been in constant contact with the pilot. They gathered as best they could, close enough to make the connections they needed to communicate, and the pilot indicated she would attempt to rebuild the ship, though it would take time. For the beings themselves, time was not a problem — as long as this planet's sun was in the sky, they would have what they needed

— but it *was* a problem for the ship. The effective charge of the hull nodes would deplete exponentially until they became inert. They could be recovered, along with fluid that formed the hull, and prepared for assembly, but primary power was the issue. Harnessing enough from the materials available might not be possible. Fifteen thousand times around the sun — the clock was ticking.

The pilot remained at the site of the crash, contained within the rock until she essentially bonded with it. The passengers dissipated into the surrounding area, close enough that they could be reached when needed. They assimilated with different features of the land, mineral, and, occasionally, organic, though only at basic levels, anchoring their presence in ways they found both effective and gratifying. Gradually, some went on to interact with other life as it came and went over long stretches of time. One life form seemed more advanced and more pervasive than the others, and the assimilated beings viewed them both as a part of nature and a threat to it. Sometimes encounters went well and sometimes they didn't, though when there was respect, there was support. Occasionally, their passage would need to be blocked, their structures taken down, or their possessions removed. Sometimes their animals would be cared for or their crops made abundant, sometimes both would be taken away. Their relationship involved guidance and retribution. The beings became known to these evolving life forms as the Vættir, and the stories grew, to the beings' amusement, to describe many forms, mainly nature spirits but also elves, dwarves, giants, and gods.

Of all the beings who landed on this planet, however, the pilot became the most connected with these indigenous life forms. Some of them stumbled into her Mountain, discovered the hull nodes, and quite by accident, repurposed them to serve their own needs. The pilot came to look on them with a sort of affection. As empowered as they became, she was still forced to intervene at times when their behaviour threatened to ruin themselves. She had hoped it would work and wanted the best for them, but she could see ahead and knew how the end would come. And when the time came, she knew it would also be the end for her in that place, because without the hull nodes they needed to construct a new vessel — having lost their charge, they were no longer effective — she and her kind would be forced to remain on this planet. She would move on from the Mountain in search of another home, another place to bond to, and perhaps another People to care for.

ABOUT MARK BURLEY

Mark is originally from Truro, Nova Scotia and now lives outside Halifax with his wife and two children. He is the author of the complete Hit the Ground Running Trilogy; Book One, *Hit the Ground Running*, and Book Two, *Flow Like Water*, are also available. You can find him at MarkBurley.ca.

WRITE FOR US

We love discovering new voices and welcome submissions. Please read the following carefully before preparing your work for submission to us. Our publishing house does accept unsolicited manuscripts but we want to receive a proposal first, and if interested we will solicit the manuscript.

We are looking for solid writing–present an idea with originality and we will be very interested in reading your work.

As you can appreciate, we give each proposal careful consideration so it can take up to six weeks for us to respond, depending on the amount of proposals we have received. If it takes longer to hear back, your proposal could still be under consideration and may simply have been given to a second editor for their opinion. We can't publish all books sent to us but each book is given consideration based on its individual merits along with a set of criteria we use when considering proposals for publication.

THANK YOU FOR READING
TAKE FLIGHT

www.ingramcontent.com/pod-product-compliance
Lightning Source LLC
Chambersburg PA
CBHW051341020726
47501CB00007B/2206